CIRCLES OF CONFUSION

JJ Grafton

Cover Design: Jacqui Jay Grafton EFIAP DPAGB BPE5*
Model: Hannah Frances Chapman

There's a yellow ribbon tied to the handle on the front door, so I walk round the side of the house to go in by the kitchen. Mummy explained to me that if the ribbon is there, she's busy and I mustn't interrupt her. I don't mind because I like being by myself. I can read a book or practice my writing – and sometimes the biscuit man will be there. I hope he's there today. Maybe he'll have Jaffa cakes, he knows they're my favourite.

CHAPTER ONE

I know every prostitute who works on Forest Road, from the Duke of Clarence pub down to the Medical Centre on the corner. There are always at least three or four of the girls standing about, even at nine o'clock in the morning.

Candice and Joanne lean against one of the ancient oak trees. They're at the end of a long night's work, still here in the hope of one more punter.

"Here, Jilly," calls Candice as I walk past. "Want to take a picture of this?"

Screeching with laughter, she pulls open her coat to reveal a pair of red frilly knickers and a tassel precariously attached to each nipple.

"You know it," I laugh, stopping to swing my camera to eye level and fire off a few shots.

"Yeah, I thought you'd like that, you mucky bugger."

Candice is delighted with the attention, particularly as a car slows down with a very interested driver behind the wheel. She makes eye contact with the punter and gets into his car.

"Stay safe, Candy!" Joanne takes a quick snap of the number plate, gives me a thumbs up and I grab another shot.

I'm going to miss these girls. I've been photographing them for a large part of my three year degree course at the Trent University. My dissertation, *Outside the Circle*, is finished and my portfolio is nearly ready to be handed in. Soon, I'll shake the dust of Nottingham off my feet and leave this phase of my life behind.

On the corner of North Sherwood Street, a red-haired girl in a skimpy dress gets out of a large car. Her eyes are red and she sobs quietly.

"You OK, Annie?" I ask. She replies with a shake of her head and rolls her eyes back towards the car. I get it. Annie's pimp has a fearsome reputation and frequently puts her back out on the street if she hasn't earned enough money. All I can do is give her a sympathetic smile and carry on down the hill towards the uni.

Halfway up the steps at the entrance to the computer building, a hand touches my arm and I turn to see Christie, my tutor. He's a tall, elegant black guy with a small goatee, always smartly dressed.Today he's wearing both a tie and a cravat in clashing colours. On him, it looks good.

"Hey, Jilly. I was just about to text you. Have you sorted out a picture for the degree show catalogue?"

"Not yet. There's no hurry, is there?"

"Well, yeah. We've got a problem. The printshop's been flooded. I've had to find an outside printer who can fit it in, but they need the finished artwork tomorrow."

"No worries. I'll choose a picture and send it to Maria in the studio."

"Can you get it to her by ten o'clock tonight? She and Charlie are pulling an all-nighter to get everything ready."

"Sure." I'm already scrolling through the thumbnails on my phone.

"If you see any of the others from your year, tell them to get their photographs in today. I'm going to get a coffee and start phoning round."

I wave absently. Christie walks away, then spins on his heel and comes back.

"Can you do me a favour, if you're not too busy?"

'Uh, maybe. What is it?"

"Oliver asked me to take a few pictures of – um – a friend of his. I can't do it now. Could you …"

He looks pleadingly at me, eyebrows raised.

"Oh, for God's sake, Christie, that guy has got you wrapped round his little finger."

"I know." He smiles sheepishly. "Anyway … she's one of the girls, used to work on Forest Road. There might be something interesting there for you."

"How on earth does Oliver know a sex worker?"

He shrugs and says, "Good … I'll get Ollie to text her, say you're coming"

"Wait, I didn't say I would …"

"Thanks, Jilly, you're a godsend."

He whirls off, thumbs working furiously on his phone. Seconds later I get a *ping* and read his message.

tina, top floor, old mill, lace market

The area that was once the centre of the lace industry is dominated by tall, red brick factories. Disused for many years, they jostle for space, most of them with five or six storeys of empty-eyed windows and crumbling brick-work. A few have spider-like scaffolding clinging to the walls, where there's been a half-hearted attempt at re-development. Few cars and no buses can manoeuvre their way through the maze of dirty streets or the one-way system although, optimistically, the council has built a gleaming car park on the edge of it.

The red dot on my phone shows the Old Mill, but I can't find it. One street leads into another with few distinguishing features. I'm about to give up, when footsteps sound behind me and I turn, ready to ask directions. A large black man, six and a half feet if he's an inch, with chest-length dreadlocks walks towards me with his hand outstretched. I clutch my camera bag protectively to my chest and give a frightened squawk.

The guy jumps back, hands held high to calm me down."It's OK! It's OK! I'm Noel."

I'm high on fear and nervous energy and blurt out, "Who the fuck is Noel?"

"Tina sent me to find you. Oliver called and said you was coming. Look – "

He points up at an open window on the top floor of one of the decrepit buildings, where a blonde woman leans out, calling down.

"Hey, are you Jilly? It's me! Tina! Noel's all right, he'll bring you up."

Noel reaches for my camera bag and I slap his hand away, unwilling to trust my precious camera to him. He shrugs and turns away. "Stay or go, suit yourself."

Slightly ashamed of the squawk, I shoulder my camera bag and follow him round the side of the building to the front of the Old Mill. I stare at the re-furbished brickwork, the shiny paintwork and the huge lacquered doors.

"What happened? Did they run out of money after they did the front?"

"Something like that," Noel throws over his shoulder, as we enter the building. "Lift's not working. Still want to carry your own bag?"

Four flights of stairs lead up to Tina's flat. Noel bounds ahead and holds the door open as I struggle up with my heavy bag. Tina greets me with a kiss on both cheeks, as though we're old mates. I don't do touchy-feely and squirm away from her. She's the complete opposite of Noel in all ways. Small, blonde and dainty – and friendly.

"You're here! Bloody hell, I thought you wasn't coming!" She talks at ninety miles an hour, doesn't wait for an answer. "I'm Tina, as if you didn't know. Here, Noel, get Jilly a Prosecco, don't just stand there."

Noel glowers and doesn't move for a few seconds, then smiles. "Coming right up, my love."

I get the feeling he's mocking Tina in some way, but she prattles on.

"I'll show you round, while that lazy sod gets the drinks."

It's only half past ten in the morning. I think fleetingly of Rob, my boyfriend. He hates the work I do with the girls, can't wait for it to be finished. Early morning drinking is certain to be added to the list of things he doesn't like. Noel presses a cold glass of bubbles into my hand and the thought melts away.

Tina and Noel have the entire top floor of the old building to themselves.

As she drags me round the apartment, Tina keeps up a running commentary. "All the other floors are empty, the developers ran out of money or something. I guess we won't be here much longer. Shame really, we've spent a lot of money fixing it up."

The different between her life and that of the girls on the street is evident. The first room she shows me is elegant and minimally furnished with low, leather sofas and coffee tables with piles of porn magazines.

"The punters sit here and wait for me," she explains. "There's no need, really, but it racks up the suspense, gets them eager, gets them out quicker."

She throws open the second door to reveal a room that's the complete opposite of the one we've just left. It's small, over-heated and dominated by a double bed, festooned with cushions and throws. The curtains are closed, the light is low and the scent of heavily perfumed candles permeates the air.

"This is where I work – my office, if you like. Although I'm open all hours, within reason. Some punters try to draw things out a bit, but Noel sees them off. Not many people will argue with him."

I look over my shoulder to where he leans against the wall, arms folded, watching us.

"So Noel is …"

"Yeah, he's my pimp, Jilly … not that the lazy bastard does much to earn his keep these days. He had to break a guy's nose once, but I have quite a few regulars now through my website, so I don't get much aggro any more."

"You work from here all the time?"

"What?" Tina cackles. "You thought I stood on a street corner and got fucked in cars for a few quid? Those days are long gone for me, ducky. Mind you, I served my time on Forest Road. I don't look down on them girls."

The last room she shows me is a small photographic studio, complete with lights, painted backdrops featuring intertwined naked bodies and a mounted camera trained on a single chair. Tina reads my silence as admiration.

"I know, brilliant, innit? I can charge more in an hour in this room than I can in the other one. I just sit there with my legs open while the dirty old geezers snap away."

I don't understand why I'm here and turn towards the

main door, an apology already on my lips, "Look, Tina, this is not my thing. I don't know what Oliver told you, but my work's been mainly with the girls from Forest Road, documentary stuff, getting to know them on a personal level. I'm sorry, but I've got a lot on today."

She stands in front of me, blocking the way.

"You're judging me, ain't you? You think I'm hard-nosed, out for all I can get. If you got on well with all the girls, what's wrong with me, then?"

"Trust me, Tina, I'm not in a position to judge any-one. It's just not for me, OK? Anyway, you don't need a photographer, you must have loads of pictures if you're on the internet."

Noel eases himself off the wall and says to Tina, "I told you this was a crap idea."

And, to me, "I'll let you out."

Tina raises a hand to stop me and lets it fall again, a gesture of defeat while Noel waits, with exaggerated pa-tience, for me to leave. He makes my mind up for me.

"OK, then, Tina. What is it you want?" I ask her, turning my back on Noel. She gives a small smile.

Are these guys scoring points off each other?

We walk across a wide hall and into a large, open area. Windows run along one wall, shedding sunlight across a wooden floor. Kitchen units are built around a din-ing nook with a scrubbed wooden table and a Welsh dresser, full of mis-matched china and delft, while the other end of the room has an array of worn, cosy-looking armchairs and a large sofa in front of a wall-mounted television. Scattered around are bookcases, an exercise bike, piles of newspapers, video games on the floor, all the clutter of a family home.

A boy of about thirteen slouches in one of the chairs,

drawing on an iPad.

"This is our son, Leon." Tina attempts to introduce him but he concentrates on the tablet, ignoring his mother.

"Leon, please." The boy stands, already taller than his mother, throws me a filthy look and walks out.

It's OK. Leave him to me." Noel is hot on the boy's heels, his angry voice booming back into the room.

After an awkward few seconds, Tina rallies.

"I just wanted you to see how I really live. Out there – that's a job, ain't it? I put on a face, give them what they want and then I come in here, this is my home."

"And Leon – he's Noel's son?"

"Yeah, Noel's … my husband. He looks out for me, protects me like. We've been together since we was at school together, married for ten years now."

I drop my camera bag to the floor. "So what is you want?"

"I want a set of pictures for in here, like – you know – normal people have. Not sexy and all glammed up for the job, just me being natural-like."

"Family pictures, you mean?"

'Yeah, that's it, exactly. Will you do it?"

"What, with Leon and …" I nod towards the door where father and son had disappeared.

Noel pads back into the room, face stony. "Do the bloody pictures for her, will you? You're here now, and I'll pay you."

The offer of money makes up my mind for me.

So we do it.

Tina changes into a series of pretty dresses and casual clothes and I follow her around, snapping away every time she pauses to strike a pose. She cracks jokes, tells *risque* stories and I relax into it. Noel is ever-present and eventually consents to being in some of the photographs. He keeps the drinks flowing, offers food and, somehow, two hours have passed and a casual observer would think we're the best of friends.

Tina insists on Noel giving me a lift home, although he doesn't seem thrilled at the idea. I wait on the street while he fetches his car from the garage. He navigates the old-style, cigar-shaped Jaguar through the narrow streets as easily as though he were on a motorway. Following my directions, he drives down through the city and out the other side, past the ice stadium, and starts to climb towards Carlton.

Noel speaks for the first time. "What street do you want?"

I hesitate. "You can just drop me on the next corner, if you like."

I gather up my camera bag, a bunch of flowers Tina gave me and a carrier bag with a few dresses she'd thrust at me, saying carelessly, "They ain't much, I know you're taller, but I think they'll fit. I know how skint students can be."

Noel glances sideways at me. "What's up, girl, you're a bit jumpy."

"No, not really," I lie. "I've just remembered I need to call in on a friend before I go home. Can you let me out here, please?"

He shrugs, slows the car down and I hop out.

"OK. Let me know when the pictures are ready and I'll come and get you."

I force a smile, "Sure thing, Noel. Bye."

The big car moves off and I hurry back the way we came, stopping only to stuff the carrier bag of clothes into a handy bin. I'd love to keep them, but Rob won't have anything to do with "prossies" in the house and he knows I don't have the money to buy new clothes.

The afternoon drags as I half-heartedly work on my computer. Unable to concentrate, my head heavy with alcohol, my head droops and I sleep.

He picks me up in a bar. It's my first week as a student and the city is full of Freshers in fancy dress, all determined to drink until they either pass out or vomit. I'm nursing a small wine and reading a book, when he sits down beside me. "That looks a bit dull, don't it? Wouldn't you rather talk to me?"

As pick-up lines go, it's rubbish and he's quite a bit older than me, maybe middle thirties. But he's nice enough, with black curls and blue eyes, a bit like that old guy, David Essex. He keeps the drinks flowing and I go home with him. In the morning, he's gone when I wake up in his empty bed, which suits me fine. There's a note sellotaped to the bedroom door.

Sorry, I'm on the early shift. Didn't want to wake you. Help yourself to breakfast and pull the door shut when you leave. I'll be in the bar tonight after work, if you fancy it.

For a guy living on his own, the place is clean and tidy. There isn't much upstairs to look at. Just the bedroom and, across a small landing, another empty room. Downstairs, the layout is the same with a tiny hallway beneath the landing and, oddly, a narrow kitchen and bathroom built on, stretching out into a walled-in back yard.

I make toast and tea, have a shower and wash my hair in the cramped bathroom. Rob doesn't appear to have a hair dryer, so I plait my wet hair in its usual style and leave it to dry naturally. It's mid-morning by the time I'm dressed – no point in going into classes late – so I have a good rummage through his wardrobe and dresser.

Work clothes are piled on the floor of the wardrobe and I remember him telling me he was a printer. The dresser has expensive aftershave, and a couple of gold chains tucked in a drawer. I briefly consider stealing them but a plan is taking shape in my mind. I meet him in the bar that night and, within a few weeks, he asks me to move in with him. After a token resistance, I move my few belongings into what will be my home for the next three years.

I don't love Rob, but I know how to play my part. We go bowling, to the races, to football matches – all things he really enjoys and I profess to enjoy. I even pretend to like his oafish friend, Nige. It's not difficult. I live rent free and Rob converts the spare bedroom into a computer room for me, buying an iMac, an Epson printer and enough accessories to ensure I never have to worry about anything. In return, I make sure he had no cause to complain.

Then I make a mistake. Rob declares his love and asks me to marry him. I should have said yes. It would have kept him happy until I leave him, as I plan to do after my Degree Show.

I say no … and I laugh. Well, more of a nervous giggle.

I blame it on the fact I've drunk too much and my guard is down.

He takes it badly, becomes increasingly morose and begins to pick fault with nearly everything I do. He goes out drinking with Nige, comes home late and rants for hours, accusing me of using him.

Of course I am.

CHAPTER TWO

Time spent in my computer room is precious; a time to be alone without thinking about which face I need to show the world. As dusk begins to cast faint shadows, I return to the present and the need to get a meal ready for Rob. He expects to find his dinner on the table and a beer in the fridge when he gets home from work.

I run down to the chippy at the bottom of the street, buy two pieces of battered fish and throw together a salad from bits in the fridge. Tina's flowers and a lighted candle make the table look a bit special, hopefully a distraction from the scratch meal.

The minutes tick away and Rob doesn't arrive. I snuff the candle, cover the salad and put the fish in the microwave, ready to be reheated when he finally comes home. If I'm lucky, he's in the local pub with Nige, his drinking buddy and the owner of the printing company where they both work. That means he will only have had a couple of beers and the night can still be pleasant, the dinner not too ruined. Or they may have walked down into the city for a pub crawl, only coming home when the pubs throw them out. Nights like that can be bad.

I sit by the window in the dark and watch the street. An hour passes, I give up on him coming home early and rise to close the curtains and turn on the light

"What the hell are you doing, sitting in the dark?"

Rob's voice, from behind me, makes me jump. One of

his little tricks is to creep up the ginnel and come in by the back door.

"For God's sake, don't do that to me! You frightened me to death."

"Aw, take a joke, can't you, Jilly?"

His face is flushed and the smell of ale is strong in the room. He's in jovial mood for now but can easily become surly, so I smile and say, "You hungry? I've got some fish, won't be a minute."

He drops heavily into a chair at the table, waiting for his food. "And what did you get up to today? You know, while I was grafting and you were swanning about, as usual."

I call through from the kitchen, as I heat up the fish. "I went to photograph a girl, Tina, who lives in the Old Mill with her husband, Noel. Christie asked me to do it, as if I haven't enough to do at the moment, without going all the way to the Lace Market. No decent photographs, just the usual bedroom stuff."

He shifts in his seat, on the edge of anger. "So you just wasted another day. Why bloody do it, then, if you got nothing out of it?"

"Well, Christie was keen and he's half promised to find me a job after graduation."

"Fucking Christie. I hate that guy, no better than a pimp himself."

I bite back a retort. Silence is the only option when Rob gets to this stage. He grunts, his meal finished, and throws himself onto the sofa to watch television. In a short while, his eyelids flutter shut and he's asleep.

Great. Time to nip upstairs and find a picture for the catalogue before he wakes up. There are over two thousand photographs on my iMac, which document the girls' lives – standing on street corners, walking into court to face prostitution charges, getting kids ready for school and doing each other's hair to get ready for a night's work.

I don't get time to settle down with my photographs. Within ten minutes, I hear Rob in the kitchen, banging doors. He comes to the bottom of the stairs and shouts up, "Jilly babes, where's my other crate of beer?"

Beer. I forgot to top up his beer. My heart sinks. There's only one way this will end.

"You finished it, Rob, remember? We're going to buy some more at the weekend."

"Why didn't you get me some more today, if you knew I'd run out?"

"Sorry, I ran out of time –"

"You ran out of time? You've got time to be on that bloody computer."

Mentally kicking myself for forgetting the beer, I turn off the computer and go downstairs. Might as well get it over with.

"Couldn't you have picked some up at the beer-off on the way home from seeing your new friends?" He shifts into another gear. "Oh no, not a thought for me."

It's not necessary for me to answer, actually wiser not to. I just have to be there so he can point out my failings.

"Is she a prossy, as well? Of course she is. Did you go in her bedroom? You didn't sit on the sodding bed, did you?"

This is familiar ground. He picks on a small detail and builds it into a major argument. If I deny sitting on the bed, he will badger me until I 'admit' it. Easier to say I did. It will shorten his rant, although not by much.

I can't remember if I sat on the bed or not, but I nod my

head anyway.

"Course you did." He pushes past me, back to the kitchen, finds a whiskey bottle, left over from Christmas. "No decent girl would even go there. But you – you sat there – who knows what goes on there with any old Tom, Dick or Harry. It makes me sick to think about it."

He drinks from the bottle, sits down and settles in to put me straight.

"You know what your problem is? You're all take, take, take. You ain't never done a real day's work in your life. I work all the hours God sends so you can waste your time at uni, pretending to be a photographer."

I'm stung into answering, "I'm not wasting my time. Christie says if I get a good result, he'll take my portfolio down to his friend's gallery in London."

"Bullshit! You spent part of your first year talking to rape victims and getting the poor cows to let you photograph them. And what happened? Eh? What happened?"

He's on his feet again, his face close to mine, as he grasps my shoulders and shakes me. I twist away from him, back up against the wall. He follows, crowds me into a corner. My better judgement over-ruled by anger, I answer him.

"OK! The pictures weren't great. I got rotten marks. Is that what you want to hear? Now back off, Rob."

"And why were they rotten? Eh? Answer me!"

This is a conversation we've had many times before and I give him the answer he wants.

"Because I didn't know what I was doing."

"Too right you didn't. If you'd been through what those poor cows went through, you'd have understood them."

He pushes me away in disgust and sits down at the table

with the whiskey bottle. I stand in my corner, silent,
hating him.

The biscuit man sits at the kitchen table, talking to Mam.

She looks beautiful, with bright red lipstick and blue stuff on her eyes. Her hair is all curly. She's just like a fairy princess.

The biscuit man says, "Hello, little Jilly. Have you had a good day at school?"

"It was all right. I wish I had some friends. Nobody wants to play with me."

"But you've got me, haven't you? I'm your friend. Look what I've brought you."

"Are they Jaffa Cakes?"

"Only the best for my Jilly. Come on, I'll open them for you."

I hesitate. "My name isn't Jilly. I don't like it."

He smiles. "OK, Jill, then."

I stretch out my hand for the biscuits.

Mam smiles and goes away.

The biscuit man has scratchy hands and he smells funny.

CHAPTER THREE

Rob is still sleeping when I slide out of bed and tiptoe across the tiny landing to the computer room. I close the door gently so he won't hear the Mac booting up. His temper had raged for nearly an hour last night, much worse than anything previously, and I didn't get any files to Maria and Charlie for the catalogue. My inbox is full of angry messages from them, telling me I have until ten o'clock this morning to get a picture across or they'll stick something in from last term.

The memory card I used at Tina's lies on the desk and my fingers hover over it. Should I take a look? Just in case? I know there won't be anything worthwhile on there, but still …. I shove the card into the reader and start downloading the photographs, impatiently waiting as the large files slowly appear. As I thought, some pretty good candid pictures of Tina, laughing and mugging for the camera, nothing out of the ordinary.

Then I catch my breath. Almost afraid to look, I backspace to the previous picture. And there it is. Tina sits cross-legged on the bed in her claustrophobic little 'office', her head thrown back as she laughs at something I've just said. A blurred Noel looms menacingly in the background, seeming to threaten the laughing girl.

And here's the kicker. Tina has no knickers on and her vagina is clearly visible to all the world. There's no doubt in my mind that this is the picture, the *only* picture, I want in the catalogue. I give it a quick edit and fire it off to Maria, just as the door opens and Rob shambles in, yawning. I hastily drag the cursor, put the computer to sleep.

"Good morning, Jilly babes, you're up nice and early."

I ignore the *Jilly babes*, which he knows I hate, relieved last night's rage has gone, if only for the moment. We walk down to the kitchen, where I scramble eggs and fry bacon for him as he talks about his upcoming day at work.

I only half-listen to him, remember to throw in the odd "Oh yeah?" and "Really?", when I catch the words *degree show* in the middle of his monologue.

"Sorry, Rob, back up there … what did you just say?"

"I wish you'd listen when I'm talking to you. Robinson's had a flood and their printing presses are down, so Nige got the job of printing your Degree Show catalogue. The artwork's coming in later this morning and I'm going to help Nige in the studio to get it ready for the press. Which picture have you got in it, by the way?"

"I was going to tell you about it. It's one of Tina –"

"Not another one of your 'conceptual portraits', is it?"

A thinly disguised sneer. I shrug and don't answer, last night's argument still fresh in my mind.

Rob finishes his breakfast. "Ah well, I'd better get off. Going to be a busy day." He pats his pockets. "Jilly, have you seen my phone?"

"Living room?" I suggest. "Maybe the bedroom?"

"Would it hurt you to help me find the bloody thing? I'm going to be late for work."

He runs upstairs, while I move cushions and feel down the back of the sofa. There it is. Just as my fingers close on the phone, I hear his footsteps in the computer room, followed seconds later by a crash as something heavy hits the floor.

"Jilly! Come up here. Now!"

My heart jumps. Please God, not another row. In the computer room, my chair lies up-ended in the corner. Rob has touched either the mouse or the keypad and woken the iMac. On the screen is the picture of Tina, where I'd left it earlier.

"What the fuck is this garbage?" He grabs my arm and drags me over to the computer. "Tell me you didn't take that … it's bloody disgusting … it's pornography." He pushes my face towards the screen and I fight to keep my balance.

"It's Tina …"

"I don't care who the fuck it is … did you take it?"

Rob's face is white with temper. I try to speak evenly, but my voice is small and shaky. "Yes, I did. I didn't know –"

He's way beyond listening to anything I have to say.

His voice rises to a scream. "Of course you bloody knew! I ain't having that filth in my house!" He hits the delete button and the picture disappears off the screen. "I ain't bloody stupid, either. Where's the memory card?"

My eyes flick to the reader. Rob follows my gaze, pulls the card out and stuffs it in his pocket.

"Let's get something straight, shall we?" He tightens his grip on my arm. "All this stuff belongs to me, even your precious camera. None of it's in your name. But I ain't attached to it like you are. Sort yourself out or I'll take a hammer to it."

Without warning, he twists my arm behind my back, and shoves me away from him. I crash to the ground, huddling there as he towers over me.

"You stupid bitch, you disgust me. I do everything I can to help you, and this is what you do. Well, they say if you lie down with dogs ... What else has been going on at Tina's?" Again, a sneer as he says her name. "Get friendly with Noel, did you?"

Rob's verbal abuse, vicious and callous, can be ridden out until he exhausts himself. This escalation into physical violence is new.

So I cry. Usually, if I cry and abase myself enough, he calms down and eventually forgives me for whatever misdemeanour I've committed.

Not this time. He walks away from me, stops by the door and mutters to himself. Just as I begin to get up from the floor, he comes back. I freeze, afraid of antagonising him further.

Rob's voice is hoarse. "No decent woman takes stuff like that. You've been round them prossies too long, you're no better than they are."

He lashes out with his foot and his heavy work boot catches me on my side, sending me sprawling back onto the floor.

I curl into a ball, fearful of another kick, and whimper, "Rob, please, don't do this." Mercifully, he stops and picks up his phone from where I dropped it.

He kneels down beside me, speaking softly, as though the violence has bled the anger from him.

"Can you see what you've driven me to? Take this as a warning, I ain't having any more of it."

His heavy boots thud on the stairs and, seconds later, the door slams as he leaves the house.

I lie on the floor, arms cradling my body against the pain, and hear his voice echo in my head.

You disgust me. You're disgusting.

My new friend, Rosemary, and I meet at the school gates every day and walk in together. Her Mummy stands with her until I get there. Mam says Rosemary's just a baby. Big girls my age don't need walking to school.

We sit together at our special desks. Rosemary is very clever, she's better than me at sums and she can spell words with six letters in them. I want her to like me, so I whisper, while Miss is talking to one of the boys who's been naughty. "I know how to get Jaffa cakes."

Rosemary's eyes light up, she loves Jaffa cakes, just like me. "Oh, tell me. I want some, too."

"Well ..." It's easier to show her, so I start to walk my fingers up her leg until they meet her knicker elastic.

"Ewww ... what are you doing? That's disgusting."

And Miss is hurrying over.

CHAPTER FOUR

The sunlight travels round the room and lands on my foot. It must be mid-morning. I heave myself to my feet, wincing against the sharp twinge in my side, and start to put the room to rights. The iMac has gone to sleep and I tap it awake. Rob forgot to empty the trash can when he deleted the picture. I retrieve it and save it to a flash card. A red dot pops up on my mailbox icon and I click on it. It's from Christie.

just seen the picture, bloody amazing, going on front cover, talk later

I read the message again, all twelve words of it. Yes, that's definitely what it says; my picture is going on the front cover of the catalogue. I say it out loud, to make it real, "The front cover, the bloody front cover!" Giddy with excitement, I do an impromptu little dance round the room. Or try to. Pain lances through my side, bringing me to an abrupt stop and I drop into my chair, now the right way up.

Oh God, what's Rob going to say when he sees it? What's he going to do?

I want to hurt him back, make him pay for what he did. For a few moments, I dwell on the pleasure it would give me to smash my fist into his sneering face. Not for long. The reality is that I'm frightened of being here when he gets home. He's bigger and stronger than me; thoughts of physical revenge are useless.

My options are few, practically non-existent. Rob likes me to spend my spare time with him, or sometimes with Nige and his wife, Lynn. I don't have any friends among the other students, who might let me crash on their floor or sofa. It's nearly the end of term, though, and some students have already left for the long holiday. Maybe I can find a vacant room, already paid for, to tide me over until after my Degree Show. There's a blackboard in the university canteen with messages scrawled all over it. It's a long shot but worth a try and I can get a sandwich at the same time.

A misty rain is falling as I leave the house. Huddling under my umbrella, I walk down the hill to the main road. The chippy on the corner has a window with postcards stuck on it. Lost cats, builder wanted, yoga classes, and occasionally a flat share pops up. I stop to have a look, but there's nothing, only a three-bedroomed house to let, which raises another problem. What am I going to do for money? Rob handles all the bills, we order groceries online and, when I need money for any reason, he'll hand over a couple of twenties.

My side aches and I regret the impulse to walk to the university. A taxi cruises the other side of the road and I flag him down, figuring I might as well spend some of the money Noel gave me.

The foyer in the main university building is heaving with students dragging suitcases on wheels. My hopes rise; maybe I'll strike lucky in my search for a room.

"Hey, Jilly, over here!" Christie calls me to his table as I push my way into the crowded canteen.

He's buzzing. "I've been up most of the night with Maria and Charlie, getting the artwork ready. Only had three hours sleep."

I smile weakly, attempt a small joke. "Come on, you love it."

"Yeah, I know, but it was hairy for a while. We had a last minute scramble this morning to change the cover, when Maria showed me your picture."

My lack of enthusiasm brings him down a bit. "What, aren't you pleased?"

Yeah, I'm delighted. Just going to get another kicking when Rob sees it.

"Yes, of course I am." *Smile.* "It's brilliant! Sorry, just a bit tired."

"Late night, was it?"

"Yeah, something like that. I'm grateful, really, can't believe I've got the front cover."

"Good, you had me worried for a minute. This could mean big things for you, Jilly. I've drawn up a mailing list of all the major photographic studios. As soon as the catalogues are posted out, we'll follow up with your c.v."

Some of my former euphoria returns. "Thanks, Christie. You're a star."

He beams. "I know! Right, I'm off to the printers' to see the proofs before the catalogue goes to press."

I wave him off and allow myself a short-lived smile at the thought of Rob having to be polite to Christie, before I check the blackboard. Nothing. I try asking a few people if they can help me, but with no luck. At least the rain has stopped when I eventually admit defeat and leave the building.

I call in to Boots the Chemists for painkillers and sit in Slab Square for a while, watching the pigeons and the buskers. Would one of the girls from Forest Road take me in? Maybe, but their lives are complicated enough already and I don't want to run the risk of crossing an angry pimp. Better the devil you know. It seems that, short of sleeping on a park bench, every line of thought leads back to the same thing. I have to go back to Rob's and try to work something out, do whatever is necessary to carry on living there for a little longer.

You can do this, you've been through much worse.

Rosemary's not at the school gate today. I wait until the very last minute but she doesn't come. Maybe she's sick. Miss shouts at me to hurry and I run to hang my coat up.

In class, Miss calls me to her desk. "You'll be sitting with Marie now, Jill. Rosemary's mummy wants her to make new friends."

I don't understand. "But I'm her friend. She doesn't need new ones."

I look round the class and see Rosemary sitting at the back. I wave, but she doesn't look at me.

She never waits for me at the school gates again.

When I tell Mam she says, "You don't need friends anyway. They just shit on you in the end."

I know Mam says bad words sometimes, but she's never said one to me. I feel big tears coming.

"And before I forget," Mam is already walking out of the room. "Your tea's in the kitchen. Stay in there until I tell you to come out. I'm going to be busy."

Today's been really horrible. Rosemary isn't my friend any more, Mam said a bad word to me, and, when I go into the kitchen, the biscuit man isn't even here.

CHAPTER FIVE

I will myself to remain calm as I wait for Rob to come home. Whatever it takes, I'm determined to make my peace with him, at least in the short term.

The house is clean like it's never been before, there's beer in the fridge and his favourite dinner waits in the oven. Instead of its usual single plait, my hair is curled loosely, falling to my waist just the way he likes it and I'm wearing a frilly, floaty dress.

The key turns in the lock. My heart sinks when Rob walks in with Nige, each carrying a six pack of beer. Judging by their breath, they've already been to the pub and are well on their way to being drunk.

"Jilly babes!" Rob is upbeat. "How's my best girl? Come and give your old man a kiss!"

What's going on? I didn't bloody imagine this morning; I can still feel the bruises on my side. I don't move, my feet rooted to the spot, but he's unfazed and envelopes me in a bear hug. Over his shoulder, Nige narrows his eyes at me in amusement, like he knows something I don't. Rob releases me and, before I can decide how to react, he and Nige sit down at the dining table.

"I've brought Nige back for dinner." Rob's smile is wide. "You don't mind, do you? His other half is off to Bingo and didn't leave him as much as a sandwich. Come on, then, get some food on the table."

I resist the urge to slam the plates down on the table as

I serve them and watch as Nige tucks in to my dinner. Neither man notices I'm not eating. As I clear the plates away, Rob suddenly says, "Beer, Jilly babes, more beer. Get one for yourself and join us."

He knows I don't drink beer, but I pop a can and sit down at the table. Nige nods at me and lifts his beer. "Cheers" He settles back in his chair, never taking his eyes off me.

"See, it's like this," Rob begins, also fixing me with a steady gaze. "Me and Nige, here, we don't know a lot about prossies, so we thought, who better to tell us about them than Jilly babes. We're interested, aren't we, Nige?"

"Very interested, Rob. I've never felt the need to be with one, myself. I'm well looked after at home, if you know what I mean." He cups his crotch in one hand. "And, then, you never know what you might catch, do you?"

"Good point, Nige. I'm glad you said that. I mean, even sitting on the bed where they do their business, you might pick up something nasty."

Their double act sounds well rehearsed, so I just sit and take it. They're both on the verge of laughter, but I know Rob's not far from losing control.

Surely he won't hit me while Nige is here?

Rob's just getting into his stride. "Well, Jilly, cat got your tongue? What about a few juicy details?" His face gets redder and the false humour begins to slip when I don't answer him.

"Nothing to say? Of course she ain't, Nige. She's got no idea about real life. I tell her all the time." He gestures towards me, spraying beer over the table. "Spends her time hanging round Women's Centres, talking to the silly tarts and then comes home to her safe little house, provided by yours truly, and forgets all about them, drinking her Prosecco –"

"Also provided by you, mate," Nige eggs him on.

"Exactly."

"I feel for you, Rob, I really do." I burn as Nige puts in another twopence worth. "I couldn't believe my eyes when I looked at that picture today. Pure filth, it was. And she sits there like butter wouldn't melt. The guys on the press were having a right old snigger."

"You think I don't know?" Rob's words begin to slur and he holds the edge of the table for support. "And then that poncy Christie turns up. He actually asked me if I were proud of her. I wanted to punch his face in."

Nige winds him up a bit more. "You should have heard the things they were saying about Jill and her prossy friends. They were wondering if, you know, Jill likes to …."

Rob caves in to the alcohol, his mood changes from belligerent to tearful and he cries, heaving great, dramatic sobs.

"Now look what you've done to him," Nige snarls at me. "You're no better than a slut and you wouldn't even make a good one of them."

With an enormous effort, I resist pouring my untouched drink over Nige's bald head. My hatred for them is strong and silent but they're oblivious, Rob on the verge of passing out and Nige puffed up with self-righteousness.

With Rob in tears, their fun is over for the evening. He gets to his feet, staggers into the living room and collapses on the sofa, where he falls asleep instantly. I know he's finished for the evening. and will probably stay there all night.

Nige leans on the door frame and stares at me speculatively, in a way he has never done before.

I open the front door. "Time for you to go, I think we've had enough drama for one evening."

For a moment I think he isn't going to go, but he walks unsteadily to the door.

"Yeah, right. I'll leave the poor sod with you. Good night, *Jilly babes*."

I double lock the door, cover Rob with a blanket and climb the stairs to get ready for bed. I stand in front of the mirror in the bathroom and my reflection looks back in contempt.

The biscuit man, Mick, lives in the back of his DVD rental shop. He looks up from his magazine when he sees me slip in by the back door.

"Jill! For fuck's sake, you can't be in here. Get out before the missus sees you."

He jumps up from his chair, grabs my arm and tries to push me back out of the door.

"Go on, then. You do that, and I'm straight round to the front of the shop to tell her all about your visits when I was a little kid. Got any Jaffa Cakes now, Mick?"

All colour flees from his face.

"Why are you doing this, Jill? Wasn't I always good to you?"

I sneer, "I'm being good to you now, keeping quiet about what you did to me."

"I can't keep giving you money, you've got to stop coming here."

"Yes, you can. How much did you pay my mam to let you wait for me in the kitchen?"

The door that leads through to the shop is closed. I stretch out a hand as if to open it.

"All right! I'll give you the money. But this is the last time, do you hear?"

I hear him, but I will *be back.*

CHAPTER SIX

A gold bag with an oversized bow – one of Rob's *I'm sorry* presents – sits on the hall table as I open the front door. Although he hasn't referred to the drunken episode with Nige, Rob has been quieter in the last week, confining himself to an odd jibe about prossies. I know he's behind the living room door, waiting for my grateful thanks. The sooner I open it, the sooner the whole sorry charade will be over, so I rip off the tape and get ready to smile in fake delight.

It's not his usual kind of gift. Instead of a floaty scarf or my favourite bubble bath, I pull out a matching bra and panties set in scarlet and black lace. The panties are crotchless and the bra has holes to expose the wearer's nipples.

Rob comes out from behind the door. "Like 'em? I thought that were more your style now. Can't wait to see you in 'em. Come on, don't keep me waiting."

There's a sly smile on his face and a look I can't pin down.

"What have you bought these for? They're tacky."

"Well, you and your prossy friends would know about that." He loses the smile. "I want you to put them on and I want you to do it now."

So he intends to humiliate me. Silly me, to think he was being remorseful. I brace myself for an afternoon in bed and turn towards the stairs. "OK, if that's what you want."

"No, not in the bedroom." He holds the living room door open. I shrug, walk past him and pull my tee shirt over my head with my back to him.

"Aww, come on, Jilly babes. Don't be a spoilsport, let me enjoy it, eh?"

He takes my arm and turns me round, eyes shining with anticipation. "Don't you like your present?"

When Rob is in this keyed-up mood, it usually means trouble for me. I hesitate, then decide to take the line of least resistance and slowly remove the rest of my clothes.

"That's my girl," he says, when I finally stand naked in front of him. "Give us a bit of a twirl, then."

My mind screams at me to tell him to fuck off. My body turns in a full circle.With my eyes fixed on the wall, I bend, pull on the panties, fasten the bra and stand mute, waiting to see what fresh hell he's got in store for me.

"Mmm, looking good, babes." He eyes me up and down. "Shake your hair out, let's get the whole effect."

It's all a bit ridiculous now, like some kind of sleazy peepshow. I choke back hysterical laughter while I undo my plait and let my hair fall to my waist. Defiantly, I throw my head back and close my eyes, striking a stolen-from-Tina pose.

Rob says, "What do you think, then?"

I open my eyes, resigned to take part in whatever his silly game is. He's looking towards the door and I follow his gaze as he repeats, "Well, what do you think? How much would you pay for it?"

Nige stands in the doorway, gazing lasciviously at my exposed body and stroking his crotch with one hand. I scrabble for my clothes, spewing out garbled curses,

"You bastards, you dirty fucking bastards –"

They both explode with laughter, slapping their knees and wiping the tears from their eyes.

"Let's see," Nige says, when he draws breath. "Maybe a tenner, although – as she's new to the job – mebbe I should get a freebie to break her in."

This piece of wit sets them off again. I resist the urge to run from the room and walk past them with as much dignity as I can muster, considering I'm wearing crotchless panties and a nipple-exposing bra. At the bottom of the stairs, my nerve breaks and I run up to the bedroom. The door doesn't have a lock and I lean my weight against it, my eyes searching the room for something to use as a barricade.

Rob calls after me, "Come on, babes, it were just a fucking joke. No hard feelings, eh?"

Nige whoops and cheers from downstairs, and calls up, "I didn't mean owt, Jill, you're probably worth twenty quid."

A few minutes later, the door slams behind them. They're off to the pub, presumably to hatch up another plan to teach me a lesson. I have a few hours respite before Rob returns, shored up with alcohol and ready to resume hostilities.

Mam and Mick's wife are sitting at the kitchen table in stony silence when I walk in. I'm halfway though the door when I see them and immediately start to back off.

"Oh no, you don't, lady." Mam springs to her feet and grabs my plait, as I try to flee. "You're not going anywhere. Mrs Coulter here wants to talk to you."

This is surreal. Mam, despised whore of this parish, has ganged up on me with the wife of one of her longstanding customers. Not to mention that she sold me to him at the age of seven.

Mrs Coulter weighs in. "You've been sneaking round the back of the shop to see my Mick. People are talking. Whatever's going on, it stops now, do you hear? I'm not having my good name ruined by the likes of you." She shoots a murderous glance at Mam. "Either of you."

"It's nothing to do with me." Mam strives for righteous indignation, but Mrs Coulter ignores her. She's said her piece, done what she came for, so she rises from her chair to leave. As she passes me, she hisses, "You're dirt, both of you."

I'm not taking that from her, not after what her husband did to me. I grab her arm, pull her close and whisper in her ear. What he did. What it cost him.

She pulls herself free and runs from the kitchen, leaving the door swinging open behind her. As she reaches the garden gate, I call after her.

"Tell Mick he owes me another twenty!"

CHAPTER SEVEN

I'm on the floor, arms wrapped round my drawn up knees. Sometime during the night, my head has fallen forward and pain lances through my head and shoulders. It takes an age to loosen my muscles as I drag myself awake. Out of the corner of my eye, I can see the despised underwear lying on the floor, where I threw it last night.

Light glimmers round the edges of the drawn curtains. Early morning, then. Where's Rob? I heave myself to my feet, jerk the chair from under the door knob and open the door. Clattering noises and the smell of frying bacon. He's in the kitchen. I have to go through there to get to the bathroom. Might as well get it over with. I clutch my dressing gown round me, push my feet into my slippers and creep downstairs.

The table in the dining room has two places laid. Rob hears me coming, and pokes his head out of the kitchen. "Morning, Jilly b– , Jill. Did I wake you? You was exhausted last night, so I slept on the sofa. Thought I'd treat you to breakfast, seeing as I was up early anyway."

He's freshly showered and shaved; his wet hair clings closely to his head and his eyes are bright and clear. As I stand bemused, he comes over and kisses my cheek. "Nip in to the shower, your food's nearly ready."

Even for Rob, this change of mood is very strange. I shuffle past him to the bathroom. A fresh towel hangs on the rail and I climb in the shower, grateful for the hot water to relax my aching muscles. After a night on the floor, my hair is tangled and messy; I give it quick shampoo and tie it into a plait while still wet.

I give myself a mental shake. Whatever new game Rob's playing, it's best to have my wits about me.

Just as he promised, a cooked breakfast and a fresh cup of tea wait for me on the table. We sit and eat in silence, my mind in overdrive as I try to work out what he's up to. I'm determined not to speak first and, eventually, he puts down his knife and fork.

"Jill, I've been a fucking idiot."

Much as I want to agree with him, I keep my eyes down and play my usual silent waiting game.

When he realises I'm not going to answer, Rob speaks again. "I don't know what to say, where to start. OK, listen, I'm sorry for what me and Nige did last night. It were stupid and we shouldn't have done it."

You got that one right.

"I ain't making excuses, but what you did, sending that picture in, embarrassing me in front of me mates –"

Furious that he's turning the blame to me, I cut across his attempt at an apology. "So, it's all my fault, as usual. Is that what you're saying?"

I brace myself for the rant that's sure to follow, but Rob checks himself, stays calm. "No, I don't mean that, honest. I just want to tell you that I'm ashamed of meself."

He's ashamed? Rob is apologising?

"Look, I know you barred the door of the bedroom last night. I crept up the stairs, thought you was in bed, and then I couldn't get in. I were shocked to think you was frightened of me."

"I wasn't bloody frightened!" I burst out. "I thought you

and Nige were coming back to have another go at me. I sat on the floor all night, trying to stay awake."

"Aww, babe." Rob reaches out and tries to take my hand, but I bat it away. He can't just say sorry and think that makes everything all right. This has gone on long enough. I push my chair back and start to rise, only to stop when I look at Rob.

He's crying.

"What's this? Another one of your games? Is Nige hiding in the other room, ready to jump out at me?" I won't be taken in by his cheap tricks. "It must be a good one, if you went to all the trouble of making breakfast."

He doesn't move or answer and I drop back down onto my chair, as my anger loses momentum. "This has to stop, Rob. I can't go on living here. I'm on edge all the time wondering what you're going to do next."

"I know." His voice is low and he looks up at me. "I'm not a clever person, Jill. Oh, I'm good at my job, one of the best, actually, ask Nige. But you – you make me feel … stupid, no, not stupid … like I'm not good enough for you, like you was looking down your nose at me."

It's been a long time since we had an honest conversation. I want to believe him. I do.

Don't be stupid, Jilly. It's a trick. He kicked you. He and Nige humiliated you.

No, he isn't going to hurt me again. I harden my face, say, "So we're back to blaming me, are we?"

Rob sighs. "All right. I deserved that. But can't you remember how good we was together when you first moved in? We had good times, didn't we? I just want to go back to them days." He tries to take my hand again and this time, I let him. "Yeah, I know, things went too far. I felt pushed away, like you was only here because I buy you stuff."

His words hit home, more telling because he's not shouting or threatening me.

"I didn't ask for any of it, did I?"

"No, love, you didn't. I just wanted to help you." Rob hesitates for a moment. "And, well, I *am* proud of your photography, really I am. It's just – I can't get my mind round the things you do with the pr– girls. Why can't you just take nice pictures of the countryside or something?"

"Oh, Rob!" I smile and shake my head.

"You see?" He takes my other hand. "We *could* get back to how it was. I'm not the bad guy here, honest."

But what happens when he gets drunk again?

I start to pull my hands away and he tightens his grip. "No, don't go, babe. There's something else. I've got the day off work. Nige said it was best I wasn't there when they printed the cover in case the guys … well, you know what they're like, taking the piss."

"And that's it, isn't it, Rob? We'll never get past that, will we? You're never going to forget that bloody picture, are you?"

"I can try, can't I? You won't be seeing those – people – any more and we'll be able to put it behind us. Here …"

He takes something out of his pocket and drops it on the table. My memory card. "Just to show you I'm going to be different."

It's an empty gesture. I have the picture of Tina safely stored on a flash card and all the others from the session on my iMac. I mutter thanks and get up from the table.

Rob isn't finished. "What I were going to say, will you come out with me for the day? Go on a date, like. Just be friends."

The long, pink limousine noses into the square, rock music blaring from the open windows. It pulls up in front of Rosemary's house and three of the guys from my class emerge in sharp suits. I watch from behind the net curtain in Mam's living room. Here come the girls, self-conscious in their glamorous evening dresses, followed by their smug mothers who record every moment on their smartphones and cameras. Balloons and streamers are tied to the ostentatious car and neighbours come out to gape at the spectacle.

Mam comes into the room behind me. "Why aren't you ready? Whatsisname'll be here soon to pick you up."

There is no whatsisname, there never was. Nobody was going to ask the daughter of the local whore to be his date. But the invention of a boy eager to take me to the prom had prompted Mam to double her customers for a few days, so she could present me with a small bundle of banknotes to buy a 'knock 'em dead' dress.

Money's good. It's my ticket out of this village. I haven't been able to save much since Mick and his wife left town.

Rosemary is crossing the square to speak to our next-door neighbour and pose for his photographs. Her blonde ponytail swings and her white dress swirls round her tanned legs as she walks. She looks beautiful and … clean. My throat closes and I sniff back tears.

I turn from the window. Mam reads my intention. "Jilly, don't." But I'm out of the door and down the garden path to intercept Rosemary.

"You look great," I choke out, no idea what to say next. She keeps walking, without even the smallest flicker to acknowledge me. As she passes me, I call her name, "Rosemary", and she hesitates for a fraction of a second before she smiles for the neighbour, who has his camera ready.

Mam tries to touch my arm when I walk back up the path,

easy tears in her eyes.
I push past her. "Don't touch me."
I don't need her. I don't need anyone.

CHAPTER EIGHT

I try really hard. We ride the Big Wheel in the city square, soaring high above the Council House and its stone lions, eat hot dogs and drink warm beer in plastic cups. Rob buys me a book of Robert Mapplethorpe's photographs in Waterstones, raising his eyebrows when I kiss him on the cheek. In the Castle, he patiently tags along as I explore the art galleries and buy postcards in the gift shop. His phone rings a few times, but he shuts it down, saying this is my day.

A group of girls blocks the pavement, cameras held aloft, photographing the old buildings. We step into the road to avoid them and Rob smiles. "See? You could do summat like that. Maybe get a job with the Council."

I return the smile, to take the edge off my words. "I know you're trying to help, but I don't want to take pictures of landscapes or buildings. Neither do I want to photograph pets or weddings, before you get to them."

His mouth turns down and I hold my breath, but he raises a smile and says, "OK, point taken. Can we pop in here for a drink?" He nods towards the pub behind us. "I want to talk to you."

There's a free table near one of the windows and Rob fetches a beer and a glass of wine while I sit down. He sinks half his pint in one go, before he starts.

"I meant what I said this morning, babe, about putting things behind us. I want to make a go of it again. It's just – don't get me wrong, you've done well with your photography, in spite of what I said – but I want you to make me a promise so we can start over, like."

"I'm not giving up photography, Rob, not after working three years to get my degree."

"No, no, I don't want you to. I'm sure you'll get a good job in a camera shop or something –"

"For God's sake, can you stop with setting up jobs for me?"

"All right." He's quick to placate me. "I'm sorry. Now can I tell you what I want?"

The good mood between us hangs by a thread and I back off.

"OK. Go ahead."

"Well, now your uni time is nearly over, will you promise me that you won't see the prossies – I mean, the girls – any more? You shouldn't be mixing with them, anyway, and I've taken enough stick at the factory over that photograph. So, what do you think? Fresh start?"

I manage to keep a smile on my face as he sits there expectantly. It's an effort not to blurt out the first words that rise to my lips. I take a sip of my wine to bring my temper under control and buy a little time. In the past few months, he's verbally abused me, kicked me, and humiliated me in front of Nige more than once. Now, he would like to control who I see?

I'll see you in hell first, you bastard.

No harm in keeping him waiting. "You bought the wrong wine, by the way. Could you just change it for Pinot Grigio, please?"

He sighs, but hustles to the bar and returns with a fresh glass of wine. "Well?"

"I don't think that's a problem, Rob. There's no need to

see any of them, now my project's over."

"Awwww, that's great, babe. I knew you'd see sense."

"No problem." Time for my little test. " While we're clearing the air, I've got a request of my own. Can we see a bit less of Nige? I don't like the way he looks at me; he makes me feel uncomfortable."

Rob drains his pint. "Sorry, babe, no can do. One, he's my boss. Two, he's my best mate. Not exactly the same as a bunch of prossies, is it?" He stands. "I'm glad we got that settled. Come on, then, I want to get a bet on before we go home."

The betting shop is located down a steep flight of stairs. I opt to wait on the street as Rob goes down to place his bets. He'll be a little while, so I browse through my apps to pass the time. Pictures of kittens and sunsets, interspersed with jokes and political rants, scroll past, but I don't really see them.

I'm mentally kicking myself. How nearly I was sucked in to the new, improved Rob. My imagination's in overdrive; I picture Rob telling Nige how easy it was to get me to toe the line. Well, two can play at that game. I calculate how long I need before I can leave the city. Three weeks to the Degree Show plus a few weeks to put feelers out for work in a studio, depending on my results. I'm gambling on a First, from hints that Christie has dropped. So, two months at the most –

My thoughts are interrupted by a light touch on my arm. I look up. It's Tina, dressed down in jeans and tee shirt. Noel stands behind her, laden with shopping bags bearing designer labels.

Tina hugs me. "Jilly! We've been wondering how you was, when we didn't hear from you."

A genuine smile tugs at the corners of my mouth. "I'm

so sorry. I should have been in touch sooner but, you know ..." I search for an excuse other than *My boyfriend kicked me in the guts.*

'Never mind, we've found you now." Tina pulls out her phone, chattering nineteen-to-the-dozen, as usual. "Give me your number and we'll sort out a time for you to come over. How did the pictures turn out? I can't wait to see them."

Rob's words ring in my ears, *you shouldn't be mixing with them*, but I can't see a way of refusing to give Tina the number, so I recite it as she keys it in to her phone.

"Yes, the pictures are great. I think you'll be pleased with them." I keep one eye on the stairs, watching for Rob's return. "I'm sorry, Tina, I'm late, got to go. Ring me, we'll definitely get together."

"Yeah, we'll do it soon," she calls after me as I rush off in the opposite direction.

A minute later, I hurry back towards the bookmaker's. Tina and Noel are gone and Rob waits on the pavement. "Where was you? I thought you'd done a runner."

"No, just doing a bit of window shopping while I waited." I feign interest in the betting slip he holds in his hand. "Anything good?"

"Nah, probably another bunch of losers. Let's go, then. I'm famished."

He takes hold of my arm and we leave the square, heading for home.

She's drunk again, slumped over the kitchen table, crying sticky, mascara tears. Nobody understands her, apparently. "The most beautiful girl in the village, I was. Men fell over themselves to take me out. I could pick and choose any of them."

I've heard it all before. "Yeah, OK, Mam. Sleep it off. You'll feel better in the morning. I'm off to bed."

Her hand shoots out and grabs my wrist as I walk past her. "You don't believe me, do you? Look, I'll show you."
She scrabbles in her handbag, sending the contents across the table and on to the floor. "Here it is!" I take the photograph from her. She's right. She was beautiful.
"Mam." I'm lost for words. For a couple of minutes, as we look at the young, vibrant woman in the battered photograph, there's no anger or resentment between us.
Then she speaks. "That's you, Jilly. Hold it up and look in the mirror. You're exactly the same age as I was then."
I recoil in horror. "No!" Because if the photograph reflects me now, what am I looking at across the kitchen table?

CHAPTER NINE

I keep my phone in my pocket, muted and set to vibrate, but Tina doesn't text or call.

Rob and I settle into an uneasy truce. He makes his usual jibes about prossies in the guise of jokes and I pretend not to notice or care. Occasionally, Nige comes home with him at lunchtime and both men are exaggeratedly polite to me. And I count off the days in my head.

On Monday, Rob is quiet over breakfast, and doesn't ramble on with his usual monologue. He rises from the table to leave for work and says, "I'll not be back until late tonight. We've got a big reprint on because the colour was wrong on one of the sections. Nige thinks it was my sodding fault, so it's a ten-hour job. Drop me off a few sandwiches in a bit, will you?"

Without waiting for an answer, he slams out of the door.

Ten hours to myself! I've been waiting for an opportunity to get some pictures to Tina. This is perfect. I make a fresh mug of tea, ignore the breakfast dishes and head upstairs to the computer room. In the next hour, I print out six pictures with a fresh, candid appeal and tape them into cream coloured mounts. I'm pleased with their natural look and I'm sure Tina will be, as well. I hesitate over the photograph that Rob hated so much, but decide against it. I haven't told Tina about it yet and I'm not sure whether she and Noel will like it.

I wrap the pictures into a brown paper parcel and go back down to make Rob's sandwiches. My hand hovers over a beer in the fridge. Rob often sneaks a can into work, but Nige has a strict rule about his operators drinking while running the machines, so I leave it there. My phone buzzes just as I'm about to leave the house. It's Rob, abrupt and bad-tempered. "Have you made my sandwiches yet?"

"Yes, I'm on my way."

"I hope you've made plenty and don't forget a couple of beers, yeah?"

"But Nige –"

"Never mind bloody Nige. I need a drink. This is a nightmare of a day."

"OK." I close the call and go back to the fridge for the beers.

It's an uphill walk to the printshop. I struggle to carry Rob's rucksack, my camera bag and the parcel of pictures for Tina. The door of the small office is open but there's no one in there. I hesitate, not sure if I should go on to the shopfloor to find Rob, when Nige taps my shoulder. Before I can stop myself, I flinch and move away from him. Perhaps I'm paranoid but he gives me the creeps.

"Aren't you the touchy one?" His smile could be a sneer, I can't tell. "Here." He shoves a carrier bag into my hand, with a few of the Degree Show catalogues inside. "I was going to give these to Rob tonight, but maybe not a good idea. I think he's seen enough of them, although all the guys want one to take home. You're quite the star, ain't you?"

I hand over the rucksack. "Can you give this to Rob? Just his lunch and a newspaper." Best not to mention the beers.

"OK." He eyes the large brown paper parcel under my arm. "Going anywhere nice?"

"No, not really, just dropping some stuff off at the uni."

"Ta ra, then. Be good."

My phone buzzes in my pocket when I'm part way down the hill.

It's Christie. "Hi, Jilly, guess what?"

He sounds so upbeat that I smile even before I hear his news. "What? Has Oliver finally proposed?"

"No! I'm going to have to ask him myself if he doesn't get his act together soon."

"What, then?"

"Have you seen *The Guardian* today?"

"You know I don't buy that rag. Come on, Christie, spit it out."

"OK." He relents and tells me. "They've run an illustrated article on censorship in the media and guess whose picture's been included?"

"Not mine? Really?" I hardly dare believe it.

"Yes, yours! It's right beside a picture of two sailors doing something impossible with their penises."

"But it can't be. How did they get it?"

He laughs. "They saw it in the publicity stuff I sent out. Get down to the newsagent and get yourself a fistful of copies, send them to all your friends."

I let that pass. I don't think Rob or Nige will be delighted to see my picture in a newspaper.

"And that's not all." Christie's on a roll now. "I've just been on to a couple of the local radio stations and I think I'll be able to get an interview for you."

"Absolutely not! No way! Don't even think about it."

"What are you talking about? This is fantastic publicity

for the university and just think how good it's going to look on your c.v."

"Hang on a minute, let me think."

Rob doesn't buy *The Guardian* so he'll probably never know anything about it. But the radio blares out all day on the shop floor. And, then, what if my mother got to hear of it? I don't want her back in my life.

"Christie, did the article mention me by name?"

"Of course it did. We always make sure students get credit for their work, you know that."

"Oh, shit! I wish you hadn't done that. I'd rather not have my name in the paper. I don't fancy being on the radio, either."

Exasperation pours out of the phone into my ear. "You're a bloody strange girl, you know that? You didn't really appreciate getting the front cover of the catalogue, when anyone else would've been over the moon. Then you're not happy about free publicity in a national newspaper. And now, you won't talk to the radio station. What is the matter with you?"

I interrupt him before he gets into full flow about the youth of today.

"I'm grateful for everything you've done for me, honestly. I know the radio station thing will be good for the university, so why don't you do the interview? You'll be much better than me, anyway. Just say I want to remain anonymous."

He's silent for a few seconds and, when he speaks again, I can tell he quite likes the idea. "All right, that could work, probably add a bit of edge. Although, your name's already in the newspaper, so I'm going to look a bit of a knob."

He cuts me off abruptly, as I'm about to thank him.

"Well, better go, lots to do." His voice is flat compared to the excitement of earlier.

"Bye, Christie."

No answer; the line goes blank and I stare at the phone. I sit down on a nearby bench, bags and parcel at my feet. Christie's not a friend; not even close, he's just my tutor. So he's disappointed in me. Big deal. Yes, it would have been good to go on the radio, to be recognised as a person with something to say. But … I did what I had to do. I don't need praise from a radio station or a newspaper. I don't need anybody.

Mam's asleep, sprawled on the sofa, snoring with her mouth open. She won't wake for hours, but I move quietly as I lift her handbag from the floor, where she dropped it. I steal the picture and leave the house.

It's my sixteenth birthday. There won't be a cake or a party, just a few maudlin reminiscences over a wine bottle, as she tries to remember who my father was. Maybe this year I'll get the truth.

Outside, the sun shines. I sit on a low wall near the bus stop, with the river at my back. My college interview is at noon in Chesterfield, just twenty minutes away.

The bus turns the corner and begins to slow down for the stop. The photograph is still in my hand. I take a last look at the smiling face of the woman who threw away her life. And mine. As I get up from the wall, I tear the picture into tiny pieces and scatter them in the river. They disappear in seconds, gone before I board the bus.

CHAPTER TEN

The lift still isn't working. and there's no answer when I knock on Tina's door. That's OK with me. The shine went out of my day a little after talking to Christie. I might as well go back to Rob's house and make the most of my free day. I prop the parcel against the door and consider leaving a copy of the catalogue, as well. Better not. I'll wait until I can give it to her personally.

The door behind me opens with a soft snick just as I reach the stairwell. I do an about-face, ready to greet either Tina or Noel. The words die on my lips. Tina is halfway out of the doorway, crouching down to pick up the parcel. Her hair is dishevelled and tears have made tracks of mascara down her face. She looks up and sees me, looks briefly over her shoulder and shakes her head. "What are you doing out there? Get back in here, now."

Tina reacts quickly to Noel's voice and slams the door shut. It's all over in fifteen seconds; it could have been a figment of my imagination.

But it wasn't. There was a red mark on her face.

I don't want to acknowledge what I've just seen. It's not my problem. But the image of Tina's face stays in my mind as I walk downstairs. She looked so frightened. She *was* frightened. I should do something.

"OK," I say out loud and set off back up the stairs. I mean to call through the letterbox, ask if she's all right. It's not the best idea in the world, but the only thing I can think of.

With my hand raised to the door, I pause. Maybe I shouldn't interfere. If she'd wanted help, she could have opened the door and let me in. A half-forgotten memory surfaces.

Mam and I sit on the floor, behind the front door.
"Sshh," she whispers, pressing a finger to her lips. "Just keep quiet and they'll go away."
I copy her with my small finger and the voice outside calls through the letterbox, "I only want to help you."
Mam smiles. "We don't need anyone, do we, Jilly?"

I lower my hand and press my ear to the door, listening. If I hear a scream, I'll call out to her. If it's quiet, there's probably nothing to worry about.

In my heart, I already know I'm going to walk away.

....

Rob's car is parked outside the front door. It's too early for lunch and he's supposed to be working non-stop all day. As I fit the key into the lock, my phone rings and Rob's picture pops up on the screen. I swipe right but, before I can speak, he asks, "Where the hell are you? Nige said you was just going down to the university."

"I'm here now. Just coming in."

He grunts and kills the call. So, it's going to be like that.

The television is tuned to a football match, the volume high, and Rob is slumped in an armchair, a six-pack of beer at his feet.

"Why are you home?" I keep my voice light. "Are you OK?"

"Do you know something?" He ignores my questions. "You were right when you said it would never end. Catalogues came back today – oh, you already know," eyeing the carrier bag in my hand.

"Nige gave them to me." I drop the bag behind his chair. "Anyway, once they're delivered to the university, you can forget about it."

"Oh, you think so? When that creepy twat off the letterpress brought in *The Guardian* and stuck the sodding picture on my machine when I were at the bogs? Yeah, you didn't think I knew about that, did you?"

"I didn't know myself until Christie told me."

"That's what you say."

Tired of his whining, I try to get a sensible answer out of him. "So what's brought you home? Did you walk out?"

"Nige sent me home. Can you bloody believe it? My best mate and he turns on me."

"What, Nige sent you home because one of the guys stuck a picture on your machine?"

"No, you silly cow. I were upset, right?"

In a foul temper, you mean. "And?"

"He caught me having a drink behind the machine, didn't he?"

"You must be crazy. You're probably going to get a written warning, as well."

Rob pops another can. "Well, if you hadn't brought the beer in, it wouldn't have happened, would it?"

I hold up my hand. "Hang on, what did you just say?"

He doesn't bother to look at me. "You heard. I told Nige you brought it in. He's coming round later to sort it out. He'll have a few sharp words for you, Jilly *babes*." The last word drips with sarcasm.

Shaking my head in disbelief, I sit down in the armchair opposite him. "But you told me not to forget the beer."

"I don't think I did." He tips his can at me with a smug

smile. "Nige knows I'd never bring alcohol into the factory."

"Well, I'll soon put him right on that."

The smile vanishes. "You'll keep your trap shut. You're the one to blame for this, so keep your nose out."

Here we go again. The short period of peace, strained as it was, is over. As clearly as if it were written in stone, I can see the next few hours stretching ahead of me – Rob's drinking, the descent into belligerence, the twisting of the facts to make it my fault, the threats and, to cap it all, the arrival of Nige later on.

Not this time.

"OK, Rob." I pretend to back off. "You spin it any way that makes you and Nige happy."

He calls after me as I leave the room, "Hey, babe, make some lunch, will you? I left mine at work."

A man hurries down the garden path, as I open the gate. He keeps his head down, brushes past me and doesn't speak.

"Hello, Mr Ferguson." I say sweetly, "How are you today?"

He mutters something under his breath and walks away. Most of my mother's customers have told their kids not to mix with me. It pleases me to make them break their own double standards.

She's at the fridge, not for food but for a bottle of wine.

"Bit early, even for you, isn't it?"

"Don't you start, Jill. I'm having a bad day already. Ferguson isn't coming back, says I'm too old."

Am I supposed to feel sorry for her? Has she even remembered it's my birthday?

I shrug and push past her to see if there's any food in the fridge. "Well, all good things come to an end, as they say. Maybe time to get a job?"

"It's not funny." Oh God, now she's crying. "That's the second one I've lost. We're going to be really pushed for money. At least you can go to work now you've left school."

"Not a chance," I say, but my heart sinks. "I've just signed up for a two year course at college. Look." I show her the gold box I've carried home. "I spent my prom dress money on a camera."

She ignores the box, opens the wine and sniffs. "Better take it back then. Didn't you heard what I said? There's no money for you to waste two years lazing about, pretending to be a student."

"But the course is free, it won't cost you anything." I can hear desperation creep into my voice.

She gulps most of the first glass of wine before she answers me. "We have to live, don't we? Do you really think I can walk into the village and ask for a job? Who's going to employ me?"

"You could go to town, register with one of the agencies –"

"Not going to happen. If you want to go to college, you'll have to get the money yourself." With that parting shot, she walks out of the room.

I pick up the wine and pour a drink, raising a toast to myself in the mirror.

"Happy birthday, Jill."

CHAPTER ELEVEN

Rob's back yard is small and, at some time, he dug up any grass that struggled to survive and laid a concrete base. It has a high wall that backs onto the street. Instead of birdsong, I hear cars and motorcycles whizzing past, the chatter of kids as they walk to the park at the end of the street and the steady boom-boom of music from next-door's open window. A small patch of sunlight reaches the end of the yard around noon and, for a short while, it's a little urban sun trap.

I sit on the ground, fish my tin out of my pocket and roll a fag. For a few blessed moments, I drag smoke into my lungs and allow my mind to empty before facing the hard facts.

I've been a fool. Rob was only ever meant to be a stopgap, a place to live while I got through college. I don't feel guilty for using him. It was a fair exchange, in my eyes. Not my fault he imagines himself in love with me. When Nige joined him in goading me, I should have walked away.

My phone rings and *Unknown Number* flashes up on the screen. I don't know many people outside of the working girls and my university contacts, so it's probably spam. My finger hovers over the red button until I remember giving Tina my number. Another few seconds tick by.

Do I want to get involved with her problems?

A picture flashes into my mind of the clothes and flowers she gave me. It was stupid to throw the clothes away – something tells me I shouldn't dismiss whatever she wants to say to me so quickly. I press the green button.

"Hi, Jilly. It's Tina!"

She sounds like her usual, bubbly self.

No trace of tears or stress in her voice so I follow her lead. "Hey, Tina, good to hear from you. Have you had a look at the pictures?"

"Yeah, that's why I'm calling. I love them all. I've sent Noel out to get a couple of them framed."

There's a small hesitation, then she says, "Why don't you come over? I mean, only if you want to. We could do coffee and cake?"

"I don't know, Tina. I've only just got back from the Lace Market. Maybe another day?"

"Please? I could do with a laugh. We had fun the last time you were here, didn't we?"

We did, if we don't count the glimpse of her tearful face this morning.

"OK, then. To be honest, Rob is in a foul mood, so it'll be good to get out of the house."

"Great! See you soon!"

In the living room, all the cans of beer are empty and Rob is asleep in front of the television. I turn down the volume, stuff one of the catalogues into my camera bag and leave him there. As the door clicks shut behind me, I smile as I hear the lock drop into place.

What's that old saying? When one door closes …

CHAPTER TWELVE

Noel stands on a chair, hammer in hand and nails in his mouth.

Tina instructs him, "Higher up, just a bit to the left, yeah, just there!"

A few minutes later, the picture is securely on the wall and the three of us stand back to admire it. The afternoon sun falls across the frame, making the colours glow. Tina has chosen one of my favourites – it shows Noel sitting on a kitchen stool with a mug of coffee in his hand and Tina nestled into the crook of his arm. They're looking at each other, laughing, completely relaxed.

"Perfect!" Like a little girl, her face scrubbed clean of make-up and her hair tied up in bunches with coloured cotton, Tina claps her hands and smiles in delight. Noel and I smile back and, just for a moment, I feel included in their happiness. I'm glad I didn't interfere earlier when I saw Tina's distressed face. People have a right to privacy and, whatever the problem was, they seem to have cleared the air.

We drift into the kitchen area of the massive living space, where Tina has piled up plates of sticky cake. Noel laughs. "Bloody hell, woman, we're not fucking children." He looks at me to include me in the joke, but I see the hurt that flits across her face and say, "Oh, lovely, I've not had cake for ages."

Noel's gaze meets mine over Tina's head as she scoops cake into napkins. His eyes narrow and I feel a prickle of unease.

We eat cake.

"So, what're your plans, now?" Tina seems genuinely interested. "Will you get a job as a proper photographer? Like weddings and babies and things?" Her face is open and guileless.

I nearly choke on a mouthful of crumbs, as I start laughing.

Exactly what Rob said!

With that thought, I see a way to turn the conversation where I want it to go.

"Sorry," I say when the giggles stop. "It just reminded me of something Rob said."

"Oh, yeah?" Tina lifts her eyebrows.

"Perhaps I shouldn't say," I begin, my head lowered and my face solemn.

On cue, Tina asks, "What's the matter, Jilly? Is something upsetting you?"

"It's just that – well, you know I've been photographing the girls for nearly three years?"

"Yeah, Ollie said you was really good."

I manage a watery smile, "Thanks, Tina. But Rob hates what I do, says I should be doing weddings and things, not prossies." I gasp and my hand flies to my mouth. "Oh God, I'm sorry. I shouldn't have said that. It's Rob's word, not mine."

She tosses her head. "I've been called worse." But her mouth tightens and her smile has disappeared.

"Anyway, he and his mate have been having a go at me, calling me names and …"

Noel chips in, his face expressionless. "Go on, then, let's

have it."

Keeping my voice low and hesitant, I tell them about Rob kicking me and how he and Nige humiliated me with the racy underwear. They're both silent as I stammer to a close. Noel could be carved out of wood for al the emotion he's showing, but Tina has her hands over her mouth, shaking with silent laughter.

"That's so funny," she splutters.

"I don't find it funny, Tina, I was really frightened. Obviously, it's a joke to you – "

"No, I'm not laughing at what Rob and Nige did, they're a pair of wankers. It's the thought of you doing a Tina-pose!"

In spite of myself, I start to grin, "Yeah, well, it seemed like a good idea at the time."

Serious again, she says, "He's a real piece of work, your Rob, ain't he?"

"I never know what he's going to do. He even took the clothes you gave me and put them in the bin."

"Bastard! They was good quality, them clothes."

A couple of sniffs and I carry on. "He's drinking again and the last time he got like this, he punched me in the head. After you called, I had to run out of the back door to get away from him."

"Fuck me, Jilly, why do you put up with it? Get out of there before he does you some real damage."

At last.

"I've tried to find somewhere, but I've no money and my savings are gone. I'll just have to put up with it and hope for the best."

Tina's pumped up with indignation on my behalf. "Oh no, I ain't having that! She can stay here, can't she, Noel?" She appeals to her husband, who looks less than happy about the idea and remains mute.

She says again, with less certainty," Noel?"

At last, he grumbles, "I don't want no trouble coming to my door."

"No trouble, I promise. Rob doesn't even know where you live." I reassure them both, but I *did* tell Rob that Tina lives in the Old Mill. Perhaps he won't remember.

"You'll have to sleep in Tina's 'office', but don't worry," Noel's voice has an edge to it. "We'll change the sheets each night."

I ignore the sarcasm and smile. "Hey, Noel, I really do appreciate this, you know?"

He gives a curt nod."Yeah, all right. If Tina's cool with it …"

The door opens and Leon slouches in, heading straight for the kitchen area without as much as a glance at his parents. Straightening up from the fridge, he snaps open a can of pop before catching sight of me. His good looks are marred by a ferocious scowl. "What's *she* doing here?"

Noel snaps at him. "Watch your manners, boy."

Tina seems nervous and places a hand on Noel's arm. "It's OK, I'll have a word with him later." To her son, she says, "Jilly's staying for a little while, Leon. Go to your room, please, until you learn to speak nicely."

Leon glares at me and slams out of the door without another word.

"Well, I suppose I'd better get into me glad rags for work." Tina says brightly, as if the interlude with Leon had never happened. "Do you want to come with me, Jilly, while I get the slap on? Noel'll bring us a nice glass of bubbly, won't you, pet?"

There's a slight hesitation on Noel's part before he nods.

As Tina and I leave the room, he touches my elbow and murmurs, "Just be careful, Jilly. I ain't Rob."

I sit at the dressing table, every part of my body trembling uncontrollably. My face, white as chalk, is framed by a frizzy mass of hair, released from its plait. I lift a hand to apply lipstick, a bright red tube belonging to my mother, but I can't hold still long enough to apply it. An off-white nightdress hangs loosely off my shoulders, trying hard to cover my naked body.

Mam takes the lipstick from me, grasps me firmly under the chin and draws a cupid's bow on my mouth.

"I don't think I can do this, Mam." My teeth are chattering and I grind them together, willing my muscles to relax.

"It's your idea, not mine. Mind you, the money would be useful, but if you've changed your mind, I'll go down and tell him."

My mind screams, "Yes!" Why did I ever think I could do this? But if I don't earn enough money to get out of here, what will become of me? Who will ever want me, the girl whose mam has sold herself to most of the village?

So I say, "No, you can tell him to come up." She gets up to do my bidding, and I hold her arm in a last, desperate attempt for help.

"Mam, how do I do this?"

She smiles, as she shakes me off.

"Get the money first."

CHAPTER THIRTEEN

I watch Tina as she transforms from the girl-next-door to a sophisticated, yet hard-faced, woman. She pouts and finishes off the look with a moist, peachy lipstick, catches my reflection in the mirror, and says, "What do you think? Will it drive 'em wild?"

"You're beautiful, Tina, it'll be wasted on your bloody punters."

She smiles and touches my hand. "I'm glad you're here, Jilly. I couldn't bear the thought of you going home to that pair of shits."

"I know, Tina. I'm really grateful to you and Noel for letting me stay. But, I have to go back to pick up my clothes and my university work. I'm afraid Rob will throw them out, and if I lose them …"

I let my voice tail off and drop my shoulders.

Tina is on her feet immediately, calling out. "Noel! Noel, come here!"

He lumbers into the room, alarm on his face. "What's the matter, Teen? What's wrong?"

"Nothing, but Jill needs to go back to Rob's to get her stuff. She can't go on her own. Will you take her?" She pulls two enormous suitcases from a cupboard as she speaks and drops them at my feet. "Here, use these for your stuff."

Noel scowls. "Me? What am I, a fucking chauffeur?"

I cut in quickly, not wanting to rock the boat. "It's OK, honestly, I can go on my own."

Tina starts to speak, but Noel puts up a hand, his eyes locked on mine. I can't read him.

He smiles. "Yeah, OK. I'll go and bring the car round. Follow me down in five minutes."

Tina holds her face up for a kiss. "Watch the make-up!"

Noel grimaces and air-kisses her before he makes for the door. He doesn't pick up the suitcases.

A little knot of worry forms in my stomach. Noel's words resound in my mind. *Be careful, Jilly.*

Tina flaps a hand at me. "Go! Don't keep him waiting."

I give myself a mental shake. I'm worrying over nothing. It was just a friendly warning.

Outside, night has fallen. Moonlight gives the buildings in the Lace Market an illusionary elegance, masking the decrepit brickwork and bringing the windows alive with soft, reflected light. I wait for Noel on the corner, a suitcase in each hand, a little nervous as I scan the empty streets. I'm not looking forward to the reception I'm going to get at Rob's house.

Noel doesn't help me with the suitcases when the car pulls up beside me, simply pops the boot open and leaves me to it. A soft retro-reggae beat pulses softly as he navigates the Jaguar through the narrow streets. He drives in silence until we reach the wider streets that lead out of the city. Just as I'm casting about for something to say, Noel reaches across and puts a large hand on my knee. I freeze.

Please, God, don't let him make a pass at me and spoil everything.

His voice is a deep rumble and, when I risk a sideways

glance, the expression on his face is stony. "Listen to me, girl, and listen good. I ain't no pushover, get it?"

His grip tightens on my leg and I nod, too frightened to speak. He registers the nod and continues. "You live in my house, you live by my rules. Tina might think you're summat special, but me? I've seen plenty of girls like you before. You're on the make and I don't like it."

Keeping his eyes on the road, he gives me a final warning. "Just don't do owt to hurt Tina, keep your nose clean and we'll get along fine. Understood?"

I nod again, my mouth dry, and he removes his hand. Five minutes later, we pull up outside Rob's house. Noel gets out of the car and gives the door a thunderous knock. When my treacherous legs are steady enough to stand, I get the suitcases out of the boot and follow him. As the door begins to open, Noel steps to one side, leaving me alone in the light spilling on to the pavement.

"Well, look what the cat's dragged home, Nige –" Rob stops the sarcasm abruptly as he sees the suitcases. Easy tears, never far away when he's drunk, spring to his eyes. "Ah, no, Jilly babes."

"What's the matter now?" Nige, irritable and sober, appears in the hallway behind Rob. He sizes up the situation and glares at me. "About bloody time you pissed off, lady. You won't need those cases, mind. You're not coming in here."

Rob turns on Nige. "Just shut it, will you? If it hadn't been for you, this wouldn't have happened."

Well, it makes a change from blaming me.

Noel cuts the argument dead by walking in front of me. "Take it inside, lads. I've not got all night."

Rob finds his voice first. "Who are you?"

Noel steps forward, his bulk pushing the two men backwards into the dining room. "It don't matter who I am, mate. Just sit down and keep quiet while she gets her stuff."

All bluster and bravado gone, Rob and Nige back up in front of Noel's menacing frame and sink into a couple of chairs. This should be a sweet moment for me but I don't stop to savour it. My nerves are still jangled from the one-sided conversation in the car and I scuttle upstairs, the cases bouncing off the steps behind me.

In the bedroom, it doesn't take long to gather all my clothes. They barely fill one of the cases. Armfuls of books, folders, memory cards and chargers, anything I can pick up, from the computer room fill the other case. I stand in front of my computer and printer, wishing there was a way I could take them with me. For a few seconds, I toy with the idea of asking Noel to put them in the car. I'm pretty sure Rob wouldn't argue, but I'm wary of Noel and

don't want to be the source of his contempt again, so I leave them there.

I carry the case full of my clothes downstairs and bump the heavier one down, step by step. Noel throws the car keys to me. "I'll stay with the boys here while you get them in the boot." The three of them watch me as I heave the cases to the door. Noel stands apart from Rob and Nige, but in my overwrought state, I see them as united against me.

At last, we're ready to leave. Noel is in the driving seat, firing up the motor, and I have the door open to get into the car, when Rob's voice halts me. He stands at the front door, with one hand held out to me. "Don't go, please, I can change."

I shake my head. Nige takes Rob's arm to draw him

back into the house. "Come on, mate, it's over. Forget her, she's not worth all this." He looks back at me, as Rob shuffles inside. I expect to see anger or triumph on his face, but he merely shakes his head and has the last word, before he slams the door. "Big mistake, Jilly babes."

Noel pulls up in front of the Old Mill.

"Hop out, then, look lively. Don't forget your stuff in the boot."

He doesn't offer to help. As soon as the cases are on the pavement, he shoots off to garage his car, leaving me on the dark street. I drag them into the lobby to wait for him. Five minutes go by before he jogs round the corner, through the main doors and straight past me.

"What, you still here, girl? Thought you'd be at the top by now. Miss Independent, ain't you? Likes to carry her own stuff."

He disappears up the dark stairwell, his laughter echoes back and I sit down on the bottom step.

Over and over in my head, Nige says, "Big mistake, Jilly."

"Name?"

"Jillian Graham."

"What course?"

"Photography."

"Oh yes. Here you are. Room 132. Hurry up, though. Induction's about to start."

My name's ticked off the list and a sheaf of leaflets pushed into my hands.

"Thank you." I beam at the woman who has greeted me at the main door of the college and set off to find Room 132.

I've made it. My first day at college and a new start. No more walking into a classroom to face sniggers, dirty jokes about my mother and – worst of all – the pitying look from the teacher. My life is a clean sheet and it feels so good.

I smile as I push open the door to join my fellow students on the course. The tutor waves me in and I'm ticked off another list. "Ah, Miss Graham, just in time. Welcome. One seat left, over there."

My smile fades as I take my seat.

For the first time in ten years, I'm sitting next to Rosemary again.

CHAPTER FOURTEEN

I'm hungry. The only thing I've eaten since breakfast is some sticky cake that now lies in my stomach like a brick. Noel sprawls in front of the giant television screen, watching re-runs of *The Sopranos*. At the other end of the room, Leon sits at the kitchen table, homework books spread out, thumbs working furiously on his smartphone when his Dad isn't looking. In between the two, I'm curled up in an armchair with a book. Nobody mentions food; in fact, nobody says a bloody thing.

It's ten o'clock. Tina's had five customers so far this evening. When there's a knock at the door, Noel pauses the television, heaves himself to his feet and ushers the man (although, once it was a woman) into the waiting area, offering coffee as though it were a social event. He lets Tina know she's required in her 'office' and sits back down to resume his viewing. Leon doesn't even raise his head.

A short while later, we hear the front door slam and Tina breezes in."You all right, Jilly? Are they looking after you?" She doesn't wait for an answer. "Good, we'll have a chinwag later, eh?" With that, she kisses Noel on the top of the head, waves at Leon, who ignores her, and dashes into the bathroom to wash off the last customer, in preparation for the next.

And silence falls again.

The footsteps on the stairs draw nearer and my stomach turns over. Oh God, I'm going to be sick. Can I get to the bathroom before he gets here? The door opens and I stare in horror. Is this some sort of twisted joke? Is Mam going to pop her head round the door and we'll all laugh, while the real customer follows them up the stairs?
Because it's Rosemary's dad.

CHAPTER FIFTEEN

Leon's asleep at the end of the table, head resting on his folded arms. Noel opens a drawer and pulls out a bundle of takeaway menus. "OK, what do we fancy tonight?"

Tina's just out of the shower and looks fresh as a daisy. "Let's push the boat out because Jilly's here. Thai! I love Thai."

Noel picks his phone up. "I know you do, Teen." He rattles off an order, without asking what we want, and pulls a couple of bottles of white wine from the fridge. "Get the glasses, then, Jills," nodding at the Welsh dresser.

I take a deep breath. *So now I'm Jills.* And smile. "Of course."

Noel settles himself at the table beside the sleeping Leon and nods for Tina and me to sit opposite him. He looks at me, his face giving nothing away, and I tense, unsure whether to speak or not. Then he smiles and tips his glass in my direction. "Mebbe I were a bit hard on you before. I been thinking since I saw those two twats. I don't blame you for getting out while the going's good." He glances at Tina. "What I said still stands, mind. Just remember that and we'll do all right."

"Thank you, Noel. It's very good of you to let me stay. I'm grateful, really." If there's one thing I've perfected, it's how to give the required answer.

"Oh, yeah. Another thing. I ain't going to charge you

rent. But food ain't free, so I'd say about fifty quid a week, OK?"

Tina nudges me under the table. "That sounds all right, Jilly, don't it?"

I just want this long evening to end and nod, stifling a yawn at the same time. My worldly goods amount to about fifteen pounds in my purse, two suitcases of belongings and my camera. Fifty quid might as well be five hundred. I haven't got it.

"Let's get your bed ready while we're waiting for our supper." Tina is on her feet with one hand under my elbow. I rise and follow her into the claustrophobic little room she jokingly calls her 'office'. The window is open wide and the curtains blow gently into the room, bringing a fresh breeze to combat the lingering smell of the snuffed-out candles. The frilly cover and the cushions from the bed are piled up on a chair in the corner and clean sheets and pillowcases are folded neatly on the mattress.

"You know, Noel ain't really as tough as he lets on." Tina gestures for me to take hold of the sheets and we bend to make up the bed. "Don't worry about the fifty quid. I know by the look on your face you ain't got it. I'll have a word with him to hold off a bit and we'll think of summat to make you a bit of money."

Tears sting my eyes at her kindness. I say, "Thank you, Tina," and this time, I mean it.

My camera bag and suitcases are stacked in the corner of the room. This is probably a good time to tell her about her photograph being on the front page of the Degree Show catalogue, while we're alone. I reach for my bag, "Tina –"

There's a knock at the door, Noel shouts, "Grub's up!"

and the moment is lost.

In spite of my hunger, I can't face the mass of contra-dictions that is Tina's family; the sullen boy, Noel who smiles as he issues veiled threats and Tina, in denial of the tearful incident this morning. I say, "If you don't mind, I think I'll just get some sleep. It's been a long day."

"No problem. You get your head down. We'll talk in the morning." And she's gone with a last wave of her fingers.

I turn off the light, close the window against the night air and lie down on the bed, too tired to take my clothes off. The pervasive smell of the candles slowly creeps back into the room, bringing with it an unbidden image of Tina lying in the bed while a faceless man labours over her. Tina's laughter in the family room meshes with the picture in my mind as I slide in and out of sleep. The man turns his head and grimaces, lost in the throes of an orgasm. I don't want to see his face. A scream bubbles up through my body and jerks me fully awake.

What the hell is happening to me?

The scream becomes a wordless moan, loud in the tiny room. Terrified Noel and Tina will hear me, I roll off the bed and stumble to the window, throwing it wide open again.

The curtains blow into the room and I cling to them, dragging in great gulps of air, afraid to let go as my vi-sion blurs and dizziness threatens to throw me to the floor. Pain blossoms in my chest and darkness creeps in at the edge of my vision. And, then, nothing.

Rosemary's dad puts his hand on my shoulder. "Take some deep breaths. That's the way. Good girl." He stays beside me, stroking my arm as I slowly calm down. I find it strangely comforting, although I don't understand what's happening. He shouts, "Sylvie, get your ass up here."

Mam appears in the doorway. "What's up?"

"Why didn't you tell her it was me? You said she was up for it. I'm not a fucking rapist."

She's unfazed. "Look, Bill, it's her idea, it's what she wants. I'm having nowt more to do with it."

She flounces off and Rosemary's dad – Bill – turns to me. "Is that true, Jilly? You really want this?"

My teeth are chattering, but I manage to say, "Yes, its just … I didn't think …"

"I know, love. It's a bit of a shock, but Sylvie and me, you know, we've been friends for many years."

"Does Rosemary know?"

His face hardens. "Let's leave my daughter out of this, shall we?" A smile, that I now know is false, creeps back on to his face. "OK, if we're both clear, let's get down to business."

This is the last second I have to change my mind.

He lays some notes down on the dressing table and walks towards the bed. I look first at the money and then at him, and say, "No, that's not enough. Sylvie –" She'll never be Mam again – "said it should be more because I'm a …" The word sticks in my throat. "… because it's my first time. I want another twenty."

I hold my breath and bargain with myself. If he refuses, then it's all over and he leaves. But if he agrees, then there's no going back.

Bill curls his lip and, for a heart-stopping moment, I think – pray – he's going to leave. Then he slaps down another note and mutters, "You really are your mother's daughter."

And the die is cast.

CHAPTER SIXTEEN

"Wake up, sleepyhead; I've brought you a cup of tea."

I peel my eyes open and squint against the sunlight. Tina sits on the end of the bed, grinning at me. "Leon's gone to school and Noel's down at the gym, so we've got the place to ourselves for a while."

Still groggy, I look down and realise I'm lying underneath the top sheet in the bed. "How …"

"Noel put you there. We heard you rabbiting away to yourself and when we came to see if you was all right, you was spark out on the floor. You must've been really plastered. Come on, up you get."

I heave myself up in the bed. I wasn't drunk, far from it. I remember bad dreams, something about a man, and being in pain, but the rest eludes me.

Still in yesterday's clothes, I roll out of bed and and carry my tea into the kitchen area. The smell of toast lingers in the air and my stomach growls.

"I'm a bloody awful cook, but I'm a fantastic toaster. OK?" The table has butter, jam and honey at the ready, and Tina keeps the toast coming until I've eaten my fill.

"So, what are you getting up to, today?" she asks, when I finally sit back from the table.

"Good question, Teen." I quickly correct myself. "Sorry, I mean Tina."

"It's all right. I answer to anything, me. Anyway, I thought we was friends?"

Friends. The word catches me off-guard and leaves me tongue-tied. I stare at my empty plate and push a few crumbs around with my knife. The silence grows until Tina breaks it. "Oh, I see. I'm not the sort you'd be friends with, is that it? You don't want – what is it Rob called me? A prossy, that's it – as a friend? But you don't mind living here, do you?" She stops talking and peers at me. "What the fuck are you crying about?"

"I'm not crying. I don't cry." That's not true. I can cry at the drop of a hat to placate Rob. But these tears have arrived unbidden and they hurt my chest.

"Yes, you *are* crying." Tina's voice is softer and she takes my hand. "Come on, Jills, out with it. You're not crying over a few tough words from me."

I smile at the pet name and more tears flow. Before I can stop myself, I blurt out the truth.

"I've never had a friend."

Except once, for a short while, many years ago.

Tina laughs, "You're joking. Look at you. You're beautiful, smart, clever. You must have loads of friends."

It's so tempting to tell her why I've never had friends. With all the will power I can muster, I stop crying and force out a laugh. "Look at me, so hung over I'm crying. Actually, it's true, I *don't* have any friends. It's just one of those things. No biggie."

"OK, if that's the way you want to play it." I can see Tina isn't convinced by my flippant remark, but she lets it slide. "So, we're friends then, yeah?"

"Yeah, friends." If only it were that easy. I gather up the plates and stack them in the sink. "To answer your question, I think I'll walk into town, see if I can find Christie. I need to put something right with him."

Tina looks a bit disappointed. "Oh, all right. I was just

thinking we could do summat together. But maybe tomorrow."

On impulse, I say, "Why not come with me? I bet Christie would love to see you again."

"What, me? Come to the uni with you? But what would I wear?"

"You're not going to visit the bloody queen, are you? Wear stockings and suspenders and tassels – that'll make their eyes water!"

We collapse, laughing, into a couple of armchairs. My sides ache and tears run down my face again. This time, I don't try to hide them.

I have a friend.

I carry my tray to a table in the canteen and say, "Anyone sitting here?" A quick shake of the head from the nearest person. I sit down. Within minutes, all the students at the table have found a reason to leave.

Conversations stop abruptly when I try to join a group. To break the awkward silence, I walk away and pretend to study a noticeboard I have no interest in.

No one ever picks me to be a partner for projects.

Rosemary never speaks to me.

I tell myself I don't care, but I'd had hopes of making friends at college. More fool me.

As usual, there's no space at any of the tables. Rosemary glances up as I walk past, whispers something to one of her friends and they burst into giggles. I hesitate, then turn back with a smile.

"Do you like my new camera bag, Rosie?" She hates being called Rosie.

A shrug and she turns away from me.

But I'm not finished. "Your dad bought it for me."

"What're you talking about. My dad wouldn't buy you an ice cream, let alone a camera bag."

"Oh, but he did, Rosie. He gave me the money for it. Ask him."

I wink at her and walk away, the laughter of her friends sweet to my ears.

CHAPTER SEVENTEEN

"Slow down, Jilly." Tina is red in the face as she struggles to keep up with me.

"I told you not to wear four inch heels, didn't I?"

"Well, I thought you was going to get a taxi. Who walks everywhere?"

I try not to laugh at her indignant answer. "Those of us who have no bloody money."

In fits and starts, with lots of swearing from Tina, we finally make it to the university building which houses the Photography department. The canteen is on the ground floor, just inside the entrance, and Tina sinks into a chair.

"That's it. I can't go any further. You go and find Christie and come back for me."

I sit down opposite her, hesitate for a moment, then ask her, "You know if you'd done something to upset somebody and you wanted to put it right, but didn't know how to, what would you do?"

She kicks off her shoes and concentrates on rubbing her feet. Without looking up, she says, "Jills, what the fuck are you on about? Can you speak in plain English?"

"I upset Christie because I didn't want to let him know about Rob – you, know, about when he hit me and what he thinks about –" I make quote marks with my fingers –

"prossies."

Tina grimaces. "Yeah, I'd still like to have my day with him about that." She leaves her feet alone for a moment. "Christie and Oliver were friends of my mum. They went to school together. I couldn't have coped when she died, if they hadn't been there for me. They was brilliant. So just tell him, straight out. He's one of the good guys."

I stand. "OK, you sure you'll be all right while I'm gone?"

"Yeah, sure, it's a bit tatty in here, ain't it? I was expecting wood panels and people wafting about in robes. And these tables need a good clean."

She's still assessing the academic world and finding it lacking, when I leave her there.

Christie is in the computer room when I finally track him down. I brace myself for a cold reception, but he smiles. "Hey, Jilly, you OK?"

"Yeah, I'm good. Just wanted to let you know I'm living at Tina's now. And to say I'm sorry about the whole radio thing." I take a deep breath before it all comes out in a rush. "The thing is, my boyfriend was giving me a hard time about me working with the girls. He hit me when he found the picture of Tina and …" I take a second to push back the tears that are threatening to spill from my eyes. "I was frightened of what he would do if he heard me on the radio."

He stops work and gives me his full attention. "He actually hit you? Yes, of course he did, if you say so. And you're right to get out of there. But … well, do you have anywhere else to go? Maybe back home, as it's nearly the end of the year, anyway?"

"What's wrong with staying at Tina's? She said you were a friend."

"That's not exactly true." He hesitates, then presses on. "I shouldn't tell you this, but she was in a fair bit of trouble when she was younger. Oliver was her social worker. Still is, if it comes to that. He managed to keep her out of prison, that's how we got to know her and her mum."

"So why say you're friends? Why lie?"

"I don't know. Tina's complicated … it's what she does." Christie's brows pull down in a frown. "I can't get involved on a personal level. You're my student, but if you'd like Oliver to have a chat with you, maybe he could help find you somewhere else to stay."

We don't need help from anyone, do we, Jill?

I shake Sylvie out of my mind and back off, sorry I had confided in him. "No, don't worry, I can take care of myself."

"Well, if you're sure." His hand hovers over his mouse, ready to start work again. "By the way, how does Noel feel about you being there?"

"He's good. Why do you ask?"

"No reason. Just wondered. He can be a bit …" His attention is back on the computer again. "Just, take care, Jilly."

Everybody telling me to take care, but nobody actually cares.

Tina looks behind me expectantly when I get back to the canteen. "Oh, is Christie not coming down to have coffee with us?'

"No, I told him you were here, but he's too busy."

Her face falls. I smile consolingly.

Through the bedroom window, I watch Sylvie stagger up the garden path. She's pissed out of her mind again, on the money I gave her, but not too far gone to see the yellow ribbon on the door handle. She heads round the side of the house towards the kitchen.

CHAPTER EIGHTEEN

I have three sessions booked today. At fifty pounds a time, I can pay Noel for this week and add some money to the little cache that's growing inside my camera bag. A tap at the door signals the arrival of my first customer. I paste a big smile on my face and fling it open.

Candice surges forward and envelopes me in a hot, perfumed hug. "When are they going to fix that bleedin' lift? I can hardly breathe." She hustles in to Tina's little photographic studio, a vision in pink frills with a feathery fascinator pinned in her hair. Two little girls trail behind her, also dressed in pink, their blonde curls tied up in multi-coloured ribbons.

It's Tina's bright idea. Over breakfast on my second day in the Lace Market, she suddenly says, "I've been thinking. You need to make some money, right?" Without waiting for an answer, she rambles on. "I bet the girls would love family pictures like mine. I never use the studio until the afternoon, so you could have it in the morning." A short pause, while she looks sideways at her large, expressionless husband. "Couldn't she, Noel?"

The question hangs in the air while Noel chews a mouthful of toast and washes it down with a gulp of tea. "She *could,* but your sex toys and whips ain't going to look too good behind the kiddies, are they?"

Tina is much quicker to read Noel's mood than me and laughs. "He's pulling your leg, Jills." And to Noel, as he gets up and walks away. "So, we can then?"

"Do what you want, you always do. Just don't ask me to help."

And that's it. All arranged without a word from me.

Every morning, we push Tina's posing chair to the back of the room, bundle the sex toys into a cupboard and drag in a loveseat and a couple of chairs from Tina's bedroom. We blow up balloons, plunder the 'office' for fringed shawls and scarves, and top the lot off with a teddy bear and a couple of dolls that Tina unearths from a cupboard.

At the stroke of noon, we reverse everything and the room is restored to its original purpose.

In the afternoon, I become the door-opener and the coffee-server for Tina's customers until Noel takes over in the evening.

Candice drones on in the background while I arrange the girls, ready for their photograph. I nod sympathetically as she tells me about her latest brush with the law.

"Yeah. This lovely car pulls up, the guy offers double the odds for a quickie. So, I get in and the bastard pulls out a warrant card, don't he?"

"I thought you knew all the cops round here? Not like you to fall for that."

She pulls a face. "Yeah, I know. He's just joined the city guys, came up from some village. He made me give him a freebie and then booked me anyway."

"Well, at least you know his car now. You'll not fall for it twice."

"Oh, no." A bitter laugh. "I'll not get caught out by Stevie again, don't you worry."

My breath catches in my throat. "Stevie? You sure that was his name?"

"Yeah, he was making a phone call when I were getting out of the car. He definitely said, 'This is Stevie.' Why, do you know him?"

"No, just thought it was an unusual name, that's all."

"OK ... oh, that looks lovely. Ready for me to stand behind them?"

I choose a moment when Noel and Leon are out to tell Tina about her picture on the front cover of the Degree Show catalogue. In a week's time, the Show will launch and the catalogues are currently being distributed to local newspapers, radio stations and art galleries to drum up publicity. It's only a matter of time before she sees one.

She has no customers this afternoon and my career as a family photographer stuttered to a halt some days ago. There are only so many working girls in the city who want photographs, but I managed to save a few hundred pounds as well as pay Noel.

"Tina, I've made coffee," I call through to the bedroom, where she's hanging up the new dresses she bought this morning. "Come through, I need to talk to you."

"Oh God, my feet are killing me." She plops down at the table and pulls the cup of coffee towards her. "I really need this."

"What have I told you about those four inch heels?"

"I know. I should give them up. Anyway, what's up? You sounded a bit serious."

"No, not really. You know it's the opening of the Degree Show soon?"

"Yeah, I'm really looking forward to it. Wait 'til you see the dress I've got." Tina rises from her chair. "I'll get it, just wait a sec."

"No." I grab hold of her wrist and she stops. "Listen. You know I've got three photographs in the exhibition? Well, one of them is a picture of you."

"What?" Her face lights up, excited and pleased, words falling over each other as she gabbles, "I'm going to be in an exhibition? Oh shit, I'd better get another dress. Which picture is it?" She gestures at the framed picture on the wall, the one of her and Noel, looking all loved up. "Is it that one? I didn't think I'd be in it, because you was finished with all your proper work before you came here."

"No, not that one. It's –"

"You bitch!" Leon's voice cuts across mine, as he hurls a catalogue on to the tale. It skitters across the smooth surface and comes to rest against Tina's coffee cup.

She gives a small scream. "Bloody hell, Leon, you made me jump. I didn't hear you come in"

Leon barrels across the room, face red with fury. He's in school uniform, his tie askew, and he sports a large bruise on his cheekbone. He screams into his mother's face, "Did you know about this?"

I reach for the book, but Tina gets there before me. She stares at the picture in disbelief and her voice is a hoarse whisper as she says, "Oh, fucking hell. What have you done? I thought you was my friend." The blood drains from her face, as another thought strikes her. "Oh my God, what will Noel say?"

The fear on her face is contagious and my stomach knots up. Noel warned me not to bring trouble to his door and this is shaping up to be big trouble.

My first impulse is to shift the blame.

"It was Christie's idea." That much, at least, is the truth.

"I begged him not to do it, but he wanted the publicity for the university. It's why he didn't come down to see you when we were at the uni last week. He was ashamed to face you." I stop for a breath. "He left it for me to tell you, but I was afraid to."

"You're a liar! You gave him the picture, you bitch!" Leon screams, red with anger. He lunges forward, his arms flailing as he takes a swing at me. I topple off my chair and we both tumble to the floor.

Tina's on her feet, grabbing at her son, trying to pull him away from me. "Leon, don't!"

"What the fuck's going on in here?" Noel's come into the room, unheard by any of us. He pushes Tina aside, grabs hold of Leon and throws him bodily into a chair. He ignores me as I scramble to my feet.

"Well? Come on, out with it." Tina and Leon are ashen and don't speak. He turns to me, face contorted by rage. "Is this something to do with you?"

I hand the catalogue to him. "I can explain –" and stop, because he's laughing.

A police car pulls up at the end of the drive and Sylvie falls out of it, hurling curses over her shoulder at the grinning cop behind the wheel. He winds the window down and laughs, "Yeah, yeah, see you next week. Better a freebie for me than jail for a few months."

He catches me watching from the window and calls her back to the car. They whisper for a few minutes before she staggers indoors.

She looks at the books I've spread across the table. "What are you wasting your time with that for? You're already earning more money than I do."

I don't bother to reply. I've told her many times before – money and education are the only way I can get out of here and build a new life.

Shrugging, she walks into the kitchen, pours a drink and comes back to stand over me. She grins, "Oh, by the way, when the cop car turns up next week, you'll be getting in it, not me."

The price for leaving home just went up.

CHAPTER NINETEEN

"This is fucking priceless. Says everything about you, don't it, Teen?"

Colour comes back into Tina's face and a glimmer of anger appears in her eyes. I back off to the other side of the table, out of their direct eyeline.

"I asked her for family pictures, not this crap." Her voice quivers, but she carries on. "That's not me, not the real me. It's just my job, don't mean any more than working in McDonald's or selling cars. It's just a job!"

Noel bends over until he's looking directly into her face. "You keep telling yourself that, Teen. But you *ain't* working in McDonald's, are you?"

He smiles. It frightens me more than Rob's bluster ever did. "Babe, you're a tart. Always have been, always will be."

His casual cruelty has stolen Tina's confidence. "But I'm your wife! That comes first, don't it?"

"Yeah, you're a good little earner." Noel dismisses her hurt, idly flicking the pages of the catalogue.

"So you don't care that she's turned *Teen* into a dirty joke?" Leon says his mother's name with such venom, I have to remind myself that he's only thirteen.

Noel crosses the room in three strides and grabs Leon by the arm. "That's enough! I've told you before," he snarls into the boy's face. "You don't talk about your Mum like that."

Leon pries at his father's fingers. "You hypocrite! And I've told you, I'd rather be in a children's home than live here. I don't want her for a Mum! And I don't want you for a Dad!"

His voice rises to a shriek. "All my mates have seen that fucking picture, even some of the teachers were laughing at it."

"Leon!" Noel warns, but he can't stop the words spewing out of his son's mouth as he fronts up to me.

"I'm sick of coming home from school, not knowing what I'm going to find. Some days there's three of the bastards in the waiting room – queueing up to screw –" He stutters to a stop and then whispers the last few words. "– to screw … she's my *mother*." His body slumps and he offers no resistance as Noel drags him from the room.

In the silence that follows their departure, Tina collapses into a chair, her head buried in her hands.

"See what you've done, Jilly? You've torn my family apart. It's your bleedin' picture that's set Leon off. He were all right, he were handling it …"

"He's never been all right and you know it." I clench my teeth, jaw rigid, to stop myself from screaming at her that being the child of a prostitute is a ticket to hell … and worse. My hands curl into claws, fingernails dig holes in my palms, every fibre of my body is rigid and I my breath hitches. The light from the tall windows fragments. Bizarrely, I think I can see yellow ribbons and there's pain in my chest …

This is not about you, Jilly.

But it is.

"Snap out of it!" A hard slap on my face. "Come on, breathe, you stupid mare!"

My breathing slows and the room steadies. "Bloody hell, Tina, that's quite a punch you have there."

"Yeah, well. You was having a panic attack. It were either that or find a paper bag. Seemed the quickest way …"

My face still throbs. "You didn't have to enjoy it quite so much."

Tina shrugs, but doesn't deny it. "This coffee's gone cold. I'll make some more."

I follow her to the kitchen area. "What I was about to tell you, before Leon came home –"

She keeps her back to me, busy with coffee cups; she's not going to make it easy. "I should have told you, asked you, there's no excuse for what I did."

"Because you know I'd never have let you use it."

"To tell you the truth, I didn't even have the right to use it because I didn't clear it with you."

"That doesn't help much now, does it?"

Tina puts two cups of coffee on the table and nods for me to sit down. "You're lucky Noel isn't mad about it. The bastard will probably get his hands on as many as he can and sell them."

"I'm sorry. You've only ever been kind to me …"

"Yeah, well, I thought you was my friend. No –" She raises a hand. "It's OK. I were wrong, that's all."

I don't argue. The moment when we could have been friends has passed. Instead, I turn the conversation back to her son.

"What I did was wrong, Tina, but it's not the reason for all this anger Leon has inside him, is it?"

She sighs. "Do you think I don't know? To be honest, he's

been like it ever since he worked out what was going on. Last week, he went into my wardrobe and took the scissors to a load of my working clothes. Noel gave him a right hiding for it."

I could almost feel sorry for Leon. At least Sylvie never raised a hand to me.

No, she did a hell of a lot worse.

Which prompts me to say, "He's seen a lot for a boy his age. I'm not judging, but –"

"What? What are you getting at?"

"Well … you don't think any of your punters might have … you know … touched him?"

Tina snorts. "Huh, I don't think so. He would have taken the scissors to *them*."

We share a glance that's nearly a smile.

"It's not my business, but have you ever thought of coming off the game until he's a bit older? I mean …" I struggle for words. "He could probably do with, I don't know, some professional help?"

Her shoulders slump. "I want to, but Noel won't have it. He thinks Leon should toughen up. I daren't push it any more."

She tugs at the neck of the kimono she's wearing. I recognise the gesture and reach across the table to push the silky material to one side. Fading purple and yellow bruises are visible on her breasts, disappearing under the kimono, towards her ribs.

"Did Noel do that to you?"

She puts a finger to her lips, stands up and says in a loud voice, "I bought some new clobber this morning, Jills, come and have a look. Try some on, if you like."

We pick up our coffees, walk through to the bedroom she shares with Noel, and sit on the double bed. Tina twists round so she's looking directly at me.

"Noel ain't that bad." I snort and she backtracks. "Not in this game, anyway. All right, he can get a bit handy with his fists if Leon winds him up, or if I don't make enough money."

"He beats you? Why do you stay?."

She fakes a laugh. "You'd still be with Rob if it wasn't for me. Didn't have many options, did you? I saw the way you looked when you were telling me about them two pieces of shit. Believe me, I've seen that look on dozens of girls' faces."

But I was pretending ... wasn't I?

I stand, look out of the window, try not to listen, but her words won't be stopped. "The thing is, girls like me, we ain't got no choice. And let me tell you something – you think you're going to get out of here, because you've got an education. Oh yeah, I know you look down on me but your chances ain't much better than mine."

Tina joins me at the window and puts an arm round my waist. It feels good and I have to fight the impulse to wrap my arms round her. She sighs. "I dunno, Jills." My eyes sting at the affectionate name. "Maybe you'll be the one that gets out and makes a life for herself but, believe me, if you thought you was using Rob, you're wrong. I ain't got an education, but I know men and he were always in charge."

I move away from her arm. She has no idea what she's talking about. I've looked after myself all my life, ever since I was seven. Nothing will stand in the way of the new life I've worked for all these years.

"So, what are you going to do, Tina?" My voice is hard. "Carry on letting Noel take his temper out on you, working when you don't want to any more?"

"Did you listen to anything I said? I ain't got a choice. Look, this place ain't cheap and, yeah, I work more hours than I want to. But what if I left Noel? I don't want to go back to Forest Road, I'm too old for that now. One day, Leon will leave – and he'll go as soon as he's able, I know that – and where will I be? No, I ain't going to be a street girl again. There's only one way that ends."

She smiles, and I see the effort it takes. "All I'm asking, is that you don't start him off again. It'll just make things worse for me ... and Leon."

"I thought you were so strong, Tina, that you'd got everything worked out."

"Funny old life, ain't it? That's what I thought about you."

We sit on the bed in silence, until it's time for Tina's first customer.

CHAPTER TWENTY

The evening drags on. Noel's restless, channel hopping on the television; Leon stubbornly refuses to come out of his bedroom. The knowledge that Noel is violent towards both Tina and Leon has unsettled me so I busy myself in the kitchen, staying out of his line of vision. I wash and dry dishes, tidy shelves and sweep the floor, waiting for Tina to finish working for the night.

I look around for something else to do, startled when a large hand clamps my shoulder. My knees threaten to buckle at the sound of Noel's voice.

"I told you, no trouble to my door."

He takes me by the arm and I stumble beside him as walks me across the room.

"Don't get me wrong, I ain't bothered about the fucking picture. It's only what she gets paid for, anyway. But you caused major ructions tonight. I don't like it and I ain't having it."

We reach the front door and he propels me out on to the landing. "

My teeth chatter with cold and fright, "I'm sorry. Noel, please, don't do this. I don't have anywhere to go."

He shakes his head and grins, bends down to me and says, "What makes you think I give a fuck?" With that, he disappears into the apartment, returning seconds later to sling my suitcases across the floor.

"Just think yourself lucky I'm letting you keep the cases,

girl. It's a small price to get rid of you."

He slams the door shut.

I stack the cases one on top of the other and sit down. Everything has happened so fast that I can't gather my thoughts. What am I going to do? If I sit here until Tina's customer leaves, perhaps she'll notice I'm gone and come looking for me. No, Noel won't let her. But still I sit, clinging on to the hope Tina will open the door and tell me to come back in, it's all a misunderstanding.

Cold seeps into my bones, stiffening my arms and legs and I walk round the landing area to loosen my limbs. After a few circuits, I'm forced to accept that Tina's door is closed to me, there will be no respite.

The first of the suitcases, heavy with books and camera equipment, is all I can manage on the first trip down the four flights of stone steps. At every landing, the light comes on for a short period, just enough time to walk down to the next stairwell before it goes out again. My slow progress with the heavy case means I navigate the last few steps of each flight in complete darkness.

My muscles scream with the effort of manhandling the luggage and I stop for a breather in the foyer, bending over with my hands on my knees while my heart slows down.

The bloody light blinks out and the foyer is plunged into complete darkness. I straighten up, waiting for my movement to reactivate it. Nothing. I swear under my breath and fumble along the wall for the manual switch. It clicks up and down but the light doesn't come back on. My heart quails at the thought of climbing the stairs in darkness but I can't leave the other suitcase up there. Noel could easily decide to throw my clothes away. Keeping my bearings by hugging the wall, I set off.

After only a few steps, my hand touches leather. A leather coat.

"Is that you, Noel?"

No answer.

"Come on, Noel. This isn't funny. You've got what you want. I'm leav–"

Unseen hands seize my shoulders and slam me against the wall. Instinctively, I try to defend myself, pushing against my attacker's body and driving my knee upwards towards his groin. He grunts as my knee hits his leg and then heaves me sideways, kicking my feet from under me.

His body weight crushes me as we fall to the ground together. I draw breath to scream and he punches the side of my head. I'm losing the battle, disoriented by the darkness and freaked by the complete silence of my attacker. He buries his hands in my hair and thumps my head against the floor. The second blow drains the fight from me, leaving only a cold fear paralysing me. My body slackens, no longer able to resist.

His breath, ripe with cigarettes and booze, fills the air above me. His bodyweight shifts as he hoists himself to his feet and I send a silent *Thank you* to a God I don't believe in.

A dim light flickers, throwing into relief the silhouette of a man with his back to me. From where I lie on the floor, he looks enormous. The light comes from a mobile phone in his hand. He's texting.

I draw my knees up in an attempt to get to my feet, but, as soon as I move, pain and nausea lance through my head and I groan. The light goes out and total darkness falls again. The last thing I am aware of is being dragged roughly across the floor, deeper into the recesses of the foyer

Night after night, yet another nameless man pushes into me, his sweat staining my body, until the final grunt as he rolls off and collapses on the bed beside me. Tonight, something's wrong. It's cold and dark. He's too rough and I can't see him, can't remember who he is.

I try to push him off and he slaps me, hard.

Shocks me back into reality.

My knickers and jeans are tangled round my feet, my legs are pushed apart and rough fingers probe my body. *Not this. Please, God, not this.*

The pain is sharp and brutal; the fingers tear my skin, as they penetrate. No way to escape them, as he pins me to the ground, an arm across my throat. I grit my teeth, force myself to stay still and start chanting in my head. *You can do this, you can get through it, you can do this …*

It goes on and on until, abruptly, he pulls his fingers out and I hear the sound of his zipper. I brace myself for what's to come, but his penis flops limply against my leg.With a roar of frustrated rage, he punches my face, my head snaps back and the darkness deepens.

....

The lights are back on, dazzling my eyes and creating a halo round the large shadow that looms over me. There is nothing but pain. It blooms in my head, courses jaggedly down my spine and explodes in my vagina. The arm no longer crushes my throat. Rough hands pull at my legs and my jeans.

I strike out, landing a feeble blow. My voice is a thin, high-pitched wail. "Don't touch me, don't fucking touch me".

The shadow materialises into Noel as my eyes adjust to the light. Tina pushes him to one side and drapes a blanket over me. "Get off, Noel, can't you see you're frightening her?"

He throws his hands up and backs off. "I was just trying to fucking help!"

I can't stop wailing. Tina gathers me up in her embrace. "Shhhh. It's all right, Jills. It's all right. You're safe now. I promise."

Her words don't register, but her voice calms me. I peer past her at Noel's retreating back. and beyond him to where Leon sits on the stairs.

Whispering through my bruised throat, I ask, "What are you all doing here?"

Tina shoots a murderous look at Noel. "He couldn't wait to tell me he'd turfed you out. Then I saw the case on the landing, so I came looking for you. You was just lying there ... I thought you was ..."

"And them?" A nod towards Noel and the boy on the stairs.

"I shouted for Noel to bring a blanket."

"And Leon just came along for the show." The words taste bitter in my mouth.

"Forget them. I've phoned for an ambulance. I know you're cold and frightened, babe, but stay where you are until the medics get here."

Not likely. I don't trust any of them.

My breath comes in rapid, shallow gasps as I struggle on to my hands and knees, using the blanket to shield my nakedness. Another effort and I've got one foot flat on the floor, my breathing now jagged. A final deep gulp and I push up on to my feet, grunting against the pain.

Tina stoops to help me pull my jeans up and I elbow her aside.

"Get away from me – and cancel that ambulance. I don't

need it."

"You're not thinking straight, you're in shock." She fusses round me with the blanket and I punch her shoulder.

"I said get away from me!"

With one hand on the wall, I hobble towards my suitcase, which still lies on the floor – and I realise what my brain has been trying to tell me.

"Tina, why are the lights on?"

"Don't worry about the lights. Just let me help you –"

My voice rises to a scream. "Why are the fucking lights on?"

She shouts back at me, infected by my near-hysteria. "They're always bloody on!"

"No. They were off, the switch didn't work."

"What are you talking about? The lights are never off, they're on a timer."

Both hands on the wall and leaning into the pain, I say again, "The lights were off. Somebody turned them off."

"You're not thinking straight." Tina attempts to soothe me. "There's nobody here but us."

So one of them did it. I shelve the argument for the moment; there's something else I need to do which can't wait.

Tina's crying now, her cheeks stained with mascara. "Come back in, Jills, please. Wait inside for the ambulance. Noel were only trying to help you, he'll stay out of the way. Come on ..." She tries to take hold of my arm, but I stay huddled against the wall.

"Just get my fucking camera bag, will you? Noel kept it when he threw me out."

At last, she runs up to the apartment, returning a few minutes later with the bag. I lower myself on to the suitcase and rummage in the pockets of the bag until I find my phone. I punch buttons and wait.

He picks up. "Yeah, what do you want, Jilly?"

"Can you come and get me? Please, Rob, I want to come home."

Tina moans, "No, Jills."

Noel shrugs and opens the large double doors.

I make no effort to look 'special', as Sylvie advises me. My hair hangs down my back in its usual plait and I haven't bothered with make-up. Plain tee shirt, short skirt and no underwear.

In and out quick, is what I hope for.

Sylvie hovers, as I wait by the front door.

"You know you're not getting paid, don't you?" she asks yet again.

"Yes, OK. You've told me a hundred times." I brush her off, too nervous to talk.

The police car glides to a stop outside the gate and waits.

"Stevie's all right. Just don't argue with him," is Sylvie's last piece of maternal advice, as she opens the door for me.

I reach the car, he leans across and opens the passenger door.

"Get in. Hurry up, don't want the curtains twitching, do we?"

Suits me. Let's get it over with.

Stevie pulls into a side road near the river and swerves among the trees, bouncing over roots and brushing against undergrowth until the car is hidden from any passing traffic. He jerks his head and I get out of the car.

"Against the tree," he says, as he shoves one hand up my skirt, propelling me backwards at the same time until the tree bark is scratching my back.

He laughs. "Oh, you dirty little slut, you've come prepared." He unzips his trousers and pushes my legs apart.

"Wait." I reach into my skirt pocket for a condom, but he knocks it aside.

"None of that shit for me," he grunts and, within seconds, his penis is inside me. He doesn't take long to finish and I breathe a sigh of relief. He zips up and turns towards the car, while I crumple up a tissue and put it between my legs.

Not long now and I can be in a hot bath to wash him away.

His hand on my chest stops me as I reach for the car door. "Oh no, you're not getting back in the car in that state. At least old Sylvie had the sense to wear pants."

Fine. I'd rather walk home, anyway.

"Just before you go," calls Stevie.

"Yes?" I turn back. An overweight, balding guy in a police uniform emerges from the trees and walks towards me.

"You need to do Barry here a little favour."

The two men high-five and Barry says, "Don't worry, love, I don't like sloppy seconds. On your knees."

I don't move.

Stevie sighs, "OK, back in the car. Let's get down to the station, get you booked in for soliciting."

"But I wasn't. You know I wasn't."

Another sigh. "You just don't get it, do you? Who do you think they're going to believe? You or Barry and me?"

I can get in the car and take my chances at the police station; or I can make a run for it, although it will only delay the inevitable.

I get on my knees.

CHAPTER TWENTY ONE

Twenty long minutes pass before a taxi pulls up at the door and Rob strolls in, his face glowing with booze and self-righteousness.

"I knew you'd come to your senses," he begins, before catching sight of Tina and Noel sitting on the stairs. Leon went back up to the apartment, under Noel's orders, but Tina refused to leave me. "What are they doing here?"

"We're waiting for you." Tina stares beadily at the man who called her a prossy. "Jills were attacked –"

Before she can say anymore, Rob drops to his knees and pulls me to him. "Babe! What's happened?"

"Don't touch me!" I shudder at the weight of my arms on my body, shrink from the smell of his cologne. "Back off. I can't breathe."

"But your head's bleeding! Who's done this to you?"

"We don't know," Tina says. "We found her at the bottom of the stairs; I've called for an ambulance."

Rob, with one of his lightning mood changes, goes on the attack. "What do you mean, you don't know? There's nobody here but you." He stands and lunges towards Noel. "Were it you?"

Noel snarls, "For fuck's sake. This ain't nothing to do with me."

Tina leaps to her feet. "Just stop, both of you! Jills don't need this." And to Rob, "It's not just a mugging, she were …"

Raped. The word hangs unspoken in the air.

Rob's face is slack with shock. He kneels again, but doesn't touch me. "Oh, Jilly. I'm so sorry." Tears stand in his eyes as he asks quietly, "Who did this? Were it him?"

He means Noel, but I can't focus. "I don't know …" My head throbs, banishing coherent thought. "There was a shadow, a tall shadow."

"Right, we need the police here, right now."

"No, Rob, what we need is to get out of here."

Tina pushes in between us. "Are you fucking crazy? You can't go anywhere with him. Have you forgotten why you came here in the first place?"

"And look how well that turned out." I push my face towards hers and hiss, "Coming here was the biggest mistake of my life."

Noel takes her arm. "Leave it, Tina. You can't help some people."

I sneer. "Help? I don't think so. How come you were the one touching me when I came round?"

"Why are you saying these things, Jills?" Tina asks. "He did nowt. I swear it, he didn't do it."

I hold Noel's gaze for a long minute.

Was it you, Noel?

Rob still hesitates, phone in hand. "I still think we should get the police."

"No!" I cut in sharply. "No police."

Noel echoes my direction – "No, mate. You're not bringing the filth round here." – and Rob drops his phone back in his pocket.

Leon clatters downstairs with my other case; he stands,

117

flanked by his mother and father, and watches while I ease painfully to my feet and hobble out of the door into the waiting taxi. Rob, now apparently sober, tries to help but I shake him off and he hurries to load the suitcases. I take one last look at Tina and her family and all I see is a small-time prostitute, her pimp and their clearly damaged son. I should never have come here. I put myself in harm's way and I've paid the price.

The wail of an ambulance echoes in the distance, as it searches the warren of streets for the incident. It won't find me. I'll see to my own healing. I'm not a victim.

I'm not.

The taxi pulls up at the gate, but the driver doesn't get out to help me with the boxes piled outside the front door. He stares out of the car window at me and waits. So do I.

Behind me, Sylvie is crying drunken tears, laced with a good helping of self-pity.

"I can't believe you're doing this – leaving your own mother with no money. How am I supposed to live?"

She gets no answer from me. Her voice rises and she shrieks, "You ungrateful little cow. I was the only one who wanted you, who looked after you when your Dad left us."

"Oh yeah? Left us?" I turn back and grab a fistful of her dress, pushing her against the door. "And which Dad was that? The soldier who got killed overseas? The farmer who had an accident when his tractor overturned? Or just one of your punters when you got careless? You can't even remember your own lies."

Letting her go, I walk down the path to the taxi, open the door and say to the driver, "Pick up my boxes and put them in the boot. Unless you want me to phone your boss and tell her that the last time I saw you was in my bed, on your knees behind me, naked as the day you were born."

He looks at me with hatred in his eyes, but he gets out of the car and does as I say.

We drive off, towards the railway station, and I don't look back.

I've paid my dues.

CHAPTER
TWENTY TWO

I sit in the small back yard every evening and watch the sky darken into twilight. Rob has double locked the gate which leads out on to the street and rigged up a light, so when darkness falls, I can dispel the shadows. I only go inside when the cold creeps into my bones. He watches me from the kitchen window. He knows not to come outside and talk to me.

The bruises to my body and head slowly heal; when the pain gets bad I self medicate with Sauvignon Blanc and a little weed I stole from Rob's cache in the bedroom. I don't think about what happened to me on the floor of the Old Mill. Occasionally, dark thoughts flood into my head, over-riding the numbness. Strangely, it's not my recent attack that haunts me, but the memory of the men who paid to own me for a short time; the ones who tried to kiss me or were rough with my still-growing body because 'it's more fun'. When I can't block them out, I count the bricks in the wall, vertically and horizontally, and make pictures out of the cracks in the concrete groundwork. I don't touch my camera, even though Rob bought me a lens I'd been hankering after for a long time. It made me almost smile. An *I'm sorry* gift from Rob when he hadn't done anything to hurt me. I sleepwalk through my Degree Show exhibition, smiling and accepting the congratulations for the First Class Honours. Christie is ecstatic with the reaction to the catalogue cover, even though he was hauled over the coals by the Dean for authorising it. At least half of the students in my year protested against the picture of Tina, piling up defaced copies outside his office. *The Daily Mail*, following in the footsteps of *The Guardian,* ran a piece on censorship, defending the use of the photograph. Christie was disappointed that I wouldn't give an interview, but issued a statement on my behalf, without any input from me.

Rob stayed away from the exhibition and from the printworks until the gossip died down about the night I was 'rescued from a pimp'. Nige has taken to dropping in occasionally at lunchtime with Rob. He's always polite and has apologised for 'maybe going too far'. Strangely, I believe him but he still makes my skin crawl. Rob no longer goes drinking with him, though.

In this way, a couple of months drift by until Spring changes to Summer and the back yard floods with sunshine. I walk to the park at the end of the street a couple of times and watch the kids kicking a football and the oldies playing bowls. The guy across the street knocks on the door, shiny blond hair and guitar in hand, and asks me to take his picture for a CD cover. And, gradually, life resumes.

CHAPTER TWENTY THREE

Monday morning, the sun is shining. I think I'll walk into town with my camera and shoot a few tourists and pigeons in Slab Square. Maybe even make an evening meal for Rob, get my life back to a semblance of normality.

My mobile phone lights up and Jim Morrison says, *This is the end*, the ringtone I've assigned to Tina. She calls every few days and I ignore her, but she keeps trying. Today, I pick up and say, "What do you want, Tina? I'm on my way out of the door."

She's silent for a few seconds and I say abruptly, "Look, I don't have time for this –"

"All right. I'm just warning you. Get Rob and his creepy mate to lay off."

"What are you on about?"

"The pizza deliveries, the fire engine, the wreathes … Noel's getting wound up and about to explode. He thought it were funny at first, but now …"

Rob, how can you be so stupid?

"Fine. I'll make sure it stops."

"Thanks." Tina hesitates, just for a couple of seconds, then says, "Are you OK?"

"As if you care. Goodbye, Tina. Don't call again."

"Wait! Jills, listen … it weren't Noel. Believe me, he

wouldn't hurt a woman for the world."

I snort down the phone in disbelief, "Come off it, I've seen the bruises, remember?"

"All right, but think about it, he's a fucking giant. You'd have known if it were him, wouldn't you?"

Her words trigger a half-forgotten memory of the tall shadow in the foyer, backlit by the mobile phone. The way he towered over me.

"I saw him, Tina." I thumb the red button to cut her off, determine not to let the past dominate my life again.

Someone knocks on the front door as I'm packing my camera bag. I peer through the small pane of frosted glass, but can only make out a vague, male outline.

"Who is it?" I don't answer the door to strangers.

"Jilly, it's me. Christie."

"Christie? What are you doing here?"

"What about letting me in and I'll tell you?"

I fumble with the chain and the locks and open the door to a vision in a flowered, silk shirt and skinny-legged black trousers, designer sunglasses perched on his head. For the first time in a long while, a real, honest-to-God smile creeps across my face. He looks like an exotic bird against the backdrop of the drab, terraced street.

"Hang on, let me get my camera." I run to grab it, while he stands patiently by the door. I pose him in the middle of the street with the sombre houses stretching out behind him and, just as the shutter drops, a grey-clad hoodie walks into view, a perfect counterpoint for the vision that is Christie. I drop to my knees to get a low angle shot, framing him against the sky.

He poses for a few more shots, then says, "So, are you going to ask me in, then?"

"Yeah, sure, do you want tea?"

The galley kitchen is barely big enough for two people, but he wedges himself into a corner as I boil the kettle and fills me in on all the latest gossip from the university. He soon has me laughing out loud at his outrageous stories.

Mugs of tea in hand, we settle into a couple of canvas chairs in the back yard and sit in companionable silence for a few minutes before I ask, "What's so important you couldn't text me?"

"Do you remember when Tom Buckley came to give a lecture on portraiture last term?"

"Yeah, I remember him. A bit surly, wasn't he?"

He shrugs. "Not really. Anyway, I showed him your work and he was interested in interviewing you, depending on your results. Then, when the catalogue came out, he was blown away by the picture of Tina on the front cover."

"And?" I hardly dare hope.

"And ... long story short, he called me this morning. He needs another assistant in his London studio and says you can have the job, if you're interested."

"If I'm interested? You know I am!"

A thought occurs to me, "Does he know about ... you know, what happened to me"

"No, he doesn't, and he won't hear it from me."

"Thanks, Christie, I appreciate that. When does the job start?"

"His present assistant leaves at the end of August, so you have a couple of months to get some good work done, impress the hell out of him."

"Oh God, yes! I have a couple of projects in my head already, sort of an extension on my Degree Show work, but in colour, not so gritty."

Before I can expand on my ideas, a car pulls up on the street on the other side of the yard wall.

"That's Rob, home for lunch. Stay and have a bite with us?"

Christie uncoils his long, lean body from the canvas chair. "No, that's OK, thanks. I'm meeting Oliver in town. We're going to book the register office for next month. We've finally decided to tie the knot."

"I'm so pleased for you, not before time, either."

Rob appears in the yard, having walked through the house while Christie and I were talking. "What's not before time?" he asks, coming in on the tail end of the conversation.

"Hi, Rob. Christie and Oliver are getting married next month. Isn't that great?"

"I suppose so, if you're into that kind of thing."

In the awkward silence that follows, Christie wiggles his fingers at me, mouths, "I'll be in touch," and disappears through the house to let himself out of the front door.

"Why did you have to do that, Rob? Couldn't you just have said "Congratulations" and let it go at that?"

He sits down heavily in one of the chairs, all his usual bluster and bravado gone, and says quietly. "Can I tell you something? These last weeks have been really good for me. I felt close to you again."

He lifts a hand as I attempt to speak. "No, hear me out. For three years, I've done all I could to support you. I didn't like the time you spent with prossies and, I admit it, I don't like Christie, either. But I love you, Jilly, you're important to me. I know I went off the rails when you turned me down and I'm right sorry for what me and Nige done."

He pauses for breath and I jump in before he starts again. "I know you are, honestly, let's just forget about it. Come on, you'd better have your lunch or you'll be late back to work."

Rob follows me into the kitchen and, while I have the fridge open looking for something to put in a sandwich, he reaches past me and plucks a can of beer from the door.

"I know, I know!"He pops the top of the can and has a long drink. "It's only one, I promise. Anyway, what were Christie doing here? I thought you was finished with all that uni stuff."

With my back to him, buttering bread and slicing tomatoes, I say, "Oh, nothing much. Just checking to see if I was all right."

"Huh! Nosy git. Still, it were nice to see you smiling again. Pity you can't do it for me."

I absorb the change in mood, but don't respond to it.

"Actually, I'm feeling a lot better. I might go into town this afternoon, take a few photographs and do a bit of shopping."

"Babe, that's brilliant." Rob perks up. "Tell you what, I'll come, too. We ain't been out together for ages. I'll just finish my sandwich and phone Nige, throw a sickie."

"No need, I'm only going to mooch about a bit."

"What? So you don't want me with you?"

"Of course I do." *Smile, you know the drill.* "I just thought you'd be bored, that's all."

"Nah, we'll have a great time. I know, I'll buy you a present to mark the end of uni. You never got a proper celebration with all the upset at that –" He stops midsentence. "Nah, no bad thoughts today, eh?"

He hustles off to phone Nige and change out of his work

clothes, pausing only to grab another beer and say, "Forget the sandwich. We'll have lunch in town."

Rob hums a tune as he disappears. His relief is palpable. I'm all 'fixed' now, no need for solicitousness or tip-toeing round me as if I were fragile. It's frightening how quickly he's reverted to the caustic remarks and the hair-trigger temper bubbling away just below the surface.

But it's not business as usual, Rob. This time I've got a Get-Out-Of-Jail-Free card.

CHAPTER TWENTY FOUR

The jeweller's shop window is a blaze of light, reflecting off diamonds and cubic zirconiums. I can't tell the difference; they're all beautiful to me. Rob has his feet planted firmly in front of the window, determined to choose a present for me. My heart sinks as I realise he is edging nearer to a display of engagement rings.

"See anything you like, babe?"

I tug on his arm. "No, not really. Let's go to Waterstone's and look at the books."

He won't budge, his eyes fastened on the trays of glittering rings. "I ain't buying you any more bloody books. Come on. We're going in."

One hand on my back, he ushers me into the shop. There are no customers inside and an assistant bustles over as soon as we enter, smile fixed and voice bright. "Good afternoon, sir." She addresses Rob and, after a brief glance, ignores me. "How can I help you, today?"

"Earrings," I blurt out, before Rob can speak. He raises his eyebrows in surprise and I hurry on. "Don't you remember, I lost one in the Lace Market?" I lay emphasis on the last two words, a hark back to the night I was attacked. When I washed the blood from my head, I discovered my ear was torn and the earring was missing. I'm gambling Rob won't want to talk about it in front of the shop assistant.

Grudgingly, he says, "Well, if that's what you want …"

I settle on a pair of plain gold earrings, similar to the cheap ones I'd been wearing for many years. I'm relieved when we leave the shop with a small bag that doesn't contain an engagement ring.

"You know, you could have had anything you wanted," Rob grumbles, all trace of his good mood gone. "Why did you have to mention that night? I thought we'd moved on and you were all right now."

I stop dead in the middle of the mall. Rob walks on a few steps before he realises I'm not with him. He looks over his shoulder, sighs, and walks back to me. "What now?"

"I've moved on, Rob, but you haven't."

He bends down to peer at me, makes a sad face. "Has little Jilly babes had her feelings hurt?" He grasps my arm and tries to pull me into step with him.

I shake him off. "No. I haven't had my feelings hurt. But I'll tell you what I have had, shall I?"

My voice rises. People stare and Rob moves in closer to me, whispers. "Be careful, babes, be very careful."

I carry on. "I've had it up to here with you." I raise a hand under my chin to emphasise the point. "I've had it with you belittling everything I do, the bullying, the threats and the stupid tricks with that bastard, Nige."

A young couple have stopped. The girl says to me, "Are you all right, love?"

"Yes, thank you for asking." I'm smiling and crying at the same time. "Just getting a few things straight."

She looks a bit uncertain. Her boyfriend pulls her away and she calls back, "Good luck!"

Aware of the attention we're attracting, Rob changes tack and adopts a worried look. "Is that what you really feel, babe? Honestly, I only want what's best for you. It's for your own good, you know that, don't you?"

"No, Rob, you're not playing the game with me again." The words pour out of me. "You've browbeat and bullied me for the last time. I don't know what drives you, but you and your mean little mind can just fuck right off, because I'm finished with you."

A woman's voice behind me, slurred and hoarse, says "You tell him, girl! Tell the bastard where to go. Men, they're all shits, every single one of them."

I'd know that voice anywhere. It's Sylvie.

I utter a mental *I'm fucked* and prepare for my world to implode. My mouth is dry and my heart hammers in my chest. As soon as Sylvie realises she's talking to her daughter, all hell will be let loose. Rob looks over my shoulder, face thunderous with rage at her interference. His jaw drops and he pushes me to one side.

"You!" he shouts at Sylvie. She screams and I turn to see her shrink back against a shop front, as Rob grabs hold of her arms and shakes her. "You bitch! You dirty fuck-ing bitch. You ruined my life."

Her face, bled of all colour, is contorted into a mask of fright.

A workman in a high-vis vest leaps forward, wraps his arms round Rob's body and drags him off Sylvie.

"Steady on, mate. Whatever she's done, you can't go around attacking women."

"Let me go!" Rob roars, struggling to get free and follow Sylvie as she hares off through the mall.

"No worries, but not until she's gone. Calm down, do you hear me?" The workman looks across at me. "Had a few beers, has he?"

I nod, unable to speak. *Rob knows Sylvie?* My legs

threaten to give way and I collapse onto a nearby bench. Sylvie is long gone and the guy releases Rob.

"You're not going to do owt silly, are you?"

Rob shakes his head, also seemingly struck dumb, and shakily sits down on the seat beside me.

"OK, I'd better get back to work." The workman slaps Rob on the shoulder. "Take it easy, mate, all right?" He nods at me and walks off.

The silence stretches between us. Rob's clenched fists rest on his knees and he's breathing heavily. An avalanche of questions crashes through my mind, without a single coherent answer for me to latch on to. The thought of Sylvie and Rob – no, I can't go there. It's just too weird. More importantly, what does he know?

Rob stands. "I need a drink."

The lunch-hour rush is over and the bar on the corner is nearly empty. I ask for a whiskey and, without comment, Rob orders a double for both of us. Ceiling fans circle lazily above our heads, not doing much to shift the warm air, yet I'm cold. I throw back the whiskey in one gulp, welcoming the heat that courses through my body, and brace myself for whatever is about to come.

"I know, I'm a bastard." Rob has his head down, staring into his glass. "Not saying it to apologise to you, don't think that. Tired of playing games and, face it – you're just as bad as me."

My denial dies on my lips, as he raises his head and I see the misery on his face. "What you and me had, Jilly, it were over long ago. I know that and I know why. And, yeah, I did want to hurt you. I was a shit. And Nige, well, who knows why Nige does things? He's just a twisted bugger. Maybe I shouldn't have listened to him."

He puts a twenty on the table. "Go and get us a refill."

When I return with the drinks, Rob stares into space, then heaves a sigh. "All right. I'm going to tell you summat I've never told anybody. Don't talk to me. Just let me get through it, OK?"

Something tells me that it probably isn't OK, but I nod anyway.

"That woman, that prossy – I went to her house once. Some village or other, Swanton mebbe, out in the sticks, anyway. It were a long time ago, on me fifteenth birthday. Me dad – he could be a right cruel bastard, at times – took me there because I'd never, you know, done sex."

I want to stand up and run out of the bar, stop him talking, anything as long as I don't have to hear any more. Rob reads the horror on my face as revulsion.

"You're disgusted, I don't blame you. I've been disgusted with meself for years. Anyway, I went through with it. Me dad was listening outside the door, shouting advice. It were me first time, like, so I'm not saying I didn't enjoy it, but ..." He shudders. "As soon as I were finished, not even got me trousers on, me dad comes bursting into the room and, in seconds, he's on top of her and the pair of them are whooping and laughing, like I was a big joke."

Please, God, make him stop.

But when did He ever listen to me?

Rob draws a ragged breath and carries on. "But that's not the worst of it. I just wanted to get out of there, get away from them and, I don't know how, but I blundered into another room. Oh God, Jilly, stop looking at me like that."

I lift my hand in front of my face, batting at the air, mutely begging him to stop talking. But Rob goes on, determined to finish his story.

"A little girl were in there, a toddler, standing in a crib. She were crying, frightened by the noise me dad and her mum was making. When she saw me, she held her hands up. I wanted to pick her up, but I felt dirty, ashamed, so I turned me back on her and ran out of the house. Me dad came out a bit later, all full of himself, telling me I was a man now, and crap like that."

And now I've got my hands clasped over my head, my eyes closed, trying to block out his words.

"No more, please, no more."

He's oblivious to me and his voice drones on relentlessly.

"He were sorry for laughing at me, mind. Because I told my mum. I left out the bit where I had the old tart, made out he'd left me waiting in the car. I didn't know it would break her heart, did I? He were gone within three days and we never heard from him again."

Rob stands, whiskey glasses in hand, and turns towards the bar. I think he's finished, but he has a final twist of the knife. "Broke my heart as well. Because he left her with a little present, courtesy of that fucking trollop. Yep, he gave her a dose of the clap. My mum, the gentlest, kindest woman I ever knew. She were dead within the year. They said it were cancer that took her, but I knew different."

A long silence; he's gone to the bar. I open my eyes and stare at the wet rings on the table. They shine in the overhead light and I think what a beautiful abstract photograph they'd make. I swirl my finger through the rings, making patterns. Two whiskey glasses slam down on the table. He's back, bringing with him a reality I'm not ready to face.

The third whiskey goes down easily and the edges

begin to blur.

....

I fall against a shop front and giggle. "Sorry, shop, didn't see you there." This strikes me as so funny, I laugh out loud. The street begins to move faster and I mutter, "Can you stop that?"

A hand under my elbow guides me to a bench.

"Here, love, I think you'd better sit down before you fall down."

I look up into a face that refuses to stay still.

"Who the fuck are you? Take your hands off me."

Another voice. "Come on, let's go. She's not our problem."

"Yeah, sod off, you sad wanker – Oh, shit! Gonna be sick –"

A pair of shoes dances backwards as I lean over and vomit up the lovely Italian lunch Rob had treated me to, along with God knows how many whiskeys. A hazy recollection of drinking snakebite starts me heaving again until I subside into dry retches.

"Oh, for fuck's sake, she's spewed all over my shoes!"

The street has stopped moving. I sit up intending to apologise. Instead, I start laughing again.

"What's so funny, you mad cow? These are designer trainers you've just ruined."

The whole world is one big fucking joke. Can't he see that?

Rob's here. Where did he come from? "Calm down, mate. She's not used to drinking, doesn't know what she's doing." He's giving money to a guy in a hoodie. "This'll buy you a new pair, OK?"

I'm tired now, my head aches and my mouth tastes foul. I don't want to laugh any more. Rob hauls me to my feet and looks round for a taxi, hoping for a driver who'll let me into his cab.

"God, you stink. What was you thinking, wandering off like that? I came back from the bogs and you was gone."

"Can we just go home, please?" It's an effort to talk. The effects of the alcohol are wearing off and there's something at the back of my mind that I really don't want to think about.

A taxi pulls up and Rob bundles me in, with a promise to the cabbie of an extra payment if I'm sick again. I loll back with my head on Rob's shoulder and close my eyes. He pats my hand. "That's it. Sleep it off. We'll talk in the morning."

CHAPTER TWENTY FIVE

It rained overnight. The roofs opposite glisten in the early morning sun and steam rises off the pavement. The guy from across the street sets off for his usual morning five o'clock run. I've been sitting by the window since two o'clock, when I woke with a raging thirst and the mother of all headaches. Rob snores obliviously in the bed behind me. He should be awake, getting ready for work, but we forgot to set the alarm clock. Besides, I want to talk to him.

Another hour ticks by. The sound of car engines rises from the street as neighbours set off for the daily grind.

Rob stirs. "Christ, my head." He sits up, swings his legs out of bed and sees me at the window. "Bloody hell, you frightened me. What time is it?"

"Too late to go to work."

He groans and falls back on the bed. "Aw, why didn't you wake me? Nige'll have a fit."

"We've got bigger things to worry about than Nige throwing a hissy fit. He'll survive without you for one morning."

Rob's face darkens. "Well, listen to you, laying down the law."

I cut him off before he can say any more. "No, Rob. You don't talk to me like that any more. Things changed yesterday. Now, I'm going downstairs to make tea and then we're going to talk."

"You'd better be very sure of what you're doing, lady. You could live to be sorry for cheeking me like this. Go on, then. Get the tea made."

I give him that one. It's going to be a long morning.

He shuffles through to the bathroom while I brew the tea and dunk a couple of painkillers in a glass of water. On his way back through the kitchen, he accepts the glass without a word and I follow him into the living room with two mugs.

"Let's have it, then." He grunts as he collapses into an armchair. "This better be bloody good, after making me miss work."

"That woman in the street, yesterday –" is as far as I get before he interrupts.

"What woman?" I wait, as recollection dawns in his eyes.

"Oh, sweet fucking hell. I told you, didn't I?"

He's horrified. This is my moment and I need to get it right.

"Rob, it's nothing to be ashamed of. You were just a kid. If anyone's to blame, it's your dad. He shouldn't have taken you there."

"Don't give me that. I bet you was loving it, hearing all my dirty secrets." He slams his mug down on the coffee table and glares at me. "If you ever tell anybody, I swear, I'll do you damage."

He shifts forward in his chair, his body tense and my headache increases as I recognise the danger signs. It takes an effort not to back off and placate him, but somehow I stand my ground and answer him calmly.

"I'm not going to tell anyone. But we need to talk about

it."

"We bloody don't." Rob rises and stalks off into the kitchen to end the conversation, but I'm on his heels.

"Yes, we do. You said something else last night, as well, do you remember? You said you knew we were finished. You apologised for what you and Nige did to me."

"Yeah, well, that were the drink talking, weren't it?"

"No, Rob, that was *you* talking. That was the real you, the guy I first met in the bar. It's my fault you changed –"

I worry that I'm laying it on a bit too thick, but he's more than happy to agree that I'm to blame.

"Too bloody right, it was you. Looking down on me, I were never good enough for you, were I?"

He looks out of the kitchen window, his back rigid. I take his arm and try to turn him to face me.

"Listen, please. If I had known about your dad taking you to –" I swallow hard. "– to that woman, I wouldn't have started working with the girls. I could've worked on something else."

Disbelief is written on his face when he finally turns towards me. "Huh, like that would have happened."

I hold his gaze, my face earnest. "But it's true. Every time I went to photograph them, came back and talked to you about them, it must have brought that memory back. I wouldn't knowingly have done that to you."

I can see that he wants to believe me. I press on, softening my voice.

"You should've told me."

He slumps against the kitchen sink, all trace of anger gone. "I were too ashamed, babes. I didn't want you to know what kind of person my dad were – or that I lied to my mum to get back at him." He avoids my gaze. "What would you have thought of me if you knew I had been with a prostitute?"

"It wouldn't have mattered. It was a long time before I met you."

I would despise you, just like I despise Rosemary's dad, Stevie and his free-loading buddies, and all the nameless, faceless men who pillaged my teenage body.

"That's true. Let's just forget it." He opens the fridge door. "What's for breakfast? I fancy a fry-up to soak up the beer."

I wonder if his favourite hangover remedy will help him to erase the memory of his drunken, self-pitying outpourings of last night. His momentary self-doubt at the kitchen window is gone, dispelled by my easy lie. I've absolved him and all's right in his world.

Time to burst his bubble.

"I'm glad we had this talk, Rob. I feel like we've really cleared the air. So, when would you like me to move out?"

"Move out? Don't be daft. That were just the beer talking."

"They say you tell the truth when you're drunk, don't they? You were right, it's time I moved on."

He straightens up from the fridge, food forgotten, and says, "I didn't mean it, you know that." He sounds uncertain, dulled by the hangover and the stress of confronting his past.

"Yeah, you did. I could tell. And you're right. We'll always be friends, and I appreciate that you trusted me with what your dad did to you." The words stick in my throat. "You deserve better than me, somebody who'll love you – and they won't know anything about – you know."

Thank God there's no sign of anger as he protests, "But

I love you, babes."

"I know, Rob, and I'm very fond of you. But I'll always be a reminder of that day, now you've told me about it. You need to forget it again. Who knows what might slip out if I get drunk?"

His eyes widen slightly at the suggestion and I ram the point home. "Can you imagine what Nige would say if he found out? After all the things he said about prossies?" I stammer a bit on the hated word and fall silent.

He lights a fag, offers one to me. I shake my head. The silence stretches as he smokes steadily until there's only the butt left. He stubs the glowing ash out in the sink and says, "Well, we had some good times, didn't we?"

I'm afraid to hope and wait for him to go on.

"I'm sorry, Jilly babes, I didn't mean to tell you when I were drunk. I was fond of you, yeah, but you spoiled it with all that prossy stuff. Pity, really."

I raise my hands in a gesture of resignation, inwardly punting the air and shouting, *Yes!*

"OK, I understand. I'll start looking for somewhere else today."

"No worries. A couple of weeks won't make much difference, but it'll be nice to get that room back."

His phone rings and he says, "Sorry, babes, I need to take this." As I walk away, I hear him say, "Sorry, Nige, it's been a nightmare here. I've had to finish with Jilly. All that prossy stuff, you know, it got to be too much … yeah, I'll be in this afternoon, tell you all about it."

I run upstairs. I've done it! London lies ahead with a shiny new start and, this time, I'll make it work. No more using people, no more lying, no more bits of my past lying in wait to trip me up. I pull Tina's suitcases out of the cupboard, might as well make a start on packing. Rob's mood could change in two weeks, so it's probably wise to be ready to go at short notice.

He calls upstairs. "Throw my dressing gown down, will you? It's on the back of the door."

"Sure thing." I pull the heavy garment off the hook and knock a coat to the floor. At the head of the stairs, I call to him, "Coming down, catch. You'll be glad when I'm gone and you can get your coats back in the wardrobe."

I hang the coat back up on the hook and feel a small sting on my finger. Sucking my finger to stem the slight bleeding, I look at the coat to see what pricked me. Stuck in the sleeve seam is a faint glimmer of gold.

It's an old, worn gold earring.

CHAPTER
TWENTY SIX

The air in the room is thick and darkness closes in. I'm back in the foyer, filled with terror, the breath crushed from my body, pain ripping through my head. I choke back a scream, afraid of another punch.

This isn't happening. It's not ...

The darkness begins to recede, pierced by a tiny star-burst of light; the gold of the earring glints in the sunshine that has broken through the rainclouds.The room explodes with light and my body is weightless, as if I could float up to the ceiling. In spite of this, my feet are leaden as I stumble across to the bed and fall heavily on to it. I sit and wait for my world to right itself. I'm numb. I dig deep inside myself and find nothing. No anger, no disbelief, no feeling of betrayal.

I wait. Time lengthens. A small spike of fear blooms inside me.

Am I losing my mind?

A manicure set sits on the dressing table, embedded with mother-of-pearl, one of Rob's *I'm sorry* presents. I can see the scissors in my mind's eye. Small and sharp. Shiny and sharp. I watch my hand as, of its own volition, it stretches out to pick up the pretty case. The scissors are cold in my hand and I give a little gasp at the sensation. I lay the coolness of the blades against my arm. How graceful they are.

My treacherous hand plunges the closed blades deep into my arm. I feel no pain and slowly pull the scissors out of my flesh. *Oh, sweet Christ!* Sharp, pure and clean, the pain races through my arm like a million shards of diamonds. Blood pulses from the wound, dropping globs on to the carpet. In the mirror, a person I've never seen before stares back at me, flushed cheeks, bright eyes, so alive I'm actually bouncing on my toes. I'm ... different. And ready for battle.

I drag one of Rob's tee-shirts from the laundry basket and wrap it round my arm.

"Rob, can you come up here?"

"What is it? Couldn't you have come down ..." He stomps into the bedroom, now fully dressed, and stops abruptly as he sees the blood on the floor. "Shit, look at that mess." A pause. "Is that my fucking tee-shirt?"

I take his arm and lead him to the door. "Do you know who owns this coat?"

He laughs, looks puzzled. "Well, yeah, I'm not fucking stupid. It's Nige's, ain't it?"

"Nige's coat?"

Rob struggles to maintain his good mood. "What's the matter with you? Did you call me upstairs to look at Nige's coat?"

Nige?

My fury is cold and cleansing. I embrace it, keep my voice even. "What's it doing here?"

"I borrowed it. Babe, are you all right?"

"When?"

"I dunno when. You're freaking me out here. Mebbe a week or two ago. Why?"

"Because –" I lift the sleeve and point at the earring. "Do

you know what this is?"

"Is that …? It looks like one one of your earrings."

I turn him to look at me. "To be precise, it's one of the earrings I was wearing the night I was raped."

'Oh, sweet fucking Jesus." He takes a couple of steps back, both hands in his head, tearing at his hair. "I don't understand. How did it get there?"

"I don't know. I thought you could tell me." I watch him closely, registering the beads of sweat popping up on his face.

He's stammering. "I guess …things were moving so fast that night … it could've got stuck when I hugged you …"

I wait impassively.

"Hang on." He sits down. "It might have been Nige who were wearing it that night."

"OK." I've got my phone. "Let's get him over here. Because one thing's for sure. Either you or Nige got pretty close to me that night. The question is, how fucking close?" My voice rises and I lean down until I'm talking into his face.

Watch it, Jilly, keep your cool.

"What do you mean by that, eh? You trying to insinuate it were me or Nige that did that thing to you?" He tries for righteous indignation, but his voice betrays him. He's frightened. "You can't believe that! OK, we did some bad things and, hands up, we shouldn't have done them. But this weren't down to us. You know it weren't. It were that black bastard. I told you to go to the police …"

"You're sweating, Rob. What's wrong?"

He's back on his feet. "Nowt's wrong! I'm not going to be blamed for something I didn't do. This is crazy! I've told you the truth and you better believe it!" He makes a grab for the coat, but I lean against the door and he can't get to it. I see the anger and confusion in his eyes and brace myself for a struggle. But he backs off and runs from the room, careering downstairs and straight out of the front door.

I haven't resolved anything, but I chalk up my first small victory. I faced Rob down and he was the one to back off. And, stone me, it felt good.

My arm throbs as I get dressed in jeans and tee-shirt, but the sensation feels good. I wonder how long this well-being, heightened senses, whatever it is, will last, as I begin to plait my hair. I stop. No. That's the old Jilly; I undo the plait and let my hair hang free down to my waist.

In the kitchen, I search through the cupboards for a black bin-bag, carry it upstairs and fold the coat into it, careful not to dislodge the sleeper. Stopping only to stick a plaster on the seeping wound on my arm, I leave the house, carrying the bin-bag and my camera bag.

As I close the door, I remember the night Rob and Nige taunted me about my work with 'prossies' and how I cowered in front of them, despising myself. I flash in on the humiliation, the hurt I lapped up and absorbed, thinking I was in control of my own life. I don't dwell on it though, because I have work to do. Somebody raped me. I'm going to make them pay.

CHAPTER TWENTY SEVEN

I walk through Slab Square, past the stone lions that guard the Council House, and turn towards the Lace Market. Maybe it's not a good idea to return to the Old Mill. My mind is in overdrive, heightened by the knowledge that, at last, I'm taking things into my own hands. I need to slow down, think about what I'm doing. My calves ache, I've walked too far, too fast, and I sit down on a bench near the tram stop, dropping the bin-bag at my feet.

Who was wearing the leather coat on the night I was raped? If it was Nige, then he had to be the man who punched and battered me. If it was Rob, then the earring could have snagged on the when he hugged me and I pushed him off – or when he attacked me. Maybe neither of them were involved in the rape and it was Noel, creeping downstairs in the dark after turning out the lights. I think of Tina's bruises, the threats I should have taken more notice of and his latent anger. The tall shadow in the foyer. Back to Rob and Nige – how would they have known the lights would be off?

A coarse voice interrupts my thoughts. " 'ere, budge up a bit, me duck." I slide along the bench, making room for a large woman wrapped up in several layers of clothing, although the day is quite warm. She parks a shopping trolly, piled high with tattered plastic carrier bags, and breathes a sigh of relief.

"That bloody hill's a killer, takes me all my time to climb it every day."

"So, why do it then?" I don't care, but she seems to expect an answer.

"This is my bench, see?"

Sure enough, there's a brass plaque screwed on to the wood. It reads *Maisie's Bench* and has a small daisy carved into it.

"So, you're Maisie?"

"I just said so, didn't I? You a bit slow or summat?"

I'm eyeing the bags in the trolley. So many bags.

"And you come here very day?"

Maisie snorts. "For Pete's sake! What's the matter with you?" She shifts her weight to get comfortable and launches into a long story about people clubbing together to buy the bench for her, ending with, "I'm not ungrateful but now I've got to come and sit on the bloody thing."

She pauses for breath and I say, "Got to go, been nice talking to you." I get up, shouldering my camera bag, and walk round the back of the bench. I bump into the shopping trolley, tipping it over, and the carrier bags scatter across the pavement.

"Look what you've done, you clumsy sod." Maisie screeches, as she tries to heave her bulk up off the bench. "That's my whole life in them there bags."

I drop to my knees, gathering up the bags and righting the trolley. "Don't worry, I'll pick them up. Sorry, just wasn't looking where I was going."

"Yeah, OK." She gives up the attempt to stand. "Make sure you get them all, I've got some valuable stuff in there."

All the bags are piled up again and Maisie is mollified, but can't resist a parting shot as I walk off. "You want to be more careful of other people's stuff."

"You, too, Maisie." I think, as I walk away. "Especially that bin-bag at the bottom of your trolley. I'll be back for it."

CHAPTER TWENTY EIGHT

Tina opens the door and I proffer the paper bag.

"Sticky toffee cake?"

"Jills, what are you doing here?"

I drop my arm, "OK, probably a bad idea, anyway."

She throws herself forward to wrap her arms round my neck. "It's a great idea! I've been so worried about you."

"I didn't know if you'd want to see me. I said some horrible things to you."

A shadow crosses her face and her arms drop away. "Yeah, you did and I didn't deserve them. I'd thought we was going to be friends."

"Maybe we still can be." I lift the paper bag again. "Coffee and cake?"

This time, Tina throws the door wide open and I walk in, looking around me warily.

"Where's Noel?"

"He's in Birmingham until this afternoon. You took a chance coming up; he's still mad at you and those two twats after ... you know –"

"*He's* mad? He's not the one who was ..." I bite my tongue. "Sorry, Tina. I'm not here to argue, although you won't like what I'm going to say."

She carries two mugs of coffee and a couple of plates over to the table. I dole out the cake, not sure where to start.

Tina makes the decision for me. "Come on, then. Out with it."

"OK. Rob and I have agreed to split –"

"Yes!" She punches the air. "About bloody time."

"Yeah, well, it's a long story." *And not one I'm ready to tell you just yet.* "The thing is, I found one of my earrings stuck in the seam of Nige's coat."

"And?" Tina raises her eyebrows and makes an open gesture with her hands.

"And it was torn out of my ear the night I was attacked."

"Oh, fucking hell, it were him! The slimy bastard. Did Rob know?"

"Wait." I put a hand on her arm. "It's not as simple as that. Rob borrowed the coat and can't remember which one of them was wearing it that night. What's more, he says the earring could have got caught up on the coat when he was helping me."

"A likely bloody story!" Tina's fired up. "You've got to go to the police now, Jills."

"No police, don't ask me why, just accept it, OK?"

She shakes her head. "Another one of your secrets, eh?"

I ignore the jibe. "The thing is, there's still a chance it was Noel."

"Not that again. I thought you just said –"

"But if Rob's telling the truth ... All I can dredge up is the darkness, the punches to my head and the pain ... and a feeling he knew me. And, then, who put out the lights?"

Tina's eyes narrow. "I don't believe this, you're making up excuses for them."

"No, I'm not." I stand and start pacing up and down. "I know one of them did it ... or else Noel did."

Her chair topples to the floor as she springs up to confront me. "It weren't Noel! I've told you and told you until I'm blue in the face."

I don't back down. "If I'm honest, it's the sort of thing Rob or Nige would do, when you think of what they got up to before. But – and it's a big but – how could they have been here at the exact time the lights went out? I didn't phone Rob until afterwards. Somebody turned the lights off, Tina. That had to be Noel, to frighten me or to show me who's boss around here."

"All right, I do think he turned the lights off, just to spite you, but that don't mean he hurt you." "Are you sure?"

I grab Tina's arm, force her to look at me, determined to ram my point home.

Before she can answer, the door opens silently and Leon walks into the room. I have to look twice before I recognise him. He's easily five foot ten. The school uniform is gone, replaced by a tee-shirt, jeans and trainers. Gold glistens at his neck and his hair is twisted into embryo dreadlocks. The anger with which he once regarded me is gone, but his expression is cold and without emotion.

He gives me a sideways glance before dropping his backpack to the floor and going to the fridge for a cold drink.

"It's you," he says. "Didn't think you'd have the balls to come back here."

I'm thrown by his likeness to Noel, both in the way he talks and the air of menace he exudes. Fuck this, no way am I going to be intimidated by a thirteen-year-old.

"It's got nothing to do with you and back off with the language in front of your mother."

"This is my home, not yours, and I'll talk any way I like."
Leon sneers and I want to knock the can from his hand.
"Besides, you'd better not be here when Noel gets back

with –"

"Leon, that's enough." Tina moves between me and her son to break up out conversation.

I'm curious, though. "With what?" And to Tina. "What's going on?"

"Nothing." She brushes me off. "He's just trying to stir up trouble."

"Am I?" Leon lounges in a chair, legs draped over the arm. "We'll see, won't we, Tina?"

He's openly insolent, almost daring Tina to reprimand him but she remains silent and sits down at the table. And when did he start calling his parents by their given names?

"I'd sling my hook if I was you." Leon's malevolent gaze is now trained on me. "Noel ain't going to like you being here. He always knew what you were, right from the start."

"I'm not afraid of him." Brave words, but maybe it's time I left.

Leon laughs. "I helped him pack your stuff. you know. Him and me, we're a team."

A team? He hated Noel's guts the last time I saw him. A small whimper escapes Tina and she rests her head on hands. Distracted by her, I almost miss Leon's next words.

"I texted him when you were in the kitchen. Whatsisname, Rob. Told him Noel was throwing you out."

"No, you didn't." I'm confident he's lying. "You don't know his number."

"Your phone was in your camera bag, no passcode. How stupid can you be?"

"I don't believe you." He's making it up. But what if it were true? Would it have given Rob time to get here while I sat on the landing and then struggled downstairs with the cases? Probably not and yet ...

"I don't care." Leon picks up his backpack and heads for the door. "Oh, hang on, you've got a picture of Donald Duck as his icon. Right?"

Right.

He has one more jibe before he leaves. "By the way, it wasn't Noel, it was me ... I turned the lights out."

Tina lifts her head. "Before you start, I didn't know."

"But–" I can't make my mind work properly. "How could he have known to turn the lights off just at the moment someone grabbed me?"

It was a set-up between two of them. It had to be. But who? Leon and Rob? Unlikely. Leon and Noel? Thinking back to how much Leon hated his father, also unlikely.

I cross the room, grab Tina's arm and force her to look at me. "Is Leon lying? Covering up for Noel?"

She screams in my face. "What? It ain't enough that you want to blame Noel? Now you're dragging Leon into it. A child? Do you know how sick that sounds?"

The adrenaline drains from my body and I feel behind me for a chair, falling into it. I don't know what to believe any more. In Tina's eyes, I see fear and confusion and a growing uncertainty.

I start slowly and quietly. "I'm not saying it was Noel and Leon. But they both have good reason to hate me, don't they? And, if Leon's telling the truth about the phone call, it could have been Rob. But why would he? I can't think straight."

Tina waves a hand at me. "Don't talk, just ... don't talk." Moving slowly like an old woman, she walks to the bathroom. The door closes behind her and I hear running water.

Ten minutes go by. The sun hasn't reached this side of the building yet and I'm cold. Shivering. I fight to hold on to the determination that brought me here, but doubts creep into my mind.

It's not too late to go back to Rob's. Forget the coat. Leave it in Maisie's trolley.

The bathroom door creaks open and Tina walks to the coffee pot, gesturing to me. I nod and she pours two mugs of dark, muddy coffee.

"You've never been honest with me, Jills." Her face is pale, scrubbed clean of make-up, and I realise with a shock that she is in her mid-forties. The girlish, bubbly facade is gone and a shattered, drawn woman faces me. I have no words. I listen mutely.

"That's OK. Why would you? But, just once, I'd have liked you to talk to me as if I were more than another prossie to add to your precious portfolio. You used me, I'm not stupid. Yeah, Noel saw what you was from the beginning. He warned me, said you'd walk all over me. And you did."

I bow my head. I can't bear to look at her. Something inside me tears loose and my head throbs in agony.

Talk to her. Be honest for once in your life.

I can't. I just can't. So she starts speaking again.

"After that night, after Rob took you away ..." She stops, takes a deep breath, and lifts her chin to look me in the eye. "He beat me, Jills. He punched me to the ground. In front of Leon." Her voice drops to a whisper. "And I could see Leon's face as I lay on the floor. He were excited ... he were getting off on my pain."

"Oh, Tina ..."

"That's what I got for sticking up for you. Because I'm so fucking stupid I still thought that, maybe, you really might be a friend." Another, ragged breath. "That night hurt me as much as it hurt you. Leon doesn't go to school any more. He goes out with Noel, comes home with new clothes, that stupid gold chain. Noel's only here when I'm working, so he can take the money."

She drains her coffee mug. "But that don't mean that Noel raped you. Or that Leon was owt to do with it." Her voice cracks on the last few words. "He's still my little boy."

I reach out and touch her hand. It's the best I can do. I say, "Teen …" and her fingers slowly curl round mine until we're holding hands.

Tina stirs. "You should go, Jills, before Noel comes back. I need to get ready for work."

"No, wait." I tighten my grip on her hand. "Doesn't Noel live here any more?"

All spirit has drained from her and she won't meet my eyes. "Some of his clothes are still here, but he ain't slept here in a long time. I think I know where he's living. Only turns up when he wants me to …"

"To what?"

"Nowt. You don't want to know."

I'm incredulous. "But why are you still working for him?"

"Don't be stupid, Jills. You've been around the game long enough to know what's what. I ain't been out of here, or even seen one of the girls, in weeks."

I look up at the framed photograph of Tina and Noel, laughing and relaxed together, remembering the day Noel hung it and how happy Tina was. None of it real.

"What's happened here, Teen? Are you going to tell me what's going on?"

Silent tears flow down her cheeks and she wipes her

nose on her sleeve. I wait. If she trusts me enough to –
The front door slams open. Footsteps and voices echo
down the hallway.

Twenty Nine

Tina's eyes, wide and panicked, meet mine. "Oh God, it's
Noel. You'd better go, quickly."
But there's nowhere to go and, seconds later, the door
opens. A young, black girl walks in. She looks barely
seventeen, wearing a tiny skirt and a strapless top.
Her elaborately made-up face is impassive as her gaze
sweeps over Tina and me without a flicker of acknow-
ledgement.
I look from her to Tina. "What the –"
She shakes her head, watching the door.
Noel follows the girl into the room, his face darkening
when he sees me. "What the fuck are you doing here?
Didn't you learn your lesson last time?"
I'm rooted to the spot, unable to move my feet, while
my brain screams at me to get away from him. Tina
moves slightly in front of me. Her voice is shaky, but she
fronts up to the man who towers over her.
"She's just going. Ain't you, Jills?" She looks back at me
and moves her eyes towards the door, then confronts
Noel again. "She came to pick up some stuff that got left
behind. I told her you wouldn't like it."
"Bloody right." He takes in Tina's tear-stained face and
casual clothes. "You look fucking rough. Why ain't you
ready? My mate's on his way over from Derby. I told him
he'd be straight in. No messing."
With no warning, he shoves her violently across the
room towards the young girl. "Hurry up, he'll be here
soon. Lainie, help her."

"Nah, you don't pay me for that. She can sort herself out." Lainie walks over to a sofa and sits down, crossing her legs. "And, if she's not ready on time, it'll cost you. I'm on the clock.."

I should get out of here. Whatever's going on, it's nothing to do with me. Except. Tina has never shown me anything but kindness from the day I met her. She gave me a home, she offered me friendship. I took all of it and gave nothing back. I look longingly at the door, take a deep breath and cross the room to stand beside Tina.

"I'll help her."

Noel's anger is now directed at me. "Why are you still fucking here?"

Tina gives me a push and whispers, "Go. I can handle this."

I waver. What am I doing? Tina's right, she can handle it, it's nothing she hasn't done before. Or is it? My gaze falls on Lainie and I blurt out, "What's she doing here?"

Noel grins. "You mean she hasn't told you about her new career?"

Tina moans, "Don't, Noel," and buries her face in my shoulder as he strides to the Welsh dresser and jerks a drawer open. "Here." He flings a handful of postcards in my face and they flutter to the carpet at my feet. "You should appreciate them, being a photographer and all. Go on, look at them!"

"No!" Tina's on her knees, scrabbling at the cards.

I bend down and pick up a handful of them. They're flyers, advertising the services of *Ebony* and *Ivory*, and graphically illustrated with photographs of Lainie and Tina. The bright, gaudy colours and glossy paper are in sharp contrast to the sordid pictures. I glimpse oral sex, dildos and, oh my God, is that an animal, before Tina snatches them away from me.

Noel jeers at me. "Make your picture look crap, don't they? But thanks for the idea."

Still trying to absorb the shock of the pictures, I stutter. "The idea? What are you talking about?"

"That picture of Tina's cunt you took? Never made a penny out of it, did you. And *she* was making rubbish money for open-leg shots. Just needed *someone*," he taps his chest, "to use their head. There's a mint to be made from the hard stuff. Ain't that right, Teen?"

Tina's gone. She fled the room as soon as she'd gathered up all the pictures.

"You bastard." I forget my fear of Noel, outraged at the comparison between my picture and the obscenities in the flyers. "My photograph's nothing to do with porn. It's been published in national newspapers, talked about on the radio –"

"Nah, don't kid yourself, woman. It's filth, not in the same league as what I'm doing, but still just summat for the punters to wank over."

"That's not true –"

"Yeah, it is. At the end of the day, we're just the same, you and me. Only difference is, I make money and you don't."

Lainie cuts in to the argument. "That's it. I'm off. I'm not doing that guy on my own." She holds out a hand to Noel. "I'll have the money you owe me."

I watch in disbelief as he scowls, but pulls out his wallet and hands over a small bundle of notes. Lainie counts it, tucks it in her bra and saunters to the door. Her voice floats back from the hallway, "See you at home."

Left alone, Noel and I stare at each other for a long moment, until he says, "How come every time I see you, my day gets fucked up?"

I should go. The urge to walk away is strong, and yet I'm still here.

Swallowing a few times to wet my throat, I say, "What did she mean? Home?"

Noel ignores my question. "Get out of my sight, you stupid bitch." He moves off through the apartment, bellowing, "Tina! Get your sorry ass out here!"

He kicks doors open, banging them against the walls, until he reaches Tina's 'office'. He rattles the doorknob."Open this fucking door." As I watch from the living area, he throws his body against the door.

I want to run, but he's between me and the front door. I'm hyperventilating, fighting off a panic attack, and stuff a fist in my mouth, frightened of attracting Noel's attention. It's only a matter of time before he breaks the door down. Tina won't stand a chance in the face of his fury. Terrified for her and now sobbing aloud, I search the room for something to use as a weapon.

Knives. Tina has a set of gleaming chef's knives in the kitchen area, never used. The thought of going after Noel with a knife terrifies me, but I can find nothing else. Somehow, I've got one in my hand and will my feet to walk towards the 'office'.

Don't be stupid. Find somewhere to hide until it's all over. It's not your problem.

I walk quietly, hugging the wall, but Noel hears me and ceases his assault on the door. His gaze drops to the knife in my hand and his anger ramps up.

"Come on, then. You think you can take me on? Give it your best shot." He opens his arms wide, offering his unprotected body, taunting me.

I back up and Noel follows me. "I'm going to bring a

whole heap of trouble down on your head, woman."

The knife slips from my sweaty fingers, hitting the floor with a dull thump. He swats at me with one large hand, catches me on the side of my head and sends me tumbling to the floor. I scrabble for the knife, but Noel kicks it away.

He reaches down and bunches my tee-shirt in his fist; the other one is raised to punch me when there's a loud knock on the front door. He drops me back on to the floor and stands irresolute, one finger pressed to his lips in a threatening gesture.

Moments pass. The letterbox is poked open and a disembodied voice calls, "Noel, mate, you in there?"

"Yeah, yeah, I'm here." Noel pulls me roughly to my feet and hustles to open the door, all smiles and fist bumps as he ushers a small, balding man into the hallway.

"Is there a problem?" the man asks, his eyes fastened on my heaving breasts.

"Nah, no problem, man. Tina's sick, but don't worry, I'll make sure you get a good time. I've got two girls in Hyson Green you'll never forget."

The customer looks unconvinced and Noel says, "Tell you what, I'll throw in a set of the new pictures, for free." He turns to me. "Just fetch me a pack of cards from the dresser. Make sure they're the shrink-wrapped ones."

I gape at him. He raises his eyebrows and lifts one fist slightly. It's enough to make me scuttle into the kitchen area and do as I'm told. When I get back to the front door, Noel is sparking up a spliff and the customer looks a bit happier. I hand the pack of cards to Noel and he bends over me, one large hand gripping my shoulder, his voice low. "Tell Tina I'll be back tomorrow, and then clear off. Don't be here when I get back." He squeezes my shoulder for emphasis, sending pain shooting down my arm.

The front door closes behind them. I run to it, slam the bolts home and lean against it, waiting for my body to stop shaking and for my breathing to slow down. I'm a nervous wreck, a pale shadow of the person I was this morning, when I confronted Rob and let my anger loose on him. The knife lies a short distance up the hallway, where Noel had kicked it. I briefly think of re-opening the cut on my arm, before rejecting the idea. That way lies craziness. Instead, I lean on the door until my breath stabilises and I trust my legs to support me.

The 'office' door remains closed. I tap on it and say "Tina, he's gone. It's OK. You can come out now."

She's almost inaudible. "Go away. Please, just go away."

"That's three times you've told me to go away." I sound resigned. "Third time lucky. I'm gone."

I make a lot of noise undoing the bolts and swinging the front door open. Cool air blows in from the landing. If I close the door and stay, I know I am going to be drawn further into Tina's problems. Noel will be back tomorrow and I'm not brave enough to stand up to him. And then there's Leon. How screwed up is he, and in what way? The temptation to find my camera bag and walk away, closing the door behind me, is very strong. I came to Tina, thinking she would be able to help me, only to find her life was just as fucked up as mine. Or worse.

I slam the door shut and walk quietly back to the kitchen where I gather up the coffee mugs and run soapy water into the sink. Minutes pass.

"You don't have to do that." Tina's voice is small, hesitant, and I keep my back turned, scrubbing the mugs long after they're clean.

"I know, just passing the time until you decided to come out."

"Why didn't you leave, now you know what I really am?"

Drying my hands on a tea towel, I swivel round to see that she's curled up into the corner of a sofa, arms wrapped round her knees, head bowed.

What should I tell her? That I don't think any less of her for taking part in the debauchery I saw in the flyers? Because it's true. The images left me completely cold. I've never seen sex as anything other than a commodity, a bargaining chip. It means nothing. The only emotion I felt regarding them was anger, directed at Noel, that he thought we were somehow the same.

I remember her fear of ending up back on Forest Road, but life on the streets is surely preferable to the degradation I saw in those pictures. Does Leon know? If the shoots were carried out in her small studio, then her son couldn't fail to be aware of what was going on. Would she do that, knowing how damaged Leon already was?

Unbidden, a memory surfaces of my seventeen year old self, on my knees in a wooded area, servicing a leering policeman while his friend watched. I didn't have to give in to them; I could have walked away, kept what small shred of dignity I had left, and taken the consequences.

But I did it. Because I didn't deserve anything better. The thought hits me from nowhere and I choke back the bile that rises in my throat. Is that what Tina feels? I give myself a mental shake. This is getting me nowhere but into a black hole I thought I'd climbed out of.

I have climbed out of.

The sun is high and dust motes dance in the shaft of light that falls across the wooden floor. The air in the room feels lighter for Noel's absence and I have an urge to get outside, to breathe fresh air and feel the sun on my face.

"Come on." I pull Tina to her feet. "We're going out."

She still won't look up, until I put a finger under her chin and tilt her face towards mine.

"I know we're in deep shit, Teen. I've walked out on Rob, after practically accusing him and Nige of attacking me. Noel is after your blood and God knows what Leon's up to. But, just for this afternoon, we're getting out of here; I want to be bloody normal and we can't be if we're cooped up in here, too afraid to open the door."

It's a brave speech. It doesn't betray the heavy, sick feeling in my stomach or the fear at the back of my mind that Noel could come back in spite of what he said.

Tina's small frame shakes uncontrollably. "I can't go out, I've got three customers this afternoon, Noel will be back to get the money."

"Sod the customers." I'm teetering on the edge of panic, but keep my voice as calm as I can. "Noel's not coming back until tomorrow. He won't know."

"But what about the money? And the punters will tell him."

I suspect that Tina has reached the end of her usefulness to Noel, but she doesn't need to hear that in her fragile condition. Somehow, with a mixture of lies and coaxing, I get her to wash her face and put on a pair of trainers.

She manages to raise a watery smile when I joke, "No

four-inch heels for you today!"

At last, we're out of the front door and on our way downstairs. I have to resist the urge to run and Tina clings on to my arm, still half-reluctant to leave the apartment. Halfway down to ground level, I realise I've left my camera bag behind and we lose another twenty minutes while I persuade Tina to give me her keys and wait on the stairs for me while I go back to get it. The final hurdle is to get her over the threshold of the main entrance and out into the street.

With many backward and sideways glances, we set off at a walking pace, heading towards the city centre. Our steps quicken until we're running, fleeing through the narrow streets, laughing out loud with more than a tinge of hysteria. We stop to draw breath at the stone lions outside the Council House, bending over to ease our aching lungs, before sitting down on the entrance steps.

Tina looks at me, half fearful, half jubilant, and says, "What do we do now?"

I re-direct the taxi away from the railway station. There's one more thing to do before I leave.

We pull up in front of a semi-detached house with a small patch of garden in front of it. A young woman weeds the flower bed near the front gate. She stands as I get out of the taxi and I see she's heavily pregnant. I pause, nearly reconsider, but walk forward until I face her across the gate.

"Good morning." She smiles. "Can I help you."

"Are you Stevie's wife?"

Her smile fades. "Yes. Is something wrong?"

"My name is Jilly Graham."

"I'm sorry," she begins, until her face changes and she says, "Oh, you're the ... um ..."

I make my voice harsh, build towards the anger I'm going to need to blow this woman's life apart. "The word you're looking for is prostitute."

She begins to back away. "You should go. My husband will be back soon ..."

I grip the gate with both hands and lean over it so she can hear me. I don't want her to miss a word as I tell her about Stevie's weekly visits; about how his demands grew more obscene as time passed; about the friends he brought with him. I give her all their names. I leave nothing out.

"He only stopped when he married you."

She leans over and vomits onto her neat little lawn. A phone falls to the ground and she leans to pick it up, wiping it clean and tapping the icons with a shaky hand.

Tears are already running down her cheeks, as she screams into the phone. "Stevie, where are you? Come home ... come home now!"

I get back in the cab and tell him to drive. As we reach the end of the road, a police car passes us, blue lights flashing, going in the opposite direction. I look back briefly before the

taxi turns a corner and it's lost to view.
I'm done. I have a train to catch.

CHAPTER THIRTY

Tina's question hangs in the air while I silently berate myself. I should have realised she would expect us to stay together. Unlike me, she's probably never made a single decision for herself in her entire adult life. I'm not sure I want this partnership. I've grown to like her, I may even admit to being fond of her, but that doesn't mean I want her around all the time.

I need time to think, but she's looking at me expectantly, so I say, "Before we do anything, I've got a couple of questions."

"Right, go for it." Tina looks relieved, as if she thinks I've got answers instead of questions.

"About Noel." As soon as I speak, she tenses and half rises from the step. I put a hand on her arm to keep her still as I continue. "He's living with Lainie; he's left you and he's poisoning Leon against you. He's becoming more violent. So, question number one, do you want to get away from him? Because if you're going back there," I nod my head towards the Lace Market, "then this is where we part company."

I give her plenty of time to answer. People mutter as they push past us on the steps, but I keep my focus on Tina until she's ready to talk.

"I'm afraid to be on my own." She lifts her head and I can see the effort she's making to be honest. "Me and Noel, we've been together since I were fourteen. I've never had to look after meself. I don't even have a bank account or a driving licence. I've only got … Noel. He looks after me."

I've never dealt with anyone who was so honest. My instinct is to back away, but there is something so raw and vulnerable in her face that, in spite of myself, I'm drawn in to what she's saying.

"I don't want to go back, Jills. I've been at this game too long. But, there's Leon. I know." She raises a hand as if to stop me speaking. "He comes across like he hates me. But, he's my baby and I love him. I don't want him to be like his dad. He were the only good thing in my life, and now … I don't even know where he is."

She's going back. Walk away. Now.

And then Tina surprises me. "Those pictures you took for me, I loved them, but they was just a lie. We've never been a real family. To tell the truth, we're not even married. He lives with me, or, at least, he did but he's got other girls round the city. Younger girls, who can make more money."

"So that's why he pushed you into doing the hard core stuff?"

"Yeah, it's a slippery slope. It won't be long until he's got me back on the streets." She grips my hand tightly. "I'm frightened he'll come looking for me – he never lets any of his girls go until he's finished with them – but I need to leave now, before …" She stops and closes her eyes for a few seconds before she says, "OK, to answer your question, yes. I'm ready to make the break. I'm bloody terrified, but I'm going to do it."

I suppose I should hug her or something, praise her for being brave, but I've still got massive problems of my own to deal with, and the moment passes.

"Right, come on." I give her a tug and we get up from the steps. "I'm hungry and I want to tell you something before the next question."

Ten minutes later, we're sitting in a nearly deserted *Frankie and Benny's*, clutching large glasses of white wine and reading the menus.

Tina is quiet, but she's calm and her face has regained some of her natural colour, after our hectic dash from the Lace Market. The sound system is playing cheesy sixties music, there's no one within earshot and I choose my words carefully.

"For as long as you live in Nottingham, you'll always be looking over your shoulder. If Noel finds you – *when* he finds you – your life won't be worth living. You know that. You'll end up on Forest Road – or worse."

"I know." Tina sinks half of her wine in one go. "I been wondering what to do. My mum were living in Clifton, last I heard of her, but God knows where she is now. She'd have a fit if I turned up at her door anyway. And probably the first place he'd look."

This is not the moment to remind her she told me her mother was dead. Then again, I have a shaky relationship with the truth myself.

"So, here's your second question. Why don't you come to London with me?"

She puts a hand over her mouth. "London? Do you mean it?"

I immediately regret the offer and start to backtrack. "I don't know, maybe it's too complicated ..."

Tina is silent again, her hands fall to the table and she says, "I thought you was serious; I might have known you wouldn't want me along."

Christ, why did I start this?

"It's not that. I just – I want to help you, but I don't want to be responsible for you."

"What are you talking about? Responsible for me? I'm bloody twice your age, or near enough."

I smile at this tiny spark of anger and resolve to lay my cards on the table. Some of them, anyway.

"When I left home, I promised myself I'd never go back. Bad things happened – maybe I deserved some of them, but when I was a kid … No –" I cut her off as she takes a breath, "I'm not telling you because I'm after sympathy. I want you to understand that, if someone harmed me, I make it my business to get even. I might have to wait a while, but I'll make them regret it."

"I don't get it. I mean, I'm sorry something bad happened to you, but what's it to do with going to London?"

"Whoever attacked me is still walking round Nottingham, thinking he's got away with it. I can't prove who it was. There's a chance it was Rob; maybe Nige was in on it, as well. I'm beginning to think there were two of them, that night. One beat me and the other one –"

I stop for a gulp of wine. "I still have a feeling it could have been Noel and – I'm sorry, Teen – but Leon is mixed up in it, as well. He phoned Rob and he turned out the lights."

"No, not Leon!" She leans across the table to glare at me. "I can believe Noel were summat to do with it, but never Leon."

I don't push it, and she sits back. "Anyway, what do you mean, get even? You going to the police?"

A shudder runs through my body at the thought. "No, not the police. I'm going after all of them. Nige is first on my list, because it'll affect Rob as well. But there'll be fall-out. If it went wrong, you could get caught up in it."

"This thing you're going to do ... is it bad?"

I nod. "Prison, if I get caught."

Tina waves the waiter over. "Bring us a bottle, will you, duck?" He brings the wine and a couple of clean glasses and she pours fresh drinks, holding hers up, inviting me to make a toast.

I shrug and clink her glass. "What are we drinking to?"

She smiles and says, "To Noel – I'd do time for him."

Whatever she sees in my face makes her laugh. "I'm in, you silly bint, We do what we have to do and then, London, here we come."

I'm pretty sure there won't be much to laugh at in the coming days, but I match her smile. We stay in the restaurant for the remainder of the afternoon, finishing the wine and eating pasta with rich sauces. By unspoken agreement, we avoid the subject of men and speculate about a future life in London. Tina doesn't mention Leon and neither do I.

As dusk gathers, we walk a little unsteadily back towards The Old Mill, apprehensive of what we might find. The whole building is in darkness, except for the foyer, where a single figure lurks just inside the glass doors.

I clutch Tina's arm. "Is that Noel?"

She peers through the doors. "No, that's Jim. He was my four o'clock appointment. Bloody hell, has he been here all this time?"

We lean against the wall, weak with relief, laughing until Jim hears us and comes out to confront Tina. "It's about time. I've been here for ages. Come on, you'd better give me a discount for wasting my time.

I step in front of him, trying to stifle my laughter. "Excuse me, sir, but I'm Tina's new manager. Sorry, but she's retired from active duty."

"What do you mean, retired? I've been waiting all afternoon."

Tina gets in on the act. "It means sod off, you dirty old bugger. Your supply's just been cut off."

He walks off, muttering about crazy bitches, and we're left in the empty street, staring up at the tall, dark building.

"Are you sure he's not coming back tonight, Jills?"

I'm not sure of anything. I only know what Noel said when he stormed out of the apartment earlier. The only thing that will bring him back, I guess, is if Tina is earning money. I answer her question with another. "How many bookings have you got tonight?"

"None. There were only the Derby guy, who wanted me and Lainie together, Jim at four o'clock and then Noel was supposed to be out tonight, making arrangements for filming tomorrow."

"That's where he'll be, then. Lainie said she'd see him at home, so I guess we're safe to go back in."

It looks like Tina's going to cry again at the mention of Lainie. As I try to think of something to say to buck her up, she marches up the steps and through the doors. With a last look up and down the street, I follow her.

"Hey, look at this!" She tries for a smile, pushing the button for the lift. "It's working!"

I hold my breath as the lift door slides open. The interior's brightly lit and empty. "Thank God." I exhale with a whoosh, we both dive inside and I press the button for the sixth floor.

The lift slowly ascends, we look at each other and I see my own fear reflected in Tina's eyes. The unspoken question hangs between us. "Will he be there?"

It's cold on the landing, there are no external windows and I shiver as Tina fumbles her keys in the locks. The door swings open, she feels for the switch and the hall lights up. One, two, three seconds ... no one appears, the apartment is quiet. I slam the bolts shut on the front door. We're safe.

Tina heads for the bathroom to fetch sheets and I walk into the living area, searching for the light switch. I can't find it, fall over a chair in the dark, and scrape my ankle.

"Shit! That hurt."

A voice comes out of the darkness. "You're like a bad fucking smell, you. What does it take to get rid of you?"

CHAPTER
THIRTY ONE

A scream bubbles up in my throat but all that comes out is a low moan. I scramble backwards and bump into Tina, who comes running from the bathroom.

"It's OK, it's OK." she says into my ear. She taps the switch and the room floods with light revealing Leon, sitting in an armchair with a glass of wine in his hand.

"Oh Christ." My heart thumps in my chest and the frustration, fright and tension of the day culminates in a full blown panic attack. My lungs scream for breath and darkness threatens my peripheral vision while pin-pricks of light flash behind my eyes. I'm cold. Very cold. Everything goes dark and I welcome oblivion.

Someone slaps my face. I moan and try to curl my body inwards, but another slap drags me back against my will. I open my eyes to see Tina's face hovering over me, hand raised for another slap.

"Enough." I shield my face and struggle to keep my eyes open.

"Thank God. I thought you was gone that time." Tina tries to hug me. I push her away and focus on Leon, croaking, "You did that on purpose, you little shit."

He snorts laughter into his wine. "Best caught I've had for ages."

I struggle to my feet, batting Tina away as she fusses

round me, and drop into a chair, closing my eyes. This has been one hell of a day; things are slipping way from me. I try to summon the courage I'd felt this morning, the clarity of the conversation over lunch with Tina, but they're gone, wiped out by a nasty little trick from a spiteful teenager. Why did I ever think I was strong enough to take revenge on Nige, let alone Rob and Noel? Not for the first time, I think longingly of my room in Rob's house. Right now, I wish I was there.

"Here." Tina offers me a glass of water and I knock it out of her hand. Ashamed of my weakness, I want to hurt her. She backs off and motions for Leon to follow her out of the room. Their voices drone on, just beyond my hearing. My eyes droop again and I sleep.

The smell of coffee and toast brings me awake. My neck is cramped from sleeping in the chair and, groaning aloud, I struggle to my feet and stretch my arms and legs. Tina and Leon are working together in the kitchen area, moving round each other easily, and smiling.

Tina glances over at me. "Ah, you're awake. We was just about to give you a shake. Breakfast's ready."

It's dark outside and I check my phone. Four o'clock. In the morning. Why is Leon smiling? Have I fallen down a bloody rabbit hole? I mumble, "Bathroom" and shuffle off, more to give myself time to think than anything else. Ablutions done, I sit on the toilet seat and pull my thoughts together. I remember Tina and Leon talking, just out of earshot, as I fell asleep; the fright I got when Leon's voice came out of the darkness. What the hell happened overnight to bring about this cosy display?

Leon bangs down a plate of toast and scrambled eggs in front of me as I take my place at the table. A few forkfuls of egg are all I can manage and I move to one of the sofas with a slice of buttered toast in one hand and a cup of coffee in the other. The atmosphere in the room is uncomfortable, but I'm determined not to be the one who speaks first.

Tina and Leon exchange glances, then she sits down beside me. "Leon and me, we've been talking. I've told him I'm finished with his dad and this life; he weren't surprised. And I told him about, you know, getting even."

My head shoots up. "What did you tell him that for? It's none of his business."

"Yes, it is." I should know Tina well by now, but I'm always surprised when she shows the steely side of her character. "He's my son. You can't just decide he's a bad lot and expect me to be all right with it."

"So what's brought this on? He couldn't stand the sight of you yesterday."

She stands and ranges herself beside her son before she answers. "We talked for hours while you was asleep. Leon came home to warn me. Noel's going to be here this morning and he's bringing Lainie with him. He's moving her in – here – to my home –"

Leon drapes an arm across his mother's shoulder. "It made me see that Mum is the victim here." He's talking to the floorboards, his head drooped, a model of contrition. Tina gazes up at him adoringly. She's got her boy back.

I snort and his head snaps up, his eyes meet mine. "I don't like you, Jilly. I wish you'd never come here, but ..." He draws in a shaky breath. "Mum has her heart set on going to London with you, so ..." He spreads his arms out in acceptance. "I'm sorry for the way I spoke to you. OK?" And now he raises the vestige of a smile.

It needs some work, he's overdone it in places, but for

a thirteen-year-old, it's a brilliant performance. I mentally applaud him. If not for the flash of hatred in his eyes, quickly concealed, I might even have believed him. Tina gives him a gentle push. "Go and pack a rucksack, we've not got much time." He drops a kiss on top of her head and lopes off in the direction of his bedroom.

Don't overdo it, Leon.

"So, he's coming with us, then?" I'm not going to tell her that her son's a lying toerag, but neither am I going to pretend to like him. I can't work why he's playing this game but, sooner or later, he'll make a mistake. I just hope he won't break Tina's heart.

"Yes, he'll be all right now he's not under Noel's thumb. You'll see, Jills. He's a good kid, really."

"I'll take your word for it, but if he gets to be a problem, then we split up and you're on your own."

She nods, but I don't think she believes me.

I eat cold toast and drink cold coffee while I wait for them both to pack their rucksacks. We'll be on foot or on public transport so we can't take suitcases. In a city full of students, three people with rucksacks will blend right in.

It's nearly half past five by the time they're ready to go. The windows are already reflecting a pale, pink light as sunrise approaches. I ask them both to sit at the table with me.

"If you want to back out, do it now." I haven't got time to wrap things up in polite language. "This is what I want … what I'm *going* to do. I'm going to spend the day in the city, maybe try to get into Rob's house for some clothes and then, after I've burned down Nige's factory, I'm going to spend a couple of days somewhere I know I'll be safe while I work out what to do next. You can both come with me, or you can strike out on your own, because after tonight, we'll be criminals."

I'm prepared for them to back out. Since the inclusion of Leon in our plans, I've begun to think I'd be better on my own.

CHAPTER THIRTY TWO

Tina's hand flies to her throat. "You're going to do what?"

I've made it very clear. No need to repeat myself.

Leon's face is suffused with excitement. "Can you do that? Burn down a whole building?"

"Wait." Tina cuts in, one hand on her son's arm to quieten him. "You said you was going to get even, not burn his bloody factory to the ground."

"It's not a discussion, Teen. Like I said, now's the time to back off."

My camera bag's at my feet. I swing it over my shoulder and wave at them. "See you, then."

Leon nudges his mother. I can see he badly wants to come with me, but Tina sits frozen to the spot. She calls after me, as I head for the front door. "You don't even know if it were owt to do with him!"

She's right. I don't. But it doesn't matter. He's part of the chain of events that led to me being punched, degraded and left traumatised. Rob, Nige or Noel – they're all part of the nightmare and I won't stop until I've hurt them all. And Leon's tucked in the back of my mind.

I undo the bolts and swing the front door open. The timer switches on the lights, the shadows flee into the far corners and memory hits me like a physical blow. I'm drawn to the corner where I had screamed and fought against my attacker. The light blinks off and my breath seizes in my throat. I reach for the switch, fingers shaking, but don't touch it; I *can't* touch it. I flee down the stairs, my hands gripping the handrails in the darkness, heart pounding and breath hitching, until the light flickers back on when I reach the next landing. I slow down and descend on legs that threaten to give way beneath me, collapsing into a heap in the foyer, which is still brightly lit although it's dawn outside.

After a few minutes, before I've gathered myself together enough to stand up, the lift door whirrs open. Tina and Leon emerge, rucksacks on their backs. If they think it's strange to find me on the floor, they make no comment, merely bend down, take one of my arms each and hoist me to my feet.

"Leon has something he wants to show you." Tina avoids my eyes, her face set and drawn, but she's on board. I guess Leon's enthusiasm, allied to her fear of Noel, has been enough to persuade her. If we were on our own, I would tell her how afraid I am right now, about my terrified flight in the dark, pursued by my memories. I won't show weakness in front of Leon, however, so I follow them out of the building and through the maze of streets until we come to a row of garages with roll-up doors. Stopping at the last one, Leon bends down and rolls the door up, revealing Noel's Jaguar.

Tina stands back, watching the streets. I ask, "He doesn't lock his garage?"

"Nah, nobody's going to mess with Noel." The boy's pride in his father is evident and, again, I feel a prickle of unease. He disappears into the depths of the garage and returns with a petrol can. He shakes it and I hear liquid sloshing.

"There you are. Boom! That'll make the job easier, won't it?" He looks at me triumphantly. What does he want? A high five? I nod curtly. He's right, but I can't shake off the feeling that he's trying to take control. In spite of her occasional flashes of independence, Tina is malleable most of the time. And, OK, I do like her. Leon, on the other hand, is a loose cannon and I still haven't worked out why he's here, helping us.

I'm thinking on my feet. "Drop the door again. We'll come back tonight and pick it up. We can't walk through the city carrying a petrol can."

He looks like he's going to argue, but my logic is sound. "What's next?" he says, his face surly.

"Next is breakfast. McDonalds?"

It's still quiet when we get to the franchise on the edge of the canal. Tina pays for breakfast, which raises another question. How much money have we got? Tina has one hundred and fifty pounds. She spread her hands and a grin glimmers for the first time this morning. "Maybe I siphon a little off when he's sleeping?" Our laughter's forced but it breaks the ice a little.

Leon and I scrape up another fifty five pounds – enough to keep us going for a few days, if we're careful.

The sun's well up now and the streets are full of commuters and students. We're just three more anonymous people among the crowds as we walk back into the city. It's time to find out where Rob is. Tina phones the factory on its landline. Leon and I listen to the ringtone on loudspeaker. She's about to give up when Nige answers the phone.

"What? I mean, Good morning, Ferguson's. How can I

help you?"

"Good morning." Tina responds. "This is the Green-holme Medial Centre. Sorry to bother you, but may I speak to Rob Knowley, please? There's a bit of a mix-up on his appointment."

Nige is grumpy, probably hungover. "Well, the shop floor guys aren't allowed to take phone calls. Can I take a message?"

Tina looks at me, uncertain how to proceed.

"Tell him it's personal." I hiss and she says, "I really need to talk to him, sir. It's sensitive."

"OK, hold on. I'll fetch him."

Nige puts her on hold and we wait until Rob's voice comes on the line. "Hello, what's all this about an appointment?"

Tina panics, forgets what we've rehearsed and says, "Sorry, wrong number." She thumbs the red button.

"It's sensitive? Wrong number?" I splutter. Tina giggles and Leon gives her a quick one-arm hug. It's a light moment and I dare to believe that we're going to be able to work together. Although I still don't trust Leon.

Tina complains constantly about the amount of walking we do. I'm afraid to use a taxi, as she asks, in case the driver knows Noel and we need to conserve our money. It's ten o'clock by the time we reach Rob's house. I check out the back yard and peer through the windows before I feel safe enough to unlock the door.

Other than a few dirty dishes in the kitchen sink and a couple of wet towels on the bathroom floor, the house is exactly how I left it yesterday. Tina and Leon wander through the rooms, laughing at the tacked-on kitchen and bathroom.

I'm quick to defend the house where I've lived for three

years and snap, "Not everybody has the money to live in an apartment in the Lace Market. Some people work for a living." They fall silent at my jibe and I add, "Go and sit down while I get my stuff. Put your feet up, we've got more walking to do."

In the bedroom, I pack jeans, tee-shirts, socks, knickers and a few toiletries into Rob's rucksack, leaving the two suitcases lying open with the clothes I haven't got room for. I look round the bedroom, checking that I haven't forgotten anything. In a moment of *deja vu*, my eyes come to rest on a note sellotaped to the door.

I can explain. If you come back and see this, ring me. I don't want you to leave me.

Bizarrely, there's a twenty pound note tucked into the sellotape.

CHAPTER THIRTY THREE

I sit down on the edge of the bed, allowing doubts to seep into my mind. What the hell am I doing with Tina and Leon? It's so hard to hold on to the idea that Tina and I are friends – should I have to keep reminding myself of it? I think of the flashes of temper I've aimed at her. Surely friends don't do that. Or do they? And then, there's the pain I felt for her, when I realised what her life was like with Leon. That counts for something, doesn't it? But I warned her. *I want to help you, but I don't want to be responsible for you.* Not to mention bloody Leon.

I leave the note and the money where it is, shoulder the rucksack and close the bedroom door behind me.

Fifteen minutes later, we leave through the back yard. The most urgent thing now is to get away from the immediate area. Rob will most likely come home at lunchtime and will know I've been in the house. There's a strong chance Noel will prowl the area; he knows roughly where Rob's house is. Tina's jumpy, frightened of being found by Noel, dreading what lies ahead tonight, but putting a brave face on it. Leon's sulking, bored and itching for action. I watch him constantly, checking to make sure he's not using his phone. We're all tired.

So we go to the cinema. Leon wants to see the latest *Avengers* film and Tina fancies *The Men in Black*. While they argue about it in the foyer of the multiplex, I buy tickets for *Prometheus*. It hardly matters because, within ten minutes of setting into comfortable seats in the back row of the over-heated cinema, they're both fast asleep. The film plays on a loop and, after I watch Dr Shaw abseil off into space for the second time, I wake Tina and Noel and we stumble outside on cramped legs.

It's dusk and we agree that, as soon as it's completely dark, Leon should go back into the Lace Market to retrieve the can of petrol and find something to break a window, while Tina and I wait in the foyer of the cinema.

While Len is at the kiosk buying chocolate, I say, "Teen, listen, we have to take his phone off him."

She laughs, as if I'm making a joke. "Yeah, right. Good luck with that."

I take her arm and lead her further away from Leon. "I'm serious. He could phone Noel and tell him where we are."

"Get off me. He wouldn't do that. He's my son, for Chrissake."

"And he's Noel's son, as well. I know you think he's deserted his dad to side with you, but what if he changes his mind?"

I can see doubt creep into her eyes and press home my advantage. "If Noel finds you, he's going to make you pay big time. We can't take that risk."

Her resistance collapses, as fear replaces doubt, and I know I've won. She walks over to Leon, leans in close to speak to him with one hand on his back and, without breaking eye contact, slips her other hand into his pocket and fishes out his phone. She saunters back, the phone now safely in her own pocket.

"Happy now?" she asks. Her eyes are hard and I stay silent. It will take a while for her to forgive me for doubting her son.

When Leon returns, nearly an hour later, he has the petrol can in his arms, wrapped up in a tartan travel blanket. A cricket bat pokes out of the folds. His face is like thunder "I've lost my fucking phone. My whole life is in there. Can you believe it?"

Tina calms him down, spins a story of how he must have dropped it. Good thing she saw it! I file away the fact that his whole life is on it.

It's time. We're ten minutes walk away from Nige's factory. It's surrounded by other last-century industrial units, some unoccupied, none with a security guard. As we climb the hill, with only a few hundred yards to go, Tina stops.

"I'm sorry." A nearby streetlight casts deep shadows across her face; she looks terrified. "I thought I were going to be all right, but now –" She bends over and vomits into the gutter. When there's nothing left but dry heaves, she straightens, wipes her face and says, "Don't do it, Jills. This is wrong. He's a nasty bastard, I know, but he don't deserve this."

"Yes, he does." I won't be deterred. "He deserves everything he's going to get." Shaking off the hand she's placed on my arm, I leave her standing there and follow Leon into the small car park in front of the factory.

CHAPTER THIRTY FOUR

The building is two storeys tall, made of red brick and has a large, double padlocked steel door, centre front on the ground floor. To the left of the door, a small, one storey office juts out, obviously built on at a later date. It has different brickwork and a sloping black roof, whose apex ends just below a row of tall windows on the upper storey.

I point at the low roof. "There's the way in. They were burgled just over a year ago and that's where the thieves got in. Climbed the roof and broke in through the window."

Three wheelie bins are lined up at the right hand side of the building. I drag one across to the office extension and scramble on to the lid. I can't quite reach the edge of the roof and say to Leon, "Give me a leg up and then pass me the petrol can and the bat."

"You sure you can do this? That roof looks slippy to me. Better if I do it."

"Just help me, will you?" My nerves are jangling. I'm sweating and chilly at the same time. Please God, don't let me throw up like Tina. He shrugs, fetches another wheelie bin and vaults on to the lid to stand beside me. Without a word, he bends, wraps his arms round my legs and heaves. Using the upward momentum, I grab the edge of the roof with both hands. Leon lets go of my legs and I swing one on the roof. I hang suspended for a moment until he pushes my other leg up and I've done it! I'm on the roof.

"Like to've seen you do that on your own." Leon mutters and drops back down to the ground. I I crawl backwards on the roof, ready for the petrol can. Leon unwraps the can from the blanket and holds it up above his head. My legs slip beneath me as I reach for the handle and I crash off the roof, landing heavily between the wheelie bins. I cry out in agony as my shoulder hits the ground and Tina comes running into the car park.

"Oh my God. Are you hurt?" she screams. I can't move my arm and shuffle away from the bins, using my feet and legs for leverage. She motions to Leon. "Help me get her out of here."

He's still holding the petrol can. "Is that what you want?" he asks. "Or are we going to finish what we started?" He looms over me, seemingly taller than usual as I crane my neck to look up at him. For a crazy moment, I think it's Noel and my insides turn to water. I raise my good arm to defend myself, then he bends down at my own level and it's just Leon.

I'm furious at myself for giving in to fear yet again. "Help me up, Leon. Let's finish this."

He nods to his mother and they each put a hand under one of my armpits to drag me to my feet. "So, what's it like up there?" Leon nods towards the upper windows.

"I've only been up there once, to help clean up after the burglary. It's the studio." I try to visualise the layout. "Just below the windows, there's a long bench with computers on it. You'll be able to jump down there. I remember the stairs are to your left. They're old and a bit rickety. Here's the best bit, they're made of wood – and so is the floor. They'll catch fire very quickly. So make sure you get out as soon as you spread the petrol. Toss this through the window." I hand him my lighter.

"And leave evidence?" He takes a box of matches out of his pocket and shakes them. "Got them at the kiosk." He tosses the lighter back at me with a withering look.

Leon dumps the petrol can and the cricket bat on one of the wheelie bins, springs up on to the other bin and transfers them to the roof. In seconds, he's jumped for the roof and swung himself up on his haunches. I watch, with Tina clinging on to me, as he crab-walks up the roof and swings the cricket bat above his head. An almighty crack splits the air as the window slowly caves in and shards of glass shower across the roof. Leon kicks in the bits of glass protruding from the frame, crabs back down to the petrol can, seizes it and disappears inside the window.

After what seems like hours, but is probably only a very few minutes, he appears at the window, straddling it as he slides open the box of matches.

This is it. The moment I make Nige pay for his humiliation of me, for his bullying. I hold my breath as I wait for Leon to strike the match. But he doesn't. He turns to look at Tina and me and whispers, so low I can barely hear him.

"There's someone coming up the stairs."

Panic grips me and I hiss, "Get off the roof, Leon."

Tina throws caution to the wind and screams at her son, "Get down, right now."

He ignores both of us and, turning back towards the window, takes a match out of the box and holds it over the striker. Now silent, Tina and I watched in horror as he slowly ignites the match and tosses it casually into the room. At first, I think nothing has happened. Leon remains perched on the roof, gazing into the studio. Slowly, light grows within the room and flames begin to appear above the window sill. Leon gets to his feet, tosses the matches, the petrol can and the cricket bat down onto the carpark. He runs down the sloping roof and leaps off it onto the ground, holding his arms above his head, punching the air in victory.

He looks expectantly at Tina and me, obviously thinking we are as elated as he is. Before anyone can speak, we are driven back towards the road as flames suddenly shoot out of the open window and lick up the side of the building. The other windows crack violently as the fire takes hold; another one collapses and more flames climb skywards. The night sky is lit up and sparks shoot up into the air.

"Holy fuck!" Leon is completely awestruck, gazing up at the conflagration, apparently oblivious to the fact that there is a person inside it. "Just look at that!" Incredibly, he takes his phone out and starts filming the fire.Tina, now hysterical, tries to pull the phone out of his hand.

While they tussle over the phone, I stand with both hands clasped to my forehead in horror. Who could have been in the factory at this time of night? There's no car in the small area in front of the factory and there were no lights on when we arrived.

"Shut up!" Tina and Leon stop at my scream. "What the fuck are you playing at?" I flail at Leon in fury and fear. "You've fucking killed someone!"

All the upstairs windows are now fully ablaze. The main doors are impenetrable. The only way into the factory is through the small office window. I shove Leon towards it. "You've got to get in there! You've got to get in and find him."

"Get off me, you mad bitch." Leon roars. "I'm not going in there."

It's a pointless struggle because the window is fitted with iron bars. We can't get into the factory. I sag against the wall, appalled at what we have done. Tina has stopped screaming and now sobs quietly. Leon's eyes glitter, his legs are jittery; he's unable to stay still, high with excitement. He raises his phone again and I push myself off the wall, tear it from his hand and throw it against the factory. It falls to the ground and breaks apart.

"For fuck's sake." He scrabbles for the pieces of his phone, inspects them and throws them back down in disgust. "It's bloody ruined How am I going to manage without a phone?"

I haven't got time for his bullshit.

"Forget the phone. Pick up the fucking can and the cricket bat. We need to run. Now."

"Jills, quick." Tina's at the entrance to the car park, looking up the hill. A small group of people is walking towards the factory, drawn by the sight of the flames shooting up into the sky. They have phones in their hands, eager to record everything and get it onto their Facebook pages.

A quick check to make sure that Tina and I have both got our rucksacks and my camera bag and I'm off, running down the street, dragging her with me. I don't look back. Fuck Leon. At this moment, I don't care if he gets caught; I don't care what happens to him; I don't care that he's technically a child. In my mind, this is already all his fault. Tina tries to wriggle out of my grasp to get back to her son, but I tighten my grip and keep running. At the bottom of the hill, I slow down as we approach the pub on the corner. Groups of people are outside, drinking beer and smoking. We mingle with them while we catch our breath. I look back up the hill. Leon is coming towards us and, thank God, he's got the cricket bat and the petrol can, wrapped up in the tartan blanket. He stands a few yards from us, sullen and suddenly looking very young again, unlike the wild, almost possessed person he'd been in the car park, his face lit up by the flames. I don't trust him and can't forgive him for taking photographs of the burning building, even though he knew there was someone inside it … Oh God, his phone! With his whole life on it.

As soon as the thought strikes me, I turn to Tina, pulling her further away from Leon.

"I have to go back to the factory." She opens her mouth to protest and I silence her, with a quick glance towards Leon. "Listen to me. Leon's phone is there. I threw it against the wall and it broke. All the pieces are on the ground, including the Sim card. It'll lead the police straight to him."

Tina moans. "He'll go to prison. We'll all go to prison. Oh God, what have we done?" She sinks on to a nearby bench, heaving deep sobs, her hands fluttering to her face.

"Get a grip, Teen." We haven't got time for this. "While I'm gone, get rid of that –" I jerk my head towards the blanket, still clutched to Leon's chest. Without waiting to see if she pulls herself together, I run back up the hill. There's a good size crowd standing in front of the factory. Trying to appear as just another rubbernecker, I ask a guy what happened. He shrugs, doesn't know but is just enjoying the spectacle. No fire engines have arrived yet.

I push my way through the crowd, keeping my head down. No one pays any attention to me, transfixed as they are by their efforts to record the blaze. The heat is intense and black smoke pours from the building. The gawkers are coughing and wiping their eyes but determined not to miss a moment of the drama. It's only when I get closer to the burning building that a few cries of "Get back, you idiot" and "What d'you think you're doing?"are thrown at me. I take a deep breath of the poisonous air, pull my tee shirt over my face and make a dive for the corner of the office. Luck is briefly on my side. I feel the broken pieces of the phone under my fingers and, seconds later, the tiny Sim card is in my hand. Just in time. Rough hands get hold of me and drag me back into the crowd.

My rescuer hisses in my ear. "You moron. Do you want to get yourself killed?" The crowd jostles me, forcing me back towards the street. I collapse on to the pavement, gratefully taking in huge gulps of slightly less toxic air until I'm able to get back on my feet.

My legs are like jelly and, halfway down the hill, I'm forced to sit down on a low wall. I'm tempted to cut down one of the side streets and just walk away from Tina and Leon. Better to split up now and go our separate ways, in case someone reports three people running away from the factory. But if I do, Leon will fly straight back to Noel like a homing pigeon once I'm gone. It will only be a matter of time after that before Noel will find Tina, wherever she is. The alternative is to get out of the city as soon as we can. And there's only one place to go.

CHAPTER
THIRTY FIVE

"Jilly, you're home!" Sylvie looks almost glad to see me. She even manages to raise a smile until she looks over my shoulder and sees Tina and Leon standing behind me. Whatever else Sylvie is, she's not stupid.

"Well, this looks like you brought trouble home with you, doesn't it?"

Nodding at Tina and Leon to follow me, I shoulder past her towards the living room and pull up short. Rosemary's dad, Bill, sits in an easy chair with a glass of beer in his hand, watching a large screen television. The room is newly decorated and the furniture looks like it has only recently been purchased.

The biggest surprise, however, is Sylvie herself. Her face is bare of make up, her hair is neatly trimmed and she's neatly dressed in a pretty blouse and a pair of tailored slacks. She looks ... normal.

"Oh Christ," I say, the words out before I can stop myself. "Don't tell me you're shacking up with him?"

Bill glowers at me and pulls himself to his feet. "No, we're not. And I'd like a word with you about what you said to our Rosemary. You caused no end of trouble between me and my wife. Ruined my marriage, you did."

"Not really." I say, stepping forward until there's only a few inches between us, as we stand on Sylvie's new synthetic carpet. "You ruined your own marriage the day you decided to pay *her* –" A nod towards Sylvie." – for what you weren't getting at home."

Bill clenches his fists and I brace myself to ward off a blow. Instead, he puts his beer down, picks up his coat and marches towards the door.

"See you later, Sylvie, when she's not here."

He pushes past Tina and Leon and the front door slams behind him.

Sylvie immediately turns on me, "Well done, Jilly. Back two minutes and you've managed to see off the only friend I've got."

It's as if I've never been away. All my pent-up anger and resentment towards Sylvie spills out as I spit at her. "Friend? He's not a friend, he's one of your regulars and was more than happy to be my first customer."

"Fuck me." It's Tina's voice, coming faintly from behind me. Muffled laughter from Leon.

What have I done? I curse myself mentally for my loose tongue; I should know better than to let Sylvie get me riled up. Tina walks round me and sits down in Bill's chair. She points at Sylvie and says, "This is your mother, right?"

I nod mutely.

"And she's a ... what's that word, again? ... oh yes, a prossy."

"I am not a prossy." says Sylvie indignantly. "Well, I was, but I'm not now."

Tina keeps her eyes trained on me. "Whatever. And, correct me if I'm wrong, Jilly, but did you just say that the gentleman were your first ... punter, that's what I'm looking for, ain't it?"

She waits for an answer from me. When she doesn't get

one, she stands up to face me.

"So, let's get this straight. You're just a prossy, too."

I can't speak. I've hugged my secret to myself for so long, believed I had built myself a better life and, all the time, my past was waiting to rear up and smack me in the face. I'm right back where I started, only worse off than before. I have no money, I can't go back to Nottingham in case the police are looking for me; I've saddled myself with Tina, who obviously hates me now, and Leon, who has always hated me. I can't bear to think how close I was to the job in London and a new start.

"You fucking hypocrite." I've never seen this side of Tina before. "You looked down on me from the day we met. You made me feel like dirt sometimes. Every time you did something nice for me, you was just pretending. You're just a whore like me. Except I don't hide it"

I've been on the receiving end of verbal abuse often enough to know that the best defence is to keep quiet. I hold her gaze and allow her to continue.

"You was so bloody righteous about Noel using me for his hard core porn, wasn't you? What were your picture all about? You exposed me to the whole world, it was in the bloody newspaper and on the radio. At least Noel kept it local."

I'm tired of all of it. My life is one big mess and I just want to put my head down and black everything out, so I simply walk out of the room and climb the stairs to my old bedroom. It looks much as it did when I left it, except the mattress is bare with no sheets. I don't care. It'll do, at least there's a lock on the door. Fuck them all. I don't care what happens to any of them. I curl up on the bed and sleep.

"Jilly! Wake up, Jilly!" Tina pounds on the bedroom

door. "Jilly, can you hear me?"

I drag myself off the bed and open the door. Tina stands there, her eyes wild. More drama.

"What is it now?"

"Oh, Jilly, I'm so sorry." Her eyes are swimming with tears and she lays one hand on my arm. I jerk away from her and snarl, "I've got no time for this, Tina. You had your say. Now piss off and leave me alone."

"No, it ain't that. It's the factory. It's on the telly." She drags me towards the stairs and I stumble after her, half awake.

In the living room, Sylvie and Leon are on their feet staring at the television set. Against a backdrop of the blazing factory stands Nige, talking to a news presenter. His voice is thick, his words barely intelligible as he struggles to speak through heavy sobs.

"I've only just got here. I don't know anything about how the fire started. But ... I've got to find Rob. He was sleeping in the office. We'd had a drink after work, he was upset because his girlfriend left him. He was too drunk to go home so I gave him a sleeping bag and left him here to sleep it off."

A paramedic appears on screen with a blanket which she drapes over Nige's shoulders and leads him gently away out of camera shot. He can be heard crying, "I've got to find Rob. I've got to find my mate."

The news presenter says, "Firefighters continue to try and put out the flames. It is too soon to know the cause of the fire, but arson is a possibility."

Someone, somewhere, is wailing. One long, high keening note. It goes on and on. I lean against the wall, try to walk, but I've lost all sense of direction. I'm not quite sure where I am. What's happening? Darkness threatens to envelop me again. The keening has subsides into a low moan. Help me, help me.

"Here, drink this."

I'm on the sofa. Tina pushes a glass of brandy into my hand; she closes my fingers around it and guides it to my mouth. I gulp some down and immediately cough as it burns its way down to my stomach. The room steadies. I look towards the television, where the newscaster still stands outside the blazing factory.

"Turn it off," I choke, my throat raw.

"Will someone please tell me what the hell is going on?" Sylvie says. "Do you know that man on the telly?"

I can't think clearly.

Rob is dead. We've killed Rob.

"Answer me!" Sylvie is losing patience. "Or, by God, I'll throw you all out. I don't need this."

Leon tells her. "We burned the factory down. It was her idea." He jerks his head towards me.

Sylvie's face drains of all colour. She totters over to sit beside me on the sofa. I keep my head down and refuse to look at her as she speaks to me.

"You burned down a fucking factory? Well, you and your friends can just pick yourselves up and clear off again. I don't want to be involved in it. Just go."

"I didn't want to come here, in the first place." Leon displays his usual belligerence. "Two hours it took us to get here, two bloody hours. Who would want to live here, anyway?" He holds his hand out to his mother. "Give me your phone, Tina. The way Noel drives, he can be here in just over an hour."

My head snaps up. "What did you just call your mum?"

He lifts one shoulder insolently, doesn't reply.

"You didn't come back to be with your mum, did you?

You were spying for your dad all the time. How could you do that? You know he'll hurt her, and hurt her badly, if she goes home."

"He won't hurt her, he told me. He lives with Lainie now, so he won't bother Tina at all, as long as she keeps her nose clean."

He infuriates me. "Oh, for Gods sake, listen to yourself. You're just repeating his words. You don't really believe that. He's just using you, the same way he's used your mum for years."

His eyes shift sideways to Tina. "Don't make me laugh. Noel told me, she's always been like it, even when he met her. She made me a laughing stock at school. Dirty notes stuck on my locker, my head shoved down the toilet."

Tina puts her hand in her pocket and takes out her phone. She's going to give it to him. I have to convince Leon to stay. He's just a boy, he can't be as hard and tough as he pretends to be.

"How old are you?" I'm right in his face, making him look at me. "I know, you're thirteen. Well, let me tell you something. When Tina – your mum – was fourteen, just one year older than you, it was your dad who ruined her life. She was an innocent schoolgirl when she met him. Please, Leon, try to put yourself in her place. Do you really think she was a prostitute when she was only fourteen?"

"Yes, I do. Noel wouldn't lie to me." Leon tries to argue back, but I can see the uncertainty in his face.

"Yes, he did. Why do you think he's suddenly your best friend? The last time I saw you together, you were screaming that you hated him. Can't you see, he's just using you to keep track of your mum?"

Tina's phone rings. She looks at the screen and then at me. "It's Noel," she says.

Before I can stop him, Leon launches himself across the room, snatches the phone from her hand and hits the green button.

CHAPTER THIRTY SIX

"Hi, Dad. It's me." Leon smirks, backing off with one arm held out to ward us off. Straight into Sylvie who whips the phone from Leon's hand and shuts it down.

Immediately, he reverts to a whining teenager. "That's not fair. You can't do that."

"I just did." Sylvie is unmoved and addresses me and Tina. "So, when – if – I throw you out, you can't go back to Nottingham, because this Noel bloke is going to come after you. Is that right?"

Tina nods. All fight seems to have drained out of her.

Leon sulks, refusing to speak.

"And what has he to do with burning the factory?"

"Nothing, that is, he's sort of involved." Numb with the horror of Rob's death and exhausted by the argument with Leon, I walk into the kitchen, straight to the fridge. There'll be wine. There always is. I line up three large glasses and fill them to the brim. There aren't any soft drinks to offer Leon. Sod him. He doesn't deserve anything.

"Come in here." I call to the group in the living room. "Not you, Leon. Turn the television on for him, Sylvie."

She grumbles. "Back two minutes and she's giving orders again." But she does as I say; she and Tina come into the kitchen, closing the door behind them, and sit at the table with me.

I'm tired. My head feels too heavy for my neck. It requires a momentous effort even to think. I lay my hands either side of my glass and stare into the wine.

Sylvie takes a breath, as if to speak, and I say, "Don't."

So they drink and wait. I don't know where to start.

So many images tumble against each other in my head – the flames shooting up into the sky; Leon saying there was someone in the factory; Nige crying, looking for his mate.

Rob, in the bookshop, laughing when I kissed his cheek.

I try to convince myself that he didn't suffer – maybe he was still drunk, thought he was having a bad dream or the smoke could have overcome him before the flames got to him.

I never wanted anyone to die. It wasn't meant to end like this. If it hadn't been for his phobia about prostitutes …

"Prossy." I lift my head and look at Tina. "That word you hate. Do you want to know why Rob used it? Why he made my life a misery? Ask *her.*"

Sylvie's jaw drops. "Me? I don't even know the man. What are you on about?"

I give her the bare bones of the story Rob told me. "Yeah, you do know him. He was fifteen when he came here. His dad brought him to have sex for the first time. He remembered seeing me in my cot. You gave his dad the clap and his mum killed herself."

Sylvie's face is blank. She has no idea what I'm talking about. Rob spent so much of his life hating her, hating prostitutes, and she can't even remember him.

"You ruined his life." The only way I can push the images of Rob out of my mind is to concentrate on my anger. Sylvie is such an easy target. "You ruined my life, as well. Did you think I wouldn't remember that you sold me to one of your customers when I was only seven?"

"I never! You wicked bitch. How can you say such a thing? What customer?" If I didn't know Sylvie better, I could believe her response was genuine, but I can remember Mick and how rough his fingers were as he pushed him into my small body.

"Mick Coulter. You left me here, in this kitchen. He brought me Jaffa cakes. You laughed when you walked out of the room."

"He was babysitting!" Sylvie screams, her face red with rage. "He was babysitting you while he waited his turn, I swear it."

I don't believe her.

"Oh, my God. That's why his wife was here that time, isn't it?" Her face is slack, she looks like she has aged ten years in the last few seconds. Her voice loses all belligerence. "Jilly, I swear to you, I didn't know."

She's wasting her time. There isn't anything she can say to change my mind; nothing she can do to take away the soiled years of my childhood.

"Tina and I need to talk some things through; we also need to sleep. I take Sylvie's glass away from her. "Can you go and make the bed up in my bedroom? Leon can sleep on the sofa, so bring some blankets when you come back down."

I wait until she's left the room, slamming the door behind her, and pull my chair round so that I face Tina. She refuses to meet my eyes.

"If you think you're going to get an apology from me, you're wrong." She shrugs her shoulders, mutely acknowledging that she's listening to me. "You don't have any right to know my life story. I didn't ask you for yours. You chose to tell me some things, I chose not to tell you some things. But I never looked down on you. I told you the first day I met you that I was in no place to judge you."

Still no answer. I pick up my glass. "OK, I'm going to finish my wine and if you still haven't spoken to me, then I'll take it that any agreement we had is over and you and Leon can leave on the next train back to Nottingham." I wait to see if she will call my bluff.

Instead, she asks me a question. "Were it true?"

" Was what true?"

"The thing about the man with the Jaffa cakes."

My anger, never far from the surface, surges back. "Oh no, you don't get to question me. I might've known you would take the mother's side."

This is impossible. We don't trust each other. Sylvie was right, all those years ago.

You don't need friends. They'll always shit on you.

The legs of my chair screech against the tiled floor; I'm on my feet reaching for the door knob when she speaks. "Don't go, Jills."

It's the *Jills* that does it. I reach blindly behind me for the chair and collapse back into it.The dam breaks. I sob aloud, half-moan, half-scream, as I grieve for the young girl in this kitchen so many years ago, for Rob, for my whole sorry life.

Tina kneels beside me, gripping both my hands, while I purge the pain from my body. My sobs cease, the room falls silent. We hold hands. It's enough.

The brief peace shatters when Sylvie flings open the kitchen door, "Here, is that bloke's name Rob Knowley?"

Tina and I follow her to the living room, where Leon has the television tuned to the twenty-four hour news. A photograph of Rob fills the screen. I took it on one of our happier days. He's in a park with deer in the background, smiling and squinting against the sun. The newsroom must have taken it off his Facebook page.

A voiceover informs us, "The body recovered from the factory fire has been identified as Robert Knowley, a printer, aged 35 years." The picture changes to show the blazing factory. "Firefighters have determined that the fire was started deliberately in the upper floor of the factory. It has not yet been established whether the perpetrator was Mr. Knowley or persons unknown. Nigel Ferguson, Mr. Knowley's friend and employer, stated that Mr Knowley was depressed because his girlfriend had left him. Police are appealing for Jillian Graham, or anyone who knows her whereabouts, to get in touch with them."

Sylvie's clearly frightened. "So this is your boyfriend, and he's dead in the fire you started?" Her eyes narrow, she looks from Leon to me to Tina. "So, which one of you did it? Who set the fire?"

Leon stands up.

Shut up. Don't say anything.

He blurts out, "I struck the match, but they told me to do it. I didn't want to, but *she*," a venomous look at me, "couldn't climb the roof so she made me do it. I told her there was somebody in there, but she told me to go ahead and throw the match."

"That's not true." I whisper, still overwrought from my emotional outburst in the kitchen and from the shock of seeing Rob's face on the television. "I did fall off the roof, but I didn't ask you to climb it."

"You didn't stop me, though, did you?"

He's trying to save his own skin, shifting the blame. For the briefest of moments, I feel empathy for him. He's lived through the same humiliations I did and, still only a child, corrupted by Noel to turn against his mother.

I shouldn't blame him.

But I do. His words snap me out of the self-pity I've been wallowing in. I can think clearly again and I know what we've got to do.

"Bill will be back tomorrow." I'm talking to Tina, but I'm watching Sylvie for her reaction. "She'll tell him everything. She won't be able to keep her mouth shut. We can't stay here."

Sylvie shakes her head. Are they tears in her eyes? "I'm not like I was when you left, Jilly. I've got a job, not much of one, but I pay my way and I've given up the life. Bill's just a friend, since his wife kicked him out. He holds a grudge against you, I can't blame him, but I swear, I won't give him anything he could use to hurt you."

"All right." I'm not fully convinced of this new Sylvie, but there's no alternative. "Tina and I are going to get some sleep. We'll leave early in the morning."

Leon's still on his feet. "What about me? Don't I get a say in what we're doing?"

"No, you don't." I'm short with him, sick of looking at his spoiled, brattish face.

Tina turns her back to Leon and Sylvie, lowers her voice and asks me, "Where are we going?"

I jerk my head towards the door, "Not here. We'll talk upstairs."

We enter my bedroom and I attempt a joke. "Welcome to my 'office'. Not as pretty as yours, is it?"

Tina sits on the bed, looks around at my teenage room,

devoid of frills or posters. "I still can't take it all in. What did you –"

"We haven't got time to swap stories, Teen." I smile to take the edge off my words. "Maybe later, if we ever get out of this."

" You're right." She hesitates, seems to come to some kind of resolution. "Look, I know you can't stand the sight of Leon. He ain't my favourite person either, at the moment. I know – first chance he gets – he'll go running back to Noel and grass on us. But he's my son. I can't give up on him. So, whatever you're planning to do, he's got to be included."

"Fine." I mean to keep Leon close by, at all costs, but if Tina believes I'm doing her a favour, it might help in getting her to agree to what I want to do. I can't delay any longer. We need to get some sleep before setting off early in the morning.

"I'm going to phone Nige as soon as we get up tomorrow."

Tina opens her mouth to speak. I raise a hand. "Let me finish before you say anything. The police are looking for me, probably only to back up Nige's story about Rob and I breaking up. They may even believe that Rob set the fire himself. But it would be the natural thing for me to do if I heard about the fire on the telly."

"All right." Tina's calmer than I had expected. "But when he asks you where you are, what're you going to tell him?"

"I'm going to tell him that I've been spending a couple of days at my mother's. He has no idea where she lives and, if the police ever check with Sylvie, she just has to tell them I arrived in the early afternoon, not in the evening."

"What about me and Leon?"

"Nobody knows we're all together." I check myself. "Although Noel could put two and two together and work out that you and Leon are with me."

"Wait, let me think." Tina paces for a few seconds. "Yeah, it's OK, even if he thinks we're with you, Noel won't go to the police, but he'll have his mates out looking for me. We'll need a good hiding place, though."

"I know. It's why we're going back to Rob's house."

She laughs. "I thought you was serious, there, for a minute."

"I am serious. Think about it, Teen. If I didn't know anything about the fire and I saw the news on the television, what's the first thing I would do?"

"Well, yeah, maybe ... But what about me and Leon?"

It would be better if I returned to Nottingham alone, with Tina and Leon following me later, under cover of darkness. I can't afford to do that. Tina isn't strong enough to stop Leon running to Noel.

"We're sticking together. Noel's probably been to Rob's already. He'll know I'm not there and he's got no reason to think I'd go back. We can hide there for a few days until we work out what to do."

She's still dubious. "It's too dangerous ..."

I'm too tired to argue with Tina. I lie down on the bed, fully clothed.

"Get some sleep, Teen. Good night."

CHAPTER THIRTY SEVEN

Sylvie whispers in my ear.

"Jilly, wake up. The police are here."

"What?" Groggy from lack of sleep, I don't react.

"They're outside." Sylvie tries to get me on my feet.

"Who are outside?"

She shakes me. "For Christ's sake, pull yourself together! The police are outside."

Her words penetrate the fog in my head and I jump up, cross to the window and peer through a crack in the curtains. A police car sits at the kerb and two uniformed officers are walking up the garden path.

"Quick." I push Sylvie towards the door. "Go and get Leon, bring him up here."

"I'm here." Leon has a gift for entering rooms quietly. "Did you know the filth's at the door?"

I don't understand how they got here so quickly. No one in Nottingham knows Sylvie is my mother. The front door bell shrills through the house.

Tina jerks awake. "What's up?" I hold a finger to my lips and point her to the window.

"Shit," she moans. "We're screwed."

"No, we're not." I've planned for this, just didn't expect it to happen so soon. "Sylvie, answer the door. Tell them I came to see you yesterday afternoon – just me, do you understand?"

"Yes." Her teeth chatter as she repeats my words. "Just you … yesterday afternoon."

"Right. Tell them they've just missed me. I left half an hour ago, had to get back to Nottingham because I saw the news about Rob. Got it?"

Oh fuck, she's crying. I grip her shoulders. "Pull yourself together. You owe me! Now go and do it."

A man's voice, just beneath the window, says, "The bell's not working. Knock the door."

The rat-tat-tat echoes up the stairs. Sylvie's visibly shaking. Tina steps forward, wipes my mother's eyes and gives her a hug. The small gesture works where my anger failed. Sylvie straightens her shoulders, walks downstairs and opens the door.

Her voice floats upstairs, as she greets the officers. "Stevie, what are *you* doing here?"

My heart picks up speed and my breath shortens, as I'm transported back to my teenage years.

Please God, not now, don't let me have a panic attack.

I've got to hand it to Sylvie. As soon as she sees Stevie at the front door, she pulls herself together and goes on the attack.

"Come for a freebie?" She sneers. "Them days're long gone, sunshine."

Stevie coughs, rallies. "Good morning, Miss Graham. We're looking for your daughter, Jilly. Do you know where she is?"

"Of course I know where she is. What do you want her for? She's got enough trouble on at the moment, without you lot sniffing around."

The second officer joins the conversation. "Miss Graham, we just need to talk to your daughter."

Sylvie's voice remains surly, but she answers him. "Of course, officer. Jilly came to see me yesterday, to stay for a while. A mother and daughter catch up, sort of thing. But she saw some terrible news on the television about her boyfriend. She's gone back to Nottingham, to find out what happened to him. You've just missed her."

Their voices fade to a murmur; she's allowed them into the house.

Be careful, Sylvie.

"Where are your things?" I whisper to Leon.

"I stuffed them behind the sofa when I saw the police car pull up."

My breathing steadies. We stand and wait. After a tense few minutes, they're back in the hallway. Stevie thanks Sylvie for her help and manages to fit in a veiled threat.

"Give my regards to Jilly when you see her again. Tell her I haven't forgotten her."

The front door clicks shut behind them and I say, "OK. Let's go."

Tina and I pick up our bags. Leon doesn't budge.

I sigh. "What now?"

He stammers, "Jilly …"

What? He's actually talking to me?

"Those cops. They might be waiting outside. I'm …"

Suddenly, I'm looking at a scared thirteen year old boy. The attitude is gone, at least for the moment. I can't find it in my heart to soften towards him; a warning voice at the back of mind wonders if he's playing games again.

"You're what?" I'm impatient to get off.

His voice breaks. "… scared."

I relent slightly. "We're all scared but staying here isn't the answer."

He gets his feet moving and we hurry downstairs to

where Sylvie stands, smiling from ear to ear, pleased with herself for seeing off the coppers.

Tina hugs her again, I mutter a thank you and Leon completely ignores her.

"Be careful, won't you?" Sylvie says, now completely on our side, buying into the drama of the moment. "Let me know when you get back. I'll be worried until I hear from you."

Sylvie in mother mode is a bit more than I can handle. I hustle Tina and Leon out of the door in front of me. As I turn to walk away, Sylvie places a hand on my arm.

"Jilly... You'll come back, won't you?"

"Maybe." It's the best I can do.

CHAPTER THIRTY EIGHT

The morning rush hour is over when we pull into Nottingham railway station. We're all on high alert, nervy and seeing things in the shadows. I had hoped there would be crowds of people so we could get lost among them.

"I'll take the first taxi in line, then you and Leon wait for ten minutes and follow me." It's not ideal, but if there are any neighbours twitching the curtains, they'll see me coming home alone. "Get your taxi to pull up at the back gate and I'll let you in that way."

Tina is visibly nervous, biting her lip and shaking, but just about holding it together. Leon's trying to look cool, but this eyes are darting everywhere.

He says, "Don't worry. We'll be careful."

I feel like asking him if he's had a head transplant, but content myself with muttering, "Yeah, well, I hope I can trust you not to leg it," before climbing in to the first cab on the rank. When we turn into Rob's street, Nige's car is parked in front of the house. He hammers on the front door and stands back, looking up at the windows. I lean forward and tap the driver on the shoulder. "Keep driving, round the next corner, and park up."

I fumble for my phone and stab at the buttons with shaky fingers. Tina doesn't pick up and I curse myself for having broken Leon's phone. I kill the connection and pay the taxi driver.

"You all right, love?" The taxi driver looks concerned when I make no move to get out of the cab.

"Yes, I'm fine. Just hang on a moment, will you?"

My brain won't work. I try to think of a way to get Nige to leave. The cabbie gets impatient. "If you're not going anywhere else, love, I need to get back to the station. Time's money, you know."

"Yeah, I'm sorry." I gather up my bags to get out of the cab. A car comes around the corner and flies past the taxi; I breathe a sigh of relief when I realise it's Nige. I apologise to the taxi driver again and he waves me off. "That's OK, duck. We've all got problems."

By the time I get through the front door, stop to lock and bolt it, run through the house, unlock the back door and the back gate, Tina and Leon's taxi has arrived.

I keep a wary eye on the street, in case Nige comes back. "Quick! Get in." They fly through the back yard and into the house, entering through the kitchen, while I re-lock the gate.

I follow them in, to find Leon already checking the fridge. "I'm starving. What is there to eat?" It's a reasonable question. We're all hungry, tired and overwrought. Everything else can wait until we've eaten. Tina finds a loaf of bread and toasts slices, Leon grates cheese and I fry eggs while the bread and cheese bubbles away under the grill. She piles up three plates of food and we move into the dining room to devour the hot meal.

"Right." I push the empty plates to one side of the table. "I didn't tell you earlier, but Nige has been sniffing around. No idea why, unless he's checking to see if I've come back. Apart from him, the biggest problem we've got is that the police could turn up. It might be better if I contact them first, say I've seen the appeal on the television."

Leon shifts in his seat. "But we'll be all right, won't we? Your mum said you were at her house, and they don't know that Tina and me were anywhere near."

He doesn't seem to have any regret or remorse for the moment he struck the match. I try to make him understand that we aren't in the clear, by any means.

"Once I talk to the police, they're going to come here and look round the house, to see if there's anything to indicate whether Rob was planning to torch the factory. And, apart from that, someone might've seen us running away."

Tina loses patience with her son. "Can't you see, we're in shit street? If the cops see us here, they'll put two and two together and, before you know it, all sorts will come out of the woodwork."

Leon's on his feet now, clearly agitated. "Well, it wasn't my idea, was it? And it wasn't your's, either. It was *her's*."

Infected by their panic, I raise my voice. "I told you not to strike the match! I told you to get off the bloody roof."

We're all on our feet, on the verge of a major argument, when there's a knock on the front door. I put a finger to my lips. Tina and Leon stand motionless. I walk into the hallway and call through the door, "Who is it?"

A female voice answers me. "Police. Can you open the door, please?"

"Of course. Hold on a second; I'll just find my keys."

Back in the dining room, I push Tina and Leon through the kitchen towards the back door. "Go out through the back yard. When you see the street's clear, go round the corner and hide in one of the alleyways."

Leon has the presence of mind to pick up their rucksacks before they go; I hastily gather up the plates and put them in the kitchen sink, before rushing back to the front door. I'm out of breath and take a few seconds to compose myself.

"Just coming," I call. A quick glance through the house to the back passageway to make sure Tina and Leon have gone and I undo the locks and take the chain off the door. Two female police officers stand in the street.

"Sorry to keep you waiting. Is this about Rob?"

Slow down. I mentally kick myself for jumping in with a question.

The taller of the two flashes a card.

"DS Peters and DC Anderson. Miss Graham?"

"Yes."

"May we come in?"

I hold the door wider and they enter, turning right into the dining room before I can usher them into the living room.

"Something smells nice." Peters takes a few steps in the direction of the open kitchen door, scrutinising the worktops. They're littered with the utensils we used but the plates are out of sight in the sink.

"Yes, I've just got back from visiting my mother. Didn't fancy the food on the train."

The two women inspect the dining room.

I babble on, "I saw the news about Rob on the television. I was just about to contact you."

Anderson speaks for the first time. "You couldn't have phoned from your mother's?"

"Yeah, it's the shock, you know? Rob and I were splitting up, but we'd been together for three years. And the

..."

I locked the back gate! Tina and Leon can't get out.

Peters, who appears the more sympathetic of the two, says, "I can see you're upset. We won't take up a lot of your time. Do you mind if we look around?"

"Not at all."

If they both go upstairs, I can run to the back door and throw my keys out.

Peters points towards the stairs door and says to Anderson, "You take the bedrooms. I'll do down here." She turns to me. "Can you show me the other room?"

There's not much to look at in the living room. Peters riffles though some papers on a small table and kicks against the small pile of beer cans on the floor near Rob's chair.

"Liked a drink, did he?"

"He and Nige had been drinking more than usual lately."

"So I gather. Is that why you were leaving him?"

"Partly. I've been offered a job in London. We sort of agreed to separate."

Anderson clatters downstairs and we walk back into the dining room to join her. She shows a picture on her phone to Peters and says," This was on the door in the bedroom. Looks like he was hoping for a reconciliation."

To me, she says, "Some nice equipment up there. Yours, is it?"

I don't bother to answer her.

Peters steps in. "So, what did he want to explain?"

"What?" I need to pull myself together, forget about Tina and Leon for the moment.

"This note. *I can explain.* What's that about?"

"He ... uh ... he hit me. He was drunk, it's why I went to

my mother's."

"Was that usual?"

"Yes – I mean no – he was a good guy when he didn't drink."

I'm not making sense. The familiar tiredness and the tingle in my fingers warn me that I'm about to lose control. Tears fill my eyes. I let my knees buckle and collapse into a chair.

"Is there anything more? I just want to ..."

They exchange glances. I hold my breath, then Peters shrugs. "No, I think we're done here." She coughs. "Sorry for your loss, Miss Graham. We'll see ourselves out."

Shouldn't I ask questions?

"Wait." The tears thicken my voice. "Is there ... do you know what happened? Why Rob ..."

Anderson raises her eyebrows at Peters, who gives a short nod. "Well, you'll find out later, anyway. We're making an appeal on the local news, asking if anyone saw a young, black male running away from the factory. We've got footage off a mobile phone. There's been a lot of burglaries and vandalism in that area by a gang of youths. He could be one of them."

"So Rob didn't ..."

"At the moment, it looks like he was in the wrong place at the wrong time. Mr Ferguson hasn't been able to access the factory yet to see if anything's missing."

I manage to choke out a *Thank you* and they take their leave. The sound of their car engine fades and, moments later, Tina and Leon come back inside.

Leon is flushed and laughing, excited by the brush with the police. "You locked the gate, we had to hide behind the bins. I nearly pissed myself. I was going to climb the wall and then we heard them come out."

I jump to my feet and scream at him. "It's not a fucking game! Somebody saw you."

He brushes me off. "Nobody saw me. I told you, the filth came out before –"

"At the factory, you bloody moron!" I round on Tina. "I told you, time after time, we couldn't trust him. We should never have taken him with us. They've got a video. What if somebody identifies him?"

"No, they won't." She tries to get me to look at her but I'm frantic, beyond reason. "It were dark. How many kids in the city look like him? Thousands! As long as he keeps his head down for a while, we'll be all right."

"Mum?" Leon backs away from me, fear written on his face. "Are the police looking for me?"

"Yes, they bloody are." I crowd him, cutting off Tina as she tries to speak. "Can't you get it through your head? We killed Rob! *You* killed Rob!"

"Stop it! For fuck's sake, stop it!" Tina's voice rises above mine. She steps in between me and her son. "No more, Jills. We all need to calm down."

There's a new authority in her voice and, my outburst over, I've neither anger nor energy left to argue with her.

"Fine." I trudge through to the back door on leaden feet, shooting home the bolts and securing the locks. As I head back towards the stairs door, I say curtly, "I'm going upstairs to lie down. Stay away from the windows and don't answer the door."

I close the curtains against the sun in the bedroom. The note stares accusingly at me, no longer legible in the gloom, but the words torture me.

If you come back and see this, ring me. I don't want you to leave me.

In my overwrought state, I give in to the waves of guilt I've been holding back.

Maybe if I'd phoned him, he wouldn't have got drunk with Nige.

Maybe if I'd never taken the picture of Tina, things wouldn't have got out of hand.

Maybe if I'd never been bloody born …

"Forget the fucking *maybes*." My voice shatters the silence in the room, loud enough to drown out the voice of guilt. I rip the note from the door and force myself to remember the vile things he did to me. The humiliation, the violence, the attack … no, not the attack – the *rape*.

But was it him?

I lean my back on the door and slowly slide down until I'm sitting on the floor. Time to be honest. The sight of my earring caught up in Rob's coat sent me into a cold fury that culminated in his death. I didn't care who was actually guilty, as long as I could make someone hurt as much as I had.

The madness of the last forty-eight hours is down to me. Yes, Leon threw the match. Yes, he's probably a psychopath in the making, if not already a full-blown danger to the world. But – I took him to the factory; I put him on the roof. I was so pumped up with the desire, the *need*, for revenge, that I used a thirteen-year-old boy. A question pushes, unbidden, to the forefront of my mind.

In Leon's place, would I have thrown the match?

I'm too afraid to answer it. My stock answer of 'It's not my fault 'doesn't seem to be available to me any more. The room is closing in on me, no longer large enough to contain the mass of emotions I'm struggling with. I'm afraid to be on my own and struggle to my feet, pounding back down the stairs, in need of a distraction.

CHAPTER THIRTY NINE

Tina and Leon are in the kitchen, washing dishes and cleaning up the mess we made earlier. I hover in the doorway, unsure how to proceed.

"I thought you was asleep." Tina smiles at me, genuine warmth in her eyes. "We're nearly finished in here. Leon, make Jills a cup of tea."

"Sure." He doesn't quite raise a smile as he obeys his mother, but the over-excitement and panic of earlier are no longer evident in his face. Instead, a hint of fear lurks in his eyes.

The calm atmosphere in the kitchen softens the edges of my heightened anxiety. My shoulders relax and I ease my neck from side to side to lessen the tension. I summon up a modicum of grace.

"Thanks ... uh, thanks, that would be nice. I'll be in the living room."

The television is on, tuned to the twenty-four hour news. I'm just in time to catch the end of the weather forecast, followed by the local news. Tina and Leon come into the room behind me and we watch as images of the burning factory fill the screen again, followed by a blurred, ten-second video showing the back of a young man running down the street. As he passes under a streetlight, a halo of small dreads can be seen encircling his head.

Leon hands me a mug of tea and asks, "Do you think people will know it's me?"

I shrug. "I don't know. What are you asking me for?"

Tina thumbs the remote and the television blinks off.

"Sit." She jerks her head at Leon and he collapses onto the sofa. In response to her raised eyebrow, I follow suit.

"OK." She grips her hands tightly together and hesitates a few seconds before she says, "I ain't stupid. I know we're in a whole heap of trouble and God knows how we'll get out of it. But we have to stop tearing each other to bits."

"You mean me and Leon, don't you?" I'm ashamed of the hostility in my voice, although it's directed at Leon, not Tina. "You're always making excuses for him."

"Excuses for me?" he shoots back. "It's you she sticks up for. I'm sick of it."

"And I'm fucking sick of both of you!" Tears stand in Tina's eyes and her face is red with frustration. "I'm sick of being in the middle." She makes a visible effort to control herself. When she speaks again, her voice is barely a whisper. "You might not believe me, Leon, but I love you, whatever your dad told you. And I love you, Jills, you're my friend, you gave me the courage to leave Noel. Can't you make an effort to get along, if only for me?"

Leon role his eyes and stares at his feet. It takes a few more seconds for her words to register with me.

And I love you, Jills, you're my friend.

"You love me?" Is that high-pitched squeak, laced with surprise and disbelief, really me?

"Of course I do, you silly mare. Why else would I put up with you?"

"Huh, I could say the same about you."

But I don't. I pick up my empty mug and head for the kitchen.

As cold water runs into the mug, I replay her words in my mind ... and smile.

It's a long time since any of us had a shower. We toss a coin to see who goes first, Tina wins and disappears into the bathroom with fresh towels.

Leon sits in front of the television, idly flicking through the channels. I stand in front of him, cutting off his vision, and talk to the top of his head as he goes into automatic sulk mode. "I don't like you, Leon, and I know you sure-as-hell don't like me. But I do like your mum and she doesn't need us tearing strips off each other."

I wait for a response, which isn't forthcoming. Fair enough.

"We're going to back off on the arguing, do you understand me?" I kick his feet, irritated by his refusal to answer.

He jerks back, scrabbling away from me. I bend down so my face is level with his. "We will be polite to each other, if it kills both of us ... for your mother's sake. Am I getting through to you?'

I rap my knuckles on the top of his head and he slaps my arm away.

"All right!" he spits out. "Now piss off."

I'm happy to do so and wait in the dining room until Tina emerges from the bathroom, wrapped in a bath towel.

"We need to talk," I say, before calling through to Leon. "Bathroom's free. Your turn."

He shambles past us on his way to a shower. I force myself to smile at him and he gives me a half-nod. It's a start.

"What do you want to talk about?" Tina tightens the towel round her and perches on the edge of the table.

I get straight to the point. "What do you say to staying here for a few days, off the radar, and just chilling? I'll do any shopping we need and answer the door, so you and Leon have effectively disappeared."

Tina answers immediately. "Bloody hell, Jills, you read my mind. I were going to suggest the same thing."

"Great!" We both laugh and I get a Tina-hug. I don't quite return it but manage a few pats on her back. She sets off upstairs and I follow, heaving our two rucksacks on to my shoulders.

"Are you OK with sharing the bed? I could make up something on the floor for me if …"

She flaps a hand at me, "Don't be daft. We'll be fine, sharing."

I leave her to dry her hair and get dressed. Partway out of the door, I turn back and say, "There's still a few of my tee-shirts lying about. Feel free to wear any of them. I guess you've only got frocks and four-inch heels in your bag."

It's not a great joke, but Tina laughs. I run lightly downstairs to chivvy Leon out of the bathroom.

As the last one in, I opt for a bubble bath rather than a shower. I finger-comb my wet hair which is a tangled mess since I stopped plaiting it, and fashion a turban out of a hand towel to blot it dry.

Tina calls through the door, "Jills, where do you keep the scissors?"

"Large ones in the kitchen drawer, small ones upstairs."

"OK! Got them."

Curious to see what she's doing, I throw on my bathrobe

and open the bathroom door.

Leon sits on a dining chair, blocking the gangway in the galley kitchen. His mother stands behind him, wielding the kitchen scissors.

"Please, Mum, don't," he begs, attempting to protect his baby dreads. "It took ages to get them started."

Tina grabs hold of a few dreads on the back of his head and hacks them off.

Her eyes widen. "Oh shit, I've scalped him." She drops a large clump of hair into Leon's lap.

I retreat into the bathroom and leave them to it.

Shortly after, Tina taps the door. "It's safe to come out now."

"Where's Leon?"

"In the living room, says he's never going to speak to me again."

She kneels down to sweep up the remains of Leon's dreads. Concentrating on the floor, she says. "Jills?"

"What?"

"Did you notice?"

I know what she means. "Yeah, I did, you're 'Mum' again."

She stands up, her eyes bright with unshed tears, and manages a shaky laugh.

"Even though I cut off his dreads, as well."

"Speaking of cutting …" I tug the towel off my hair and it falls wetly down my back. "Fancy having a go at this?"

"Oh, I don't know, it must've taken a long time to grow it."

"Most of my life, but I want it gone now. Just cut it up to my shoulders, it'll be fine."

I drag the dining chair back into the kitchen and sit down, handing the scissors to Tina.

She takes them reluctantly, says, "All right, but it's on your head if it goes wrong," and we collapse in giggles.

I close my eyes, listening to the snip-snip of the scissors and the occasional, "Oh, bugger" and "Oh, shit." Hair falls on my nose, making me sneeze.

"OK, you can look now." Tina gives a final snip and it's done. My head feels light as I walk to the mirror. She's given me a long bob with a thick fringe just clearing my eyebrows.

"I look like Cleopatra!"

"Don't you like it?"

"I bloody love it."

Tina lets out a long breath. "Oh good, I were worried there, for a minute."

Back in the living room, Leon's got the television tuned to the twenty four hour news again. I switch channels and cut off his protest.

"No, we're taking a break from that. Have a look at Rob's films, see if there's anything you fancy."

He sizes up my new hair-do and says, "I see she got to you, as well."

Aware of Tina anxiously watching us, I afford him a small grimace which could pass for a smile.

We pass the rest of the afternoon watching television, dozing and drinking tea. None of us has the energy to do anything else.

Teatime approaches and we debate whether to scratch a meal together or order a takeaway. There's a knock at the door, just as I agree to fish and chips.

In the hallway, I can see the outline of a man's head through the small pane of frosted glass. He knocks again and shouts, "Miss Graham? Are you there?"

Seconds tick by. I remain motionless in the hallway.

Tina and Leon hug the wall in the living room, one on either side of the window so they can't be seen from outside.

"Miss Graham?" He doesn't give up. "It's Rick Palmer from the *Evening Post*. Can we have a word with you?"

A shadow appears at the living room window and a second voice says, "The telly's on. There's somebody in there."

"Go round the back, see if she's in the kitchen."

"Nah, I'm not climbing that wall."

"Oh, for Chrissakes, I'll do it myself."

From where I stand in the hallway, I can see the kitchen darken as a shadow falls across the window. Minutes later, the first voice is back at the front door.

"Jilly? Come on, Jilly. We just want to know your side of things."

A few more minutes and suddenly a business card pops through the letterbox.

"OK, call me if you change your mind."

And they're gone. I think. No takeaway, though, to be on the safe side. Scratch meal it is.

The rest of the evening is quiet. Leon moans a bit about having to sleep on the sofa, only slightly mollified when he finds it opens up into a bed.

"Can I watch telly?" he asks Tina and she says, "Yeah, just keep the sound down. Don't bother the neighbours."

Not the answer I would have given but I bite my tongue.

He pushes his luck. "Jills?"

Jills? He must want something.

"What?"

"Can I go on your computer tomorrow? Just to catch up with my mates. I really miss my phone."

He doesn't say, "You know, the one you smashed," but the implication is clear.

Does he think I'm stupid? He'd be straight on to Noel. Before I can answer him, Tina touches my arm and shakes her head in silent entreaty.

I back off, mutter, "Goodnight."

Leon shrugs and turns back to the television.

CHAPTER FORTY

Tina snuffles in her sleep, tiny little breaths that disturb the strands of hair across her face. I watch her for a moment, then slide out of bed and tiptoe downstairs. Leo is awake, sitting up in the sofa-bed, watching cartoons.

He doesn't see me, leaning on the doorframe, until I say, "Have you been up all night?"

The remote control hits the floor as he whirls round, startled, "Do you have to creep around like that? And, no, I've not been up all night. Just woke half an hour ago."

"OK, just asking. Do you want tea?"

"Yeah, all right." A pause. "Thanks."

I line up three mugs and wait for the kettle to boil. Leon pads past me on his way to the bathroom and there's the faint thud of Tina's feet hitting the floor upstairs. The house feels different – looser somehow, less tense.

Tina walks into the kitchen. "Morning, Jills, why is it so quiet? Ain't you got no music?"

"No, Rob doesn't like noise in the morning –"

Rob's dead. I killed him. I'm never going to see him again.

"Careful!" Tina pushes me to one side and grabs the kettle, turning the plume of steam away from my suddenly nerveless hand. "Let me do this."

Rob has an old-fashioned sound system in the corner of the living room. I've never seen it used in the last three years. I plug it in and fiddle with the controls, while Tina makes the tea. The radio booms into life – somebody's riding through the desert on a horse with no name – and I turn it down, wary of upsetting the neighbours.

Tina comes running when she hears the music. "Oh, I love this old stuff."

Leon is close on her heels and mutters, "It's like a bloody old people's home in here."

"Well, your mum likes it, so you'll just have to put up with it. Sort your bed out so we can sit down, will you? And turn the telly off."

He grumbles under his breath as he bends over to do as he's told, more in a pain-in-the-ass teenager way than the cold, casual cruelty we're accustomed to.

We plan the day, which amounts to making a shopping list. After warning Tina and Leon again to stay away from the windows, I unlock the front door, open it and nearly walk into Nige's raised fist. He jumps back, as surprised as I am.

"God, you frightened me to death," he says. "I didn't know you were back."

My heart hammers in my chest and a sweat breaks out on my face. My armpits are prickling. I pull the door shut behind me and turn the key in the mortice lock.

Loudly, to alert Tina and Leon, I ask, "What do you want, Nige? I haven't got time to talk."

"That's all right. I've just come to pick up a couple of bits I left here."

No condolences: tears for his drinking buddy?

I keep my back to the door. "I can't let you in now. I've got to be somewhere."

He dangles a bunch of keys in front of me. "You don't need to, I'll let myself in. Don't worry. I'll lock up afterwards."

I recognise the heavy gold-coloured keyfob. They're Rob's keys. I fight back the bile that rises in my throat and struggle to make sense of this.

"Where did you get the keys?" I tighten my grip on the door handle, determined not to let him in.

"The police gave them to me. They found Rob's dad in York and he authorised it, so I could keep an eye on the house. He can't get here until August."

"August? His son's dead and he can't be assed to come down for two months?"

Further along the street, I catch sight of Leon, hoodie pulled up over his head, balanced on the back yard wall. He drops down, puts his hands up and mimes a push. What the hell is he doing?

I'm half listening to Nige while trying to work out what Leon wants.

"He's a guest of Her Majesty. A bit of breaking and entering, so I understand." He waves the keys at me. "Now, if you don't mind?"

Leon gestures again, more urgently, and I get it. Nige turns his body slightly away from me to see what I'm looking at. I shove him as hard as I can and he falls back against his car at the kerb. Leon sprints along the pavement and snatches the keys from Nige's hand before careering round the corner.

Nige roars, "You little fucker!"

By the time he struggles upright and gets to the corner, Leon has disappeared. I'm back on the doorstep as Nige rounds on me.

"What did you do that for, you stupid bitch?"

"I thought he was going to mug you so I pushed you out of the way."

"Did you see what he looked like?"

"Uh, no. He had a hoodie."

"Useless, don't know what Rob ever saw in you. Anyway, let me in so I can go and get my stuff."

"Tell me what you want and I'll get it together. You can pick it up later."

He shuffles his feet, looks up and down the street, before saying, "Not much, most of it doesn't matter, anyway. Just –" His eyes shift sideways, then he appears to come to a decision. "Er … I think I left my leather coat here."

I try, and fail, to keep the smile off my face."You mean the leather coat I gave to the charity shop? Didn't Rob tell you? It had a rip on the sleeve, he said you wouldn't want it back."

We both know I'm lying. I savour the moment, as conflicting emotions chase across his face.

"Put it this way, Nige, I don't think you should come round here again, do you?"

He blusters, "I don't know what you mean."

"Yeah, you do," I wait a beat and say, "I know."

"How did you –" He stops, realises what he's just blurted out and fishes his car keys out of his pocket.

"Don't bother with that stuff, it'll keep for another time."

Nige bleeps the remote to open his car and halts with his hand in the door when I call to him.

"Maybe I didn't take the coat to the charity shop. It's such a small thing stuck in the sleeve, isn't it?"

"You bitch." Anger suffuses his face and he spits at me. "All right, maybe I know something, but you had it coming."

And there's the truth, at last. Bile rises in my throat, the bitter taste choking me. I cough until tears stream down my face. All the while, Nige watches me, a sneer on his face. Wiping my mouth, I lean on the door for a moment, buying time to think.

Somehow, I manage to get a smile of sorts on my face.

"Thanks, Nige. I *didn't* know. Very kind of you to tell me. And, by the way, the coat's gone so you didn't need to make your confession."

"You think you're so fucking clever." Fury at being tricked turns his face uglier than usual. A vein throbs in his temple. "I thought it was a bloody stupid idea in the first place, but Rob was like somebody mad when the kid phoned to say you were at the prossy's place and the black bastard was throwing you out."

Now he's started, the words come spewing out of him. "I was in the *Angel* at the time, just round the corner from the Old Mill. Rob called, he wasn't making sense, said to keep you there, whatever it took."

I remember the dark silhouette, backlit by the light of a smart phone.

"Oh my God. You ... it was you ... you punched me in the head ..."

He briefly looks ashamed then belligerence reasserts itself. "I didn't want to hurt you. But I didn't know what to do to keep you there. And then the lights went out – it just got out of hand."

Leon, his childish desire to hurt me, encouraged by Noel, had played right into Nige's hands.

Suddenly, I'm weary of listening to Nige. "Stop. Just shut up."

I can't bear to know if he was still there when Rob attempted to rape me, whether he witnessed Rob's impotent rage when he failed to penetrate me. The impulse to scream into his face that I torched his factory, that Rob has paid the ultimate price for what he did, is almost overwhelming.

I choke out, "Just go. Get away from me."

He slinks to the other side of his car, opens the door and fires a parting shot, cocky again now he thinks the coat with the damning earring is gone.

"You deserved all you got, you tramp. You destroyed his life."

His tyres shriek as he tears off up the street, breaking the speed limit.

CHAPTER FORTY ONE

Minutes pass. My hands are clasped tightly together, the knuckles white, blue veins standing out. I press harder and harder until pain starts to spread up my arms, into my shoulders. More pain blooms in my neck and at the back of my head. Eyes tightly shut. I press harder to increase the agony, but I can't blot out the words repeating over and over in my head.

Rob raped me. I deserved it.

"Jilly!" Leon passes a hand in front of my face.

Leave me alone.

"Shit! What's the matter with you?" Leon shakes me violently. My muscles begin to ease and reluctantly, I let the world back in, staggering against the door as my vision clears.

"Hang on," he mutters, fumbling with Rob's keys to get the door open, calling for Tina. Between them, they manhandle me back into the house and lock up again.

"Fetch her a glass of water, Leon." Tina sits beside me on the sofa and draws me into her arms, soothing me as if I were a child. "There, there, it's OK. I could hear him, the bastard. Let it all out."

But I can't cry. Perhaps I'd always known, in some hidden corner of my mind, that Rob was my attacker. I'd built a case against Noel because I didn't want to face the reality, be forced to look at. the chain of events that led to that terrible moment in the foyer of the Old Mill. The lies I've told, the damage I've done to myself and others, the life I took. Using a thirteen year old boy.

I free myself from Tina's arms. If I stay beside her, I'm afraid of where my thoughts might lead me. It's an effort to stand, my muscles still sore from the panic that engulfed me in the street.

Leon gives me the glass of water and saunters off into the kitchen. Seconds later, he's back.

"I thought you were going to the shop?" he asks. "If we're going to be cooped up, at least get some crisps and chocolate. Oh, and some coke."

I hate to admit it, but he's a clever little sod. His snarky comment penetrates the self-pity that threatens to engulf me. My legs are unsteady, there's an emptiness in my chest with pain nibbling at the edges of it, but I'm on my feet.

Tina shoots a filthy glance at her son. "Don't be so selfish, she ain't in any state to go shopping."

He shrugs, "I'm going to watch telly, nothing else to do." He nudges Tina off the sofa and says over his shoulder, "Cheese and onion."

The sound of their argument rises and falls behind me as I make my way to the bathroom. A few splashes of cold water on my face, followed by a vigorous scrub with the towel, sets my blood zinging again. I run on the spot for a few moments, punching the air, to start adrenaline coursing through my muscles. The pain in my chest subsides. I'm ready to go.

With a quick prayer that there won't be anybody outside the front door, I unlock it and open it cautiously. The street is empty. The pent-up air whooshes out of my lungs.

Tina rushes into the hallway and grabs my arm. "No! What are you thinking?"

I shake her off and nod at Leon, who stands behind her. "He's right. We need crisps. Here –" I hand her Robs's keys – *no, the spare keys* – "Lock the door behind me. I won't be long."

There's a supermarket on the main road that runs across the bottom of the hill. It's almost devoid of customers and I take my time, filling the trolley with bread, butter, eggs, cheese, vegetables and frozen chicken. The silence is broken only by the distant hum of the fridges and the occasional burst of laughter from one of the assistants as she serves a customer. I pause at the gondola stacked with beer and reach for a six pack of the kind that Rob favours, only to draw my hand back as if stung. *No more beer. Ever. Rob's gone and he won't be coming back.*

I wait for the familiar tingling in my arms, for the darkness to threaten my stability, for the pain in my chest. It doesn't happen. For the first time since the night of the fire, I'm able to allow Rob into my mind without some kind of panic attack. I'm free from that particular fear, of dreading what new humiliation will be waiting for me when I get home, of dealing with the aftermath of his final brutality.

I pass a shelf with photograph frames, china ornaments and knick-knacks cluttered together. When did I last take a photograph for the sheer joy of it, for the buzz it gave me when I created an image to be proud of? I don't count the girls and their children. That was for money to pay Noel and required nothing more than repeatedly pushing a button.

If I die today, my last creative picture will be the one that inadvertently led to Rob's death.

"Are you all right, love?"

A shop assistant touches my arm, his eyes anxious. I don't know how long I've been standing here, but dredge up a smile.

"I'm fine, just day-dreaming. Sorry to have worried you."

"No problem." He returns my smile and, as he moves away, I call after him, "Can you tell me where the chocolate and crisps are?"

"Sure, they're on aisle eleven, beside the checkout."

Moving quickly now, as an idea forms in my head, I top up the trolley with several bottles of wine and coke before throwing in a selection of chocolate bars and bags of crisps, not forgetting cheese and onion. I've bought so much that I have to make two trips up the hill to get it all home, running the gauntlet of Tina's fretting and Leon's demands for crisps.

I collapse into a chair in the dining room, panting for breath. "If I've forgotten anything, we'll just have to do without."

Leon's poking in the carrier bags I've dropped at my feet. I give him a nudge, "Pack that lot away, will you? And just one bag of crisps; we have to make it last for a while."

Eager to start work on my idea, I assess the dining room. It's roughly square, with a large window set in the wall that opens on to the street. The wall at a right angle to it has the kitchen door and a tall, narrow window, which opens on to the back yard. I fish out my phone and tap on the compass, pointing it at each window in turn. Brilliant!

"This is going to work," I tell Tina.

She shakes her head and laughs, "I don't know what you're talking about, but yeah, whatever."

"Help me move the table and chairs."

It only takes a minute to drag the furniture across the room. It fits perfectly underneath the window on to the street, leaving a blank wall opposite the narrow window.

I shout through to Leon, "Can you have a look in the kitchen drawers, find me a hammer and some tacks? I think they're in the middle one."

Upstairs, I drag a white, kingsize sheet out of the airing cupboard and shake it out. It's creased but I'm too impatient to iron it and run back down to the dining room. Tina and Leon sit on the table, watching the empty wall as if something was going to happen.

Leon clutches a hammer and a small box of tacks. I say, "Come on, then. Help me."

We work together, under my direction, and tack the sheet across the wall at just above head height. It falls down the wall and spreads across the floor for a couple of feet.

Tina claps her hands. "I've got it it! I know what you're doing."

I can't keep the grin off my face, as I haul my tripod out of the cupboard and set it up. Another minute and I have my camera mounted on it, facing the sheet.

There it is. My makeshift home studio, complete with natural light from the large south-east facing window and a fill light from the north-east facing narrow window.

Leon is suitably unimpressed and sits back down on the table next to his mother. I ignore him and keep my attention focused on Tina.

"That photograph –" I stop for a second to check she knows what I'm talking about and move on swiftly. "It happened because you asked me to take pictures of the 'real' you, family pictures like everyone else has, right?"

She moves restlessly. "Yeah, but –"

"No, wait. I didn't know that wasn't the 'real' you, that Noel was …" I glance at Leon but he's studying his fingernails. I plough on. "And, you've had a few bad experiences with photography with, you know …"

Shit, this is awkward. They both look like they'd rather be anywhere but here.

I forge on. "All I want to do, in the time we're going to be here, is try and wipe out the memory of that photograph and …all the things that followed."

Leon jumps down from the table. "It'll take more than a few shitty pictures to make everything all right." His back rigid, he stalks from the room, slamming the door behind him.

He's right. It's a stupid idea. Nothing can wipe out the past.

"I'm sorry, Teen. I'll take it down."

"Don't you dare!" She shoots about a hand to stop me from dismantling the camera and tripod. "It ain't a stupid idea. Come here." She pats the table and I sit down beside her.

"This ain't easy to say. I'm not clever like you." Tina chews her lip, makes a couple of false starts and says, "These last few days – yeah, I've been terrified for most of the time, for all of us, but – there's another side to it. I feel like a girl again, does that make sense?"

I have no idea what she's on about, so stay silent. She watches my face, waits for an answer that doesn't come.

She sighs.

"What I mean is ... ever since I were fourteen and met Noel, there's always been a man ... I never had a choice, sometimes it were two of them. I did it because Noel loved me, needed the money ... only later, it were all lies, and I wasn't the only one ..."

Mutely, I reach out and gather her into my arms. Her words are muffled against my shoulder, but I hear them.

"It's like ... my body belongs to me again. I can almost imagine my life were ... like I dreamed of when I were a kid. Husband, couple of kids, happy ..."

"No more." I whisper in her ear. She doesn't need to go through this. I can't bear it. I'm afraid it will open floodgates in my mind and I won't be able to close them. So, I whisper, "No more, it's enough. I know."

Soon, she quietens, but the pain of unshed tears in my throat takes much longer to retreat.

CHAPTER FORTY TWO

We all slept late this morning and I hurry us through breakfast, eager to make a start in my little studio. Tina sits in a chair against the white background, now free of some of the creases. She's stiff, self-conscious. I'm not worried. We have a long way to go. After a few frames, where she stares into the lens like a rabbit in headlights, I announce a break and make tea, carrying a mug through to Leon, who's glued to the television and refuses to acknowledge me. We've been here before. I leave him to it.

I sit on the floor and chat to Tina as we drink tea, asking her how I should look after my new hairstyle. She's animated as she describes the process and mimes how to use straighteners. As if I ever would. All the while, I click away with the remote control, capturing her with her hands in the air, her eyes alight as she laughs at my dumb questions, or her own hair flying out as she turns her head to illustrate a vital part of the procedure.

Leon walks through, on his way to the bathroom, and grumbles, "Glad you two are having fun. I'm ready to rip my fingernails out, watching that bloody telly."

Tina immediately says, "Yeah, he must be bored stiff. I'd better go and spend a bit of time with him."

I'm reluctant to stop, but she's got a point.

"Hold on, I think I can fix that." I get to my feet and, when Leo comes back into the room, I say, "Come upstairs and help me for a minute, will you?"

With much eye rolling and sighing, he follows me to the computer room. I set about unplugging the iMac while he leans on the door, sullen and disengaged.

"OK, carry that down and put it on the table."

He obeys, moving as slowly as he can get away with. I follow him down, plug in the computer, check that the Wifi is working and gesture towards it.

"All yours."

He drops the petulant front and a smile lights up his face. "You mean it? I can go on the internet?"

I grin at his evident pleasure. "Yep. Browse a bit, games, the works. Just ..."

"I know, stay off the social media."

I don't need his promise, nor am I ready to trust him. I've angled the computer so he has to sit at one side of the table, ostensibly to keep him out of the light that falls on Tina's face, but actually so that I can see the screen and monitor what he's doing.

Tina mouths, "Thank you" and winks as I resume my seat on the floor. Click.

The morning flies by in the little studio, as the sun moves the shadows round the room. Tina is comfortable as long as I use the remote control so we can maintain eye contact. In the afternoon. I download the morning's work on to the iMac, while Tina sits in the backyard with Leon. Through the open back door, I catch snippets of their conversations. Sometimes their voices are raised and I tiptoe to the back door to warn them to keep it down. Most of the time, though, they seem at peace with one another and I give an inner fist-punch for Tina, as she slowly makes friends with her pain-in-the-ass son.

In the late afternoon, someone taps lightly on the small pane of glass in the front door. I jerk my head towards the kitchen and wait while Tina and Leon make their way through to the bathroom, closing the door behind them.

"Who is it?" I ask the blurred silhouette who stands on the pavement.

A discreet cough. "Good morning. I'm Gerald White-house of Bennett Solicitors. Is Miss Jillian Graham there, please?"

"Who sent you?"

"Sent me? Nobody sent me." He's a little tetchy. "Is Miss Graham there or not? I'm a busy man."

"I'm Miss Graham, but I'm not opening the door. What do you want?"

"Oh, for goodness sake! I haven't got time for this."

A few seconds later, an envelope shoots through the letterbox and lands at my feet.

The voice, now decidedly huffy, says, "I'll bid you good day. Our contact details are in the letter."

The envelope is thick and cream coloured with a fancy crest embossed on the top left corner. I rip it open and take out two sheets of matching notepaper. The top sheet is a covering letter to advise me that I will find at-tached the Last Will and Testament of Robert Knowley. It further informs me that Mr Knowley Snr is a tempor-ary resident of HMP Full Sutton, near York and he has requested that I make the funeral arrangements until such time as he can travel down to Nottingham.

The attached will is short, dated one day after the at-tack at The Old Mill. Rob has left his house and worldly goods to me and asks to be buried at Wilford Hill, beside his mother.

Softly, so softly I can barely hear myself speak, I say, "Oh, you bastard. You rotten fucking bastard."

This is the ultimate 'I'm sorry' present. The only thing missing is the gold coloured bag tied off with a ribbon. How deep his guilt must have been to drive him to this, not even twenty-four hours after he brutalised me.

I take a deep breath and scream it out. "Fuck you, Rob!"

Tina and Leon come charging out of the bathroom and I feel a pang of guilt at the fright on their faces. I push past them, the letter crushed in my hand, and head for the fridge to pour a large glass of wine.

"I give you a toast to Rob. He rapes me one day and makes it all right the next day by giving me his fucking house."

I know my anger is driven by guilt and make an effort to control it. Unsuccessfully, as a second glass of wine follows the first one down my throat.

"Jills, please." Tina reaches out to me. "Getting drunk ain't the answer."

"You don't want me to get drunk? Fine, I won't drink!"

I hurl the glass into the kitchen sink. It shatters on impact, shards flying up into the air, peppering my face with tiny stings. The explosion, shocking in the small kitchen, cuts through my violent outburst and I slump against the worktop.

"You're bleeding." Tina dabs at my face, leading me away from the mayhem I've created in the kitchen. I've still got the letter in my hand, stained with spilt wine and speckled with tiny pinpricks of blood.

"Read it."

She takes the letter from me, her eyes widen. "You own

the house? But, why are you angry?"

I can never make her understand the emotions I felt when I read Rob's will. Hell, I don't even understand it, myself.

Leon's in the kitchen, picking up glass. He mutters, just loud enough to be heard, "It's because she's a fucking nutcase."

"Takes one to know one."

Yeah, but you've had longer to practice."

Tina smiles – a bit uncertain, but it's a smile – as Leon and I get into one of our arguments. "You two. You're like brother and sister when you get started."

"God forbid!" I keep the joke going, in an effort to lift the mood.

Leon stops picking at the glass. "Yeah, but you know, we've a lot in common, don't we?"

Before I can stop myself, I snap back, "What, you think because we both had a prossy for a mother, we're joined at the hip?"

The words hang in air. Tina's eyes are huge with hurt.

"Oh Christ, Tina, I'm sorry. It just came out."

"I thought we'd got over all that, after everything we've been through." She stops, brushes away a tear. "How could you?"

"She didn't mean it, Mum." Leon pushes me towards his mother. "Tell her you didn't mean it."

"Teen …" I falter, lost for words. She walks out of the room, one hand shielding her eyes, and closes the door behind her.

"Best leave her alone for a while." Leon boots up the computer and immerses himself in YouTube. I watch him, to make sure he isn't contacting Noel.

Without looking up, he says, "You don't need to do that

any more, you know."

I believe him, or maybe I'm too shattered to argue. Either way, I leave him and take over cleaning the kitchen. I mop up the last of the wine splashes and wash my hands. My minds is in overdrive, trying to find a way to put things right with Tina, when Leon shrieks from the studio.

"Jilly! Quick! She's gone."

CHAPTER FORTY THREE

Leon is already out on the street by the time I get to the front door. He runs to the corner, turns, pounds to the back gate, peers down the alleyway, his eyes wide with fear.

"Where did she go?"

"For Christ's sake, get back inside!"

"But, my mum … we need to find her."

"I'll find her, I promise, but you've got to get off the street."

He allows me to drag him back into the house.

"Leon, listen to me. You *must* stay indoors. You've been outside twice now, somebody could recognise you and phone the police."

I give him a shake. "Do you understand?"

"Yeah, yeah … I hear you, but find her, Jilly."

"I'm going. Lock the door, don't open it for anybody but me or Tina."

I stand outside the door until I hear the key turn in the lock, then race down the hill towards the main road. Buses pass along here frequently; she could have boarded one to head into the city, assuming she had money. Several people stand at the nearest bus stop, none of them Tina.

Out of breath, I gasp, "Please, have you seen a blonde

woman in the last few minutes? About five foot two, in jeans and a tee shirt."

Most of them shake their heads, a couple don't even look up from their phones and a smartass says, "No, but if you find her, send her my way."

Throwing a 'Fuck off' his way, I dart across the road to the supermarket. A security guy is closing the shutters and answers my frantic question with a shake of the head and a muttered, "Sorry, duck."

It's hopeless. She could have flagged down a taxi, be hiding in one of the alleyways or have run into the rabbit warren of streets behind Rob's ... *my* ... house.

I spend a couple of minutes listening to the recorded message on Tina's phone. Of course she isn't going to answer me, and Leon no longer has a phone.

The March Hare, a small local pub, sits several hundred yards up the road in the opposite direction to the city. It's a long shot, but I sprint along the pavement, through the customer car park and into the bar. Two young men shrug when I show them Tina's picture on my phone, turning back to their game of darts.

A young barmaid, out from behind the bar to wipe a few tables, stops to look at the picture.

"Pretty, ain't she? Have you two had a row, then?"

"No," I lie. "What makes you say that?"

"She's in the beer garden at the back, bawling her eyes out. I gave her a glass of water, not two minutes ago."

I follow the long, dark corridor to the door which opens on to the euphemistically named beer garden. A couple of benches are bolted onto flagstones and multiple ashtrays are dotted round the small enclosure. The only signs of foliage are two hanging baskets with plants already choked by cigarette smoke.

Tina, expressionless, watches me come through the door.

"I hope you ain't come to say you're sorry."

I'm out of breath and can feel cramps tightening the muscles in my legs as I limp over to the other bench. I had intended to apologise but, looking at Tina's stony face, I decide to keep my distance and hold my tongue. While I'm searching for a way to make my peace or at least get her to talk to me, I send a quick email to my iMac, hoping Leon will pick it up.

Found her. Don't worry. Back in a little while.

His reply comes back immediately.

Tell the silly cow to come home.

I reach forward and show the screen to Tina. She glances at it and her face softens for a fraction of a second, only to become impassive again.

"He's come a long way in the last few days, hasn't he?"

She drinks from the water glass, ignores me.

"I mean, he's still a stroppy little bugger, but without Noel's influence ..."

Her body stiffens and she turns slightly away from me. I blunder on, "I – we – were worried in case you'd gone back to the Lace Market."

"Don't be so bloody stupid."

At least, it's a response.

"Don't blame Leon for what I said –"

"I don't."

I want Tina to be angry. I can cope with that. God knows, I've had enough experience of manipulating my way through Rob's rages in order to survive another day. I know what lies to tell, how to dissemble and, if all else fails, how to abase myself until the storm passes.

What I can't handle is this coldness, this distance.

"OK." I stand up. "You don't want to talk to me and I'm not allowed to say I'm sorry. Your choice. I'm going home and you'd better come with me until you make up your mind what you want to do. It's not safe to be out here on your own. Noel might do a drive-by; he's bound to be still looking for you."

As I knew it would, this gets Tina on her feet and she sullenly follows me out of the beer garden and up the hill towards home. In spite of the waves of hostility coming off her, I have to hide a smile at how much she looked like Leon when she glared at me.

Safely indoors, she makes a beeline for Leon and hugs him. "I'm sorry if I frightened you."

He shrugs it off. "That's OK, I wasn't worried."

Over Tina's shoulder, his eyes meet mine and I pantomime his nose growing longer. He gives me an honest-to-God grin and says to his mum, "You guys OK now?"

Tina looks at a point on the wall and says, "Hope nobody minds if I run a bath? Think I'll get an early night."

I'm weary of it all. Every time we achieve some sort of normality, one of us offends one of the others; or the door knocks and we're plunged into another drama; and now this chase round the streets, putting us all in danger of discovery.

"You're being childish." I put one hand on Tina's arm and try to turn her to face me. She's stiff and unyielding. "Go and have a bath if you want one and stop talking to the bloody wall."

She stalks off to the bathroom and Leon shuffles his feet. "I guess I'll go and open up my bed, watch telly for a bit." Two seconds after he leaves the room, he shouts through to me, "Thanks for bringing her back."

I'd like to say, No problem, but everything's a fucking

problem at the moment. Instead, I boot up the iMac, open a new folder and label it *London Portfolio*, and buckle down to choose some photographs to accompany my CV. Time to look ahead.

CHAPTER FORTY FOUR

"Jilly, wake up. Have you been down here all night?"

I lift my head. God, that hurts.

Leon hunkers down to peer into my face. "What are you doing on the floor?"

"Uh, I was working til late. Didn't want to disturb your mum."

I have a vague recollection of Tina standing beside me, as I worked on the computer. Maybe she was waiting for me to speak. After she disappeared upstairs, I believe that's when I opened the wine.

"Help me up." Leon hoists me on to my feet. Every bone in my body complains.

I hobble through the kitchen and the back passageway to the bathroom and stand under the shower, dialling the water down to the lowest temperature I can stand. I towel myself dry and get dressed in yesterday's clothes. My hair is a tangled mess. I have no idea how to fix my new hairstyle, in spite of Tina's instructions from yesterday, and finger comb it until it lies flat.

Tea waits for me on the worktop in the kitchen. I nod a grateful thanks to Leon and ask, "Is your mum up yet?"

"She's watching nature stuff on the telly."

I want to go into the living room to talk to Tina, but my pride and my annoyance at her standoffishness won't let me. And, yes, resentment because she's still sulking over a throwaway remark. I didn't really mean it. Why can't she see that?

As if he can read my mind, Leon says, "Stop worrying. She'll come round in the end."

"Yeah, whatever."

Leon's idly playing a card game on the computer and, over his shoulder, I catch sight of my *London Portfolio* folder on the desktop. Underneath the icon, it says 40 images. I'm impressed with how much work I managed to do before succumbing to wine and sleep.

"Move over." I nudge Leon off the chair, ignoring his grumbles, and click the folder open. Eight rows of five thumbnails spring into focus. Unlike the monochromatic pictures I used for my Degree Show, they're all in colour and each one features a laughing family group.

"I don't get it," Leon says. "They're OK pictures, but they're just ordinary. Why would you take them to London?"

"They're not finished. I was sorting out the ones that would lend themselves to diptychs."

"Dip-whats?"

"I'll show you – look."

I open up a picture of Candace on a sunlit street, laughing with her little girls. The children have minirucksacks with fairy tale princesses on them. Beside it, I position a monochrome photograph of Candace, standing underneath an oak tree on Forest Road. It's dark, fog creeps in round the heavy branches and rain drips off the leaves on to her umbrella. She looks weary and dispirited.

"Oh, I see. You're showing real life beside ..." Leon stops, starts again. "So, which one is real life?"

"You tell me. Is she a mother who turns tricks to support her children?" I don't mention the pimp who takes most of the money. "Or is she –"

"Just a prossy who's got kids?"

"Let's not use that word anymore, eh?"

He hoists himself up on to table, sits looking down at me.

"So, why didn't you do nice pictures with my mum? Why make fun of her?"

Oh, shit.

"A couple of things. I'd already finished this project. It was signed off, ready for mounting in the exhibition. And, the picture on the catalogue cover, well … it was an accident that she was flashing, you know …"

I wish he would say something, stop staring at me. He sits there, waiting, expressionless.

So like his mother.

"I should have deleted it as soon as I saw it. Your mum didn't give me permission to use any of the pictures. It was wrong, and I told so many lies to justify using it. I didn't even think about what effect it might have on Tina, on you …"

I swallow and whisper, "I'm sorry."

He ignores my apology and goes off on another tack. "Hmmm, so if you were still doing the project, would you have done one these dip-things with me and my mum?"

An image flashes across my mind of Leon's face, suffused with hatred as he screamed at his mum and dad. When I first knew him, he couldn't bear to be in the same room as his parents.

"Um, probably not." I leave it at that and get up from the chair. "I need a drink. Want one?"

"Sure, a coke'll be OK, thanks."

I pop a couple of cans and return to the studio to find him sat on the floor opposite the camera. He grins, looks nervous, says, "Do some of me, then."

"What, you want me to shoot your ugly mug?"

The insult relaxes him a bit. "Yeah, it'll be cool."

It takes a few minutes to shorten the tripod legs so the camera is level with his face, check the battery and memory card and drop down to floor level, remote control in hand.

"How does work, then? Do you give me instructions, like?"

"No, just relax and be yourself. There's no rush. Tell me something about yourself, anything … music, games, books, school …"

Leon's face shuts down immediately. "Nah, I don't like talking about myself. It's boring. How about I do some stuff?"

He falls into a series of poses, does jazz hands, pulls silly faces, hands clasped over his mouth, his eyes wide in pretend horror. I humour him, clicking every time he changes position, knowing there's nothing here I will keep. He'll have some funny shots for his FaceBook timeline, maybe encourage him to make friends with kids his own age.When this is all over. Wherever we are. When we both stop pretending it's cool, he slumps against the wall. I do the same and, for a little while, we don't talk.

He breaks the silence first.

"Jilly?"

"What?"

"You know that thing you said … that we both had a – uh, a sex worker – for a mother?"

"Yeah." So now we're sex workers. How terribly PC. I almost prefer prossy.

"How … how did you handle it? You know, day to day. School and stuff."

He doesn't like talking about himself? It's OK, though, to ask *me* questions about a past I keep hidden, even from myself.

"I don't think I want to go there, Leon."

He starts to scramble to this feet. "I'm sorry, I shouldn't have asked …"

"Wait." I hold up a hand and he slides back down the wall, his face a mask of confusion.

I'm sure my face mirrors his. I've begun to like this strange, prickly boy. On the other hand, I allowed myself to like, maybe love, his mother and look how that's ended up. The good moments were so intense, giving rise to emotions I'd never felt before, but when things went wrong, it was so fucking painful. Maybe it's better to keep a cap on feelings, keep others at a distance.

I don't know, but something unlocks inside me and I answer him.

"It wasn't a case of dealing with it. I can't remember a time when things weren't … not quite right. I had a friend once, but my mother … you've seen her, she isn't anything like yours … allowed one of her customers to …" My throat is full, perhaps I won't be able to carry on. But, somehow, I do. "She allowed him … access to me."

Such a stupid, stilted phrase for the moment that defined my whole future.

"Fuck, man. That's .." Leon searches for words.

"After that, I can't remember why, but I no longer had any friends. "

"How old …?"

"Maybe seven."

"Shiiiit."

"Yeah."

"What about your dad?"

"Never had one."

Leon launches into the longest speech I've ever heard him make. "Sometimes I wish I'd never had one. In some weird way, I guess he thought it was like I was going to take over the family business."

"You didn't know your mum was …?"

"Nah, I just thought she had a lot of friends, you know?"

I nod. "Yeah, I know."

It seems like neither of us wants to continue picking at the scabs, so I say, "You can come in now, Tina." I know she's been standing by the half-open door for quite a while. The sound of the television has stopped and a faint shadow falls across the carpet, picked out by the pane of glass in the front door.

She slips into the room and sits down beside Leon. In a white, oversized tee-shirt which once belonged to Rob, bare-legged and make-up free, she looks beautiful. The compliment trembles on my tongue, but remains un-said.

Leon reaches out and takes his mum's hand, their fingers intertwine, and she rests her head on his shoulder. Instinctively, I pick up the remote control and make a small gesture in Tina's direction. She nods, a small smile lights up her face, and I click.

Leon grins. "You guys OK now?"

Tina and I exchange glances and nod. We will be OK. It'll take time, but we'll get there.

For the rest of the morning, the three of us sit on the floor, getting up only to fetch crisps, chocolate or drinks. Leon tells his mum about the dip-things I'm doing for my London job and we make tentative plans for the future. Tina wants a job in a clothes shop or selling make-up. She doesn't want an education, that's for Leon. He fancies being something in IT. We're all buoyed up, fantasising about the new start, and all the while I keep clicking.

The sunlight moves round the room until, just after noon, soft shadows creep across the floor and we reluctantly call a halt to the photoshoot. Leon begs Tina to go out into the backyard with him as he works off the cramps in his legs. I listen to their chatter as they walk through the kitchen, knowing that, when they come back inside, I'm going to kill the good mood of the morning.

I wait in the living room until they come to find me. They're still talking about London, but fall silent when they see my serious face.

"What's up, Jills?" asks Tina. I smile at the affectionate nickname and motion for them to sit down.

"Tomorrow, we're going to start putting things in place for when we leave. It's not going to happen unless we work at it."

"I know we ain't got much money left. Maybe enough for tickets, but after that ..."

"It's OK, Teen. Money's the least of our worries. I'm going to sell the house; in the meantime, I'll let it out to get some cash. That's something you can do, Leon. Browse the local estate agents, see which ones deal in property like this."

"On it, boss." Leon's excited, pleased to be included in the plans.

"While you're doing that, I'll email Tom Buckley, to

finalise my starting date. I'd like to see Christie before we go, as well."

Tina asks, "So why the long face? It all sounds good to me."

"I'm going to phone the police tomorrow, to find out when they're releasing Rob's body. I've decided to do as his father asked and organise the funeral. Somewhere in the next couple of days, I'll have to fit in a visit to the solicitor's to sort out the legalities."

"If there's owt I can do to help you with any of it, just ask."

"Thanks." I hesitate, unsure how to proceed. "There's one more thing. Leon, what did you do with the petrol can?"

"Why do you need to know?" The brightness has fled from his face.

"Because it's a loose end. We can't leave it out there. I'm sorry."

"It's OK. I get it. It's just ... I try not to think about the fire, try to tell myself it never happened."

He looks at his mum, "I'm so sorry, I wish I'd never done it."

"I think we'd all like to go back and –"

Tina speaks at the same time as me. "It's like we was crazy – but it's over, ain't it?"

It'll never be over, not as long as we carry the guilt of what we did, but I don't say that.

"Leon?" I wait.

"Across the road from the pub, there's a derelict site with a wire fence. I peeled up the corner and shoved everything into the scrub. It's all right, nobody's going to find it. I can't even remember exactly where I put it."

"No, it's not all right. When they start work there,

they'll find it. There'll be fingerprints on it, You have to go and get it. I'll come with you, help look for it."

"Jills, no! He can't go back there, we can just leave it."

I can't bear to look at her agonised face. "I'm sorry, but we've got to do it. Leon?"

"I don't want to." He buries his head in his hands. "But, if it was found ..."

I reach out a hand to him and, in a gesture that touches me, he squeezes my fingers briefly and lets go before saying, "I'll do it."

CHAPTER
FORTY FIVE

Dusk falls just before nine o'clock. Leon and I are ready to go, dressed in black, worried because there's a bright moon in a clear sky. Tina's face is ashen. We've stopped trying to reassure her. There's no point. We're more frightened than she is.

One last check that she's got the spare keys, one last reminder not to open the door to anybody and we slip out of the front door. Leon won't leave until he hears the key turn in the lock.

"OK, lets go." I'm jittery, anxious to get this over with.

The streets are nearly deserted and we set a brisk pace, driven by urgency and fear, hugging first hedges and then buildings as we near the city centre.

Leon speaks only once. "What if ..."

"I don't know."

In the cool of the evening, there are no revellers on the pavement tonight and a light cloud drifts over the moon, throwing shadows and darkening the street. I drift over to stand on the corner outside the pub, suppressing a shudder at the memory of the last time we stood there. Leon waits for my nod that the coast is clear, and prowls the perimeter of the disused site, peering through the wire fence. He reaches the end, looks across at me and spreads his hands.

"Keep looking," I hiss.

Halfway back along the fence, Leon stops and tugs at his leg. His jeans are caught on a piece of wire. He bends down to free himself and his body stiffens. I catch my breath.

Please, God, let him find it.

Nearly a minute ticks away until he straightens, now holding something bulky. He jerks his head in the direction of the city and hurries off. I have to run to catch up with him and pull on his sleeve.

"Slow down. You'll get stopped if the police see you."

"I've only got the can and the blanket. The cricket bat's gone."

"Can't be helped. Some little toe rag probably stole it, it'll have his fingerprints all over it now." I fish a carrier bag out of my pocket and we slide the can and the blanket into it. "We'd better not walk beside each other now and I'll carry the bag. We can't risk a stop and search."

"Yeah." Leon starts to walk ahead of me.

I call him back. "Wait."

"What's wrong? Come on! We've done it."

"Not yet." I turn right, in the direction of the Lace Market, beckoning him to follow. "We're going to Noel's garage, to put the can back where we found it."

He digs his heels in, stock still on the pavement. "No way! I'm not going back there."

I draw him into the shadow of a nearby building. "Listen, Leon. That petrol can is the only thing that can link us – you – to the fire. It's got your fingerprints on it, but it's got Noel's, as well."

"What are you getting at."

"Don't you see? If the police were to find that can, it puts suspicion on Noel. Your fingerprints can be explained away, because you used to fetch petrol from the garage for your dad."

He's thinking it through. "Yeah, but why would they go to the garage in the first place?"

"Nige and Rob always blamed Noel for the attack on me to cover their own backs. He's made a statement to the police and he'll have spun the same story."

Is he wavering?

"I'm doing this to protect you, Leon. Your mum need never know, she'd worry. And then we can have our new start."

He still looks dubious, but follows me as we emerge from the shadows.

"Are you sure …"

"Yes, it's the logical place for the can to be; it may never be found, anyway."

"Right."

He strides off in the direction of his old home. I breathe a sigh relief, give him a couple of hundred yards start and follow him, carrying the can and blanket.

You know you wouldn't have got away with that if Tina'd been here.

I push the thought out of my mind. It's a bit late to grow a conscience. It's true, though. Tina would never have let her son walk into danger if I had told her what my intentions were.

But we're not in any danger. And it's insurance for the future. For all of us.

I'm out of breath, falling further behind Leon. Looking back, he sees this and sits down on a bench as I struggle up an incline.

"Jilly?" he says, as I collapse beside him.

"What?"

"I'm scared."

He's a child, no matter how tall he's grown or how tough he talks. I'm scared, too, but I can't let him do this. "Change of plan." I stand, one hand on his shoulder to keep him seated. "I'll do it. Even if someone did see me, I'm not as recognisable as you. It's no problem, I'll be back in two ticks."

I can see the relief on his face.

"Are you sure?"

As I walk away, a small plague on the back of the bench catches my eye. *Maisie's Bench* and a small, etched daisy. *Look after him for me, Maisie.*

The Old Mill stands silent and dark. The one remaining streetlight has expired and I stumble though the streets to the garage in near total darkness. The large front doors of the block where Tina lived are shut and there's a notice pinned to them. I can't read it and daren't turn on the torch on my phone.

The garage door is ajar. I stand watching it for several minutes, convinced that Noel lurks inside, ready to attack me. Aware that Leon waits, exposed to passers-by, on Maisie's bench, I creep forward. Panic chips at the edges of my mind; I throw the petrol can into the entrance. The hollow sound of it bouncing off the floor echoes through the silent street. I take to my heels, as if the devil were after me.

In sight of Leon, I slow down and stuff the carrier bag into a waste bin. Before we walk away, back towards home, I throw the tartan blanket over the bench.

"Is that wise?" asks Leon. I don't answer, but smile inwardly. I know a lady who will be delighted to find it.

We cut through Slab Square, past the silent stone lions, up Queen Street and start the walk home along Parliament Street.

"Do you think we're going to be able to move on, now?" asks Leon.

"Yep, the worst's behind us."

He gives a whoop and leap-frogs over a bollard. I grin as he follows up with a cartwheel and think of Tina, waiting at home for us. My head is bent over my phone to contact her, to tell her we won't be long, and Leon is still capering about, releasing tension. Neither of us sees the long cigar-shaped Jaguar slow up at the other side of the wide street, only becoming aware of it as Noel screeches to a halt.

"Leon!" I scream. "Run!"

We join hands and fly into a nearby alleyway.

"Shit, we're trapped." I moan. It's a dead end, with large cartons of rubbish and waste bins piled up against the wall that barricades us in. I turn back towards the street, push Leon behind me, and scream for help. There's no one to hear, but it doesn't matter. Noel isn't there.

"Maybe he didn't see us," Leon whispers.

He did, though. We reach the entrance to the alley in time to see the Jaguar do a U-turn and pick up speed towards Sneinton. Towards Tina.

Leon takes off running. I shout after him, "Take Bath Street. It's quicker." I can't keep up with him, but follow as fast as I can, thumbing my phone frantically.

"Pick up, Teen, please, pick up." Why doesn't she answer? I push the redial button, my breath coming in gasps, pain in my side as I stagger on. The number's engaged. Shit, she's trying to phone me back.

"No, Teen, no. Hang up, we're coming."

The stitch in my side lances pain through my body. Noel

will have reached the house by now. I keep running, keep thumbing the phone.

Tina answers, "Hi, Jills. I were in the bathroom. Are you –"

"Get out of the house!" I can barely speak, my breath ragged. "Get out, Teen, he's –"

I hear a solid thump-thump-thump at the other end of the phone.

"Teen, run –"

Noel says, "Sorry, wrong number."

And the line goes dead.

CHAPTER FORTY SIX

I run, every breath painful, my chest raw, my lungs protesting with every step. But I run. My legs turn to jelly and threaten to buckle underneath me. And I run. Along a narrow street, across a wider road, every step nearer to Tina. Until I can't. My legs give out. I sink to the ground at the bus stop, opposite the supermarket, now wreathed in darkness.

Come on, you're nearly there. Get up.

A tiny red light glows in the darkness. A man in black clothes, smoking a cigarette, comes towards me.

"Help! Please help me!" I gasp in an agonised wheeze and grab the side of the bus shelter in an effort to get back on my feet.

"What's up, duck? Had one too many?" He puts his hands underneath my armpits and hoists me up on to the seat. "There you go, not going to be sick, are you?"

"Not drunk." I fight to get my breath steady again, to make him understand I need help.

His phone rings. He straightens to answer it and, as he walks away, I hear him say, "No, it's all right. I'll be there in a minute. Just helping some lass, she's right bladdered."

"No, please, come back ..."

My legs prickle with pins and needles and I attempt to

stand.

A car halts at the bottom of the hill that leads up to my house. Its indicator blinks in the direction of town and the driver navigates out on to the main road.

A Jaguar with the interior light on.

Noel slows as he reaches the bus shelter and winds the window down. "Thanks for looking after her for me."

Tina sits beside him, staring straight ahead, her hair matted with blood.

"No!" My throat constricts and my scream comes out as a hoarse whisper. I lurch forward, not daring to let go of the bus shelter. "Don't do this, please. You don't need her, let her go, I'm begging you."

He bares his teeth in a horrible parody of a smile as the car accelerates away. I throw myself forward in the crazy hope of stopping him, my treacherous legs refuse to hold me up, and I collapse on the ground.

She's gone. My beautiful Tina's gone. Tears engulf me, my sobs echoing through the night air. Footsteps approach, hesitate and walk away.

Yeah, walk on, you bastard. Don't make yourself late for the pub.

The unseen person's callousness and my bitter thoughts prod me into choking back the tears. Again, I pull myself up on the bus shelter and hang there for a few minutes, while feeling returns to my legs, before setting off up the hill.

The front door hangs off its hinges and light pours out into the street. Leon sits on the doorstep, leaning against the shattered frame, ignoring the few neighbours who stand about, gossiping.

"Come on, Leon, let's get you inside." I'm grateful when he acquiesces and disappears into the house, because I haven't got the strength to get him to his feet.

A small woman, in her dressing gown, says, "It were a big black guy. He broke the door down like it were plywood." She pushes forward, trying to see into the house, and I block her view. "He dragged the woman out, she could hardly walk." Her eyes widen, feeding off the drama. "I've phoned the police, don't you worry, they'll get him."

"OK, thanks," I mutter. "I'll take it from here."

The door's heavy but I get it propped up against the ruined frame to give us some privacy from the gawking neighbours.

"Fucking ghouls," says Leon, when I find him in the studio. "What happened to the door?"

"What happened to the …? Leon, what's the matter with you? Noel did it! He took your mum!"

I'm frantic, exhausted mentally and physically, and can't make sense of his attitude.

"Right." He sits down at the computer. "How do you turn this thing on?"

"Leon!"

He flinches. "Oh, hi, Jilly. What happened to the door?"

"What the fuck is wrong with you?"

"Can you turn this on for me?"

Gently, fearful of startling him, I turn him away from the computer.

"Leon, has something happened to you?"

Before he can answer, there's a knock on the door and a voice calls, "Police, can we come in?"

"Yeah, come in."

Two male officers edge their way round the door.

"What's happened here, then?"

Their curious eyes take in the makeshift studio. With

one hand on Leon's shoulder, I follow their gaze. Everything's in place, no sign of any disturbance. I bend to Leon and tip his chin up to see his eyes. He blinks a couple of times, but I'm not sure that he's focusing on me.

"Listen, mate, I have to go in the other room for a minute with these guys. Can you promise me to stay in the chair until I come back?"

He smiles but doesn't answer. I turn the computer on for him, hoping it will keep him quiet for a few minutes.

"Can you come through here?" I say curtly to the officers and lead them though to the living room. I'm not prepared for the sight that greets us and give an involuntary moan, quickly stifled. The television screen is shattered, one of the chairs lies up-ended and, worst of all, there's a smear of blood on the corner of the marble fireplace.

"For the second time, what's happened here, Miss ...?"

"Don't you have to show me some identification?"

With exaggerated patience, they produce warrant cards and hold them out for my scrutiny. Sergeant Wilkins and Constable Taylor.

"Graham, Jillian Graham. My friend's been assaulted and taken away against her will."

Wilkins does all the talking. "What's your friend's name?"

"Tina Lloyd."

They exchange glances before Wilkins asks, "What do you think has happened to her."

"I know what happened. Her husband broke the door down and dragged her to his car. I saw them drive off towards the city."

"Were you here when the incident occurred?"

"No. Leon and I were out."

"So, Ms Lloyd was here alone. Does she live here?"

Taylor hunkers down to look at the bloodstain.

Frustrated at their lack of urgency, my voice rises. "Look, this is just wasting time. I can tell you where Noel, her husband. lives. You need to go and get her back. He's dangerous."

"Were Ms Lloyd and her husband separated?"

"Yes, she's staying here for a while. She's afraid of him. You don't know what he's like."

Taylor straightens up and says, "Oh, we know Noel and Tina very well, don't we, Sarge."

Wilkins glares at his subordinate, turns back to me and says, "What we have here, then, is a domestic dispute that got a bit out of hand."

"Domestic dispute? Are you crazy? He'll kill her!"

He sighs. "When you saw them in the car, was Ms Lloyd struggling? Did she call to you for help?"

"Well, no …"

"Exactly. You don't want to get mixed up in other people's troubles, Ms Graham. You've got enough of your own, haven't you?"

I let that slide. "What are you going to do? You can't just ignore it."

Wilkins takes a last look round the room. "No, we'll pop over to the Old Mill and pull Noel in. He'll only get a rap on the knuckles, a waste of our time."

"But he's not at the Old Mill." I burst out. "It's closed up."

"Oh yeah? And how do you know that? It was open yesterday."

"Um … I think somebody told Tina."

He considers me for a moment but doesn't pursue it.

"That's it, then. We'll find him. Taylor, get that door,

will you?"

In the hallway, waiting for the door to be manhandled to one side. Wilkins looks through to Leon, who sits unmoving in front of the computer, his hands in his lap.

"There's something wrong with that lad."

"I know. I'm going to get help for him."

I'd've done it by now if I hadn't wasted time with you two wankers.

"Bad things seem to happen to people round you, don't they, Jilly?"

Jilly?

Taylor props the front door open and unlocks the police car. Wilkins follows him, leaving the door open for me to wrestle with. He pauses on the pavement, one finger on his lips.

"There was something else. What was it, now? Oh, yes. Stevie says hello."

For a long moment, I think Stevie's in the car, then fear gives me strength to heave the door closed, Wilkins laughter ringing in my ears.

They're not going to do anything.

Close to despair, I kneel in front of Leon. "What happened to you? Can you tell me?"

He frowns, "What's wrong with the door>"

Through my tears, I whisper, "It's all right. You're going to be all right," and punch 999 into my phone.

"Ambulance, please." I give the operator the information she asks for and she tells me to stay on the line until the paramedics arrive.

Just before I disconnect, I say, "Please, ask them to hurry, he's acting strangely."

I'm consumed with guilt. What if something happens and they can't find us? I repeat my mantra to Leon, "It'll be all right," and dial Christie's number.

Thank God, he answers after the first ring.

"Jilly, great to hear from you. Are you all ready for London?"

"Christie, I need help." No time for niceties. "Is Oliver with you?"

"Yes, he is. What's wrong?"

"Leon, Tina's son, is here. Something's wrong. I've called an ambulance."

"Slow down. You're not making sense." He sounds alarmed. "What's Leon doing there? Is Tina with you?"

"Somebody has to go to the hospital. I thought … Oliver knows Tina, he's a social worker. Please, just come."

"Yeah, OK. We're at the uni, just let me lock up and we'll be there. What's wrong with Leon? Can't you go with him?"

His questions chip away at the last few shreds of my endurance. Hardly aware of what I'm saying, I sob down the phone, "There's no door. He broke the door …"

I drop down on the floor at Leon's feet, the phone slipping from my nerveless fingers.

Twenty minutes later, the room is bathed in a pulsing blue light. The ambulance is here. A fist hammers on the door and a voice calls, "Are you in there, love?"

Pain shoots through my legs, cramped from sitting on the floor in one position and the frenzied run home. It takes me nearly a minute to hobble to the door and heave it open for the medics.

A young woman, slim and with blonde hair in a topknot, breezes in and takes up my position, kneeling in front of Leon. I listen, as she goes through the 'Can you hear me, can you tell me your name?' routine, without getting a response.

"Leon, his name's Leon."

A voice outside says, "Shit, look at that door!" Christie rushes into the room, followed by a short, balding man, whose stomach strains against his shirt buttons. He holds out a hand to me. "I'm Oliver."

I shake the proffered hand and say, "Thanks for coming."

A second medic is in the room with a collapsible stretcher. Christie confers with them in a low voice then joins us.

"It looks like he's concussed. They're going to take him in. Are you OK to go with him, Ollie?"

"Sure." He turns to me. "Where are Leon's parents?"

His kindly tone starts my tears flowing again. The only thing I can think of in answer is, "Not in the picture."

"All right. We can talk more about that in the future. You realise that Social Services will have to be involved?"

"No, I ..." Of course I don't. I can't cope with this any more. All my life, with good reason, I've avoided contact with figures of authority. In the last few days, I've had to cope with police, a solicitor, paramedics and now the threat of Social Services.

Six people in this small room, all taking at once. What are they all doing here?

I whisper, "Get out, all of you. Get out." It feels good, so I say it louder, building for a scream.

"It's OK. I've got you." Christie's arms are round me and we're in the kitchen, I'm drinking water and my world has gone quiet again. He opens the kitchen door to show me the studio, silent and empty.

"Look, they've gone."

"I'm sorry, Christie. I don't know what came over me.

They were all trying to help."

"Jilly, tell me to mind my own business, if you like, but what the hell's been going on to put you in this state? Who did that to the door?"

My head aches, I'm having trouble forming coherent thoughts and I need to get some of the pain and anger out of my system. So I tell him the truth. Some of it.

I cover the day Tina, Leon and I fled from the Old Mill because of Noel's violence; how we went to my mother's, where we heard the dreadful news about Rob.

This prompts Christie to say, "I'm really sorry about Rob. I know you two had your problems, but you'd been together a long time. It must have been a terrible shock."

"We'd agreed to split up and remain friends, but the way he died …"

I paint a picture of the few days we'd been holed up here, taking photographs and chilling, keeping our heads down, avoiding any chance of coming across Noel. And then, the terrible events of tonight, how Noel saw Leon and I in the street, drove here and took Tina away.

"There's blood, in the other room. He must've hit her or she fell, I don't know."

Christie's eyes are wide with shock. "Did you call the police?"

"They're not really interested, said it was a domestic dispute, but they'll try to find Noel."

"That's disgusting. Did they at least call out the emergency carpenter to board up the front door?"

"No, they were quite … hostile. They already knew Noel and Tina."

"Right. I'll get on to that. You make us some tea and sit

down."

"Actually, there's something I need to do first."

While Christie's on the phone, I half-fill a bucket with warm, soapy water, find some cleaning cloths and carry them through to the living room. On my hands and knees, I scrub at the blood smear. The water turns an ever deeper pink but, in spite of my best efforts, the marble won't let go of the memory of Tina's blood. I admit defeat, sit back on my heels and let the tears flow.

"Jilly?"

Christie pops his head round the door and says, "The carpenters are on their way. They'll make the door secure until you can get it replaced."

"Thanks, Christie, you and Oliver have been brilliant."

"I'm glad we could help. Don't worry about Leon, I'm sure Ollie will sort something out for him until Tina turns up." He touches my arm. "You look wiped out. I wish I could stay, but I need to pick him up from the hospital."

"What about Leon?"

"They're keeping him in for a few days. You can go to see him tomorrow."

Another hug, more reassurances from me that I'm OK, and he's gone.

The night has cooled. The house is silent. I wander through to the studio and sit on the floor, facing the sheet, still pinned to the wall.

I project two mental images onto the backdrop, as sharp and clear as if I had shot them on my camera. One of Tina, bloodied, battered and devoid of hope, in Noel's car, as he drove her away. Leon, confused and lost, his eyes unfocused, all the teenage snark stolen from him. I view them side by side until they're burned into my brain, then close my eyes and let them go.

The police aren't going to do anything.

But I will.

CHAPTER FORTY SEVEN

I block out the world for half a morning.

The radio in the living room is still tuned to the 'golden oldies' that Tina loved – loves – so much. I dial up the volume to fill the empty house and make a start on restoring order. The Eagles urge me to take it to the limit while I drag the heavy television out to the back yard and straighten up the living room, resisting the urge to look at the pink stain on the fireplace. Dismantling the studio and restoring the dining table to its original spot takes very little time, as Meatloaf roars in my ear about being a bat out of hell. The neighbours keep time, banging on the communal wall, shouting at me to 'turn down that fucking racket'.

The fridge is bare except for milk, a few vegetables and half a sliced loaf in the small freezer compartment. Tea and toast it is, then. I carry my makeshift breakfast through to the living room, turn off the radio, and sit down to eat. Alone. In silence.

A text pings from Christie.

Leon at the QMC. East Block. Go at any time.

The Queen's Medical Centre is enormous and nearly impenetrable. The paper map is useless and I circle the corridors twice before I find Leon's ward. He's sitting in an armchair beside his bed and jumps up when he sees me.

"Hey, Jilly! Am I glad to see you. Can you get me out of here?"

We half-hug and dance awkwardly round each other until we settle down, Leon sitting on the bed, me on the chair.

He's insistent. "I mean it. I want to come home with you. Have you seen this place?"

"What's wrong with it?" I look round the ward and, for the first time, notice the decals of hedgehogs and bunny rabbits. There's a big rainbow painted across the ceiling. "It's the fucking *children's* ward."

"Well, you're a child, where else would you be?"

It's hard not to laugh, seeing Leon surrounded by pictures of cartoon characters, but one look at his agonised face sobers me.

"I'm not a child, I'm fourteen next week."

"OK, hang on. I'll see if I can find someone to talk to."

The nurses' station is deserted. I track the sound of voices to a waiting area and discover two women in uniform drinking out of plastic cups. On hearing my request, one of them accompanies me back to the nurses' station and makes a phone call. After a few minutes, she replaces the receiver.

"I'm sorry, love, Leon's been admitted into the care of the Social Services. Apparently, there's a meeting this afternoon to see where he's going to be placed. I'm afraid he can't leave, anyway, he's under observation until at least tomorrow."

The news doesn't go down well, when I relay it to Leon. His face turns sullen and he shouts towards the nurse, "You can't keep me here."

"Yeah, they probably can," I tell him. "It's for the best, after what happened to you. Can you remember what happened, yet?"

"Some of it." He sits back down on the bed and I take the chair, hitching it closer to him, so we won't be overheard.

"He was already in the house by the time I got there. The door was smashed in. I could hear him shouting at Mum. She was ..." He bites at a fingernail, his eyes focused inwards, reliving the moment. "... sort of, whimpering, making these ... sounds."

I get off the chair to sit beside him, one arm round his shoulders; after a few seconds, he starts again.

"They were in the living room. I tried to get to her, I really did, but he had his back to the door. And she kept making these noises ..."

"It's all right, take your time."

"I banged on the door, said I'd call the police. And ... all of a sudden, he pulled the door open and pushed me back. He had hold of her with his other hand. I saw her, Jilly ..." Tears clog his nose and throat; his voice is thick. "She had blood all down her face and on her top. He was pulling her out to the car. I tried to stop him ... honestly, Jilly, I tried."

Leon falls silent. I give him a handful of tissues from a box on his locker. He's a little calmer when he carries on.

"I can't remember how she got in the car, but, somehow, she did. She was screaming, but I couldn't hear her. And – the neighbours were just standing there. I shouted for them to help her, they just stood gawking – how could they do that?"

"I was hanging on to his arm, I wanted him to take me, as well, so I could look after her..."

My heart breaks for Leon; I burn with fury and hatred for Noel.

"He didn't even speak to me. I think he shook me off, or something. The next thing I remember is seeing those fucking hedgehogs." His small attempt at bravado starts him crying again.

"Find my mum, Jilly."

My throat constricts. The last time Leon said that to me, I answered, "I promise."

This time, I tighten my grip and hold him until he exhausts himself and the sobs stop.

I stay for another thirty minutes, unpacking the crisps, chocolate and coke I brought for him, until a nurse indicates that I need to leave.

Leon walks to the ward door with me. "I'm frightened. Mum's gone and I don't know where they'll send me." He holds my sleeve to stop me leaving. "You're not going to leave, as well?"

"Don't worry. Wherever they put you, I'll find you."

This time, I add, "I promise."

CHAPTER FORTY EIGHT

It's nearly noon by the time I enter the Central Police Station.

"I've come to report a missing person … uh, a kidnapping." I tell the duty sergeant, a grey-haired woman who reeks of cigarette smoke.

She pulls a form towards her with yellowed fingers.

"Which is it, then? Missing or kidnapped?"

I go though my story again. When I get to Tina's name, she hesitates and glances at me from under lowered brows.

"What? Why are you looking at me like that?"

"Just trying to help you, madam. How long is it since you saw Ms Lloyd?"

"Maybe eleven-thirty last night. I'm not sure."

"Barely twelve hours. Are you sure she's not at home, making it up with her husband?"

"I'm sure. I've just left her son; he witnessed his father beating his mother. Please."

I'll beg the snotty cow if I have to.

She softens slightly. "I'll pass this through to one of our patrol cars, ask them to go round there and check. Although, if the building is closed up …"

"What about Sergeant Wilkins? Didn't he go round there last night?"

She consults her computer. "Last night? There's no record of Sergeant Wilkins visiting you last night. I can see a call-out just before midnight but it was a prank call. No action taken."

Why am I not surprised?

"But you'll take action, now?"

"I've said."

I have no choice but to leave and hope she will do as she says.

"Wait," she says. "How well do you know Tina?"

No longer Ms Lloyd.

"She's my friend."

"So you know she has a long history of accusing her husband of assault and battery, then dropping the charges?"

"Well, uh ..." I rally. "That doesn't mean she's not in danger, does it?"

She shakes her grey head and goes back to her forms. I'm dismissed.

A police car sits outside the boarded-up front door. when I get home I brace myself for another round of hostilities from Stevie's sidekicks, but DS Peters gets out, holding a large Jiffy bag.

"Ms. Graham, glad we caught you." She looks at the door. "What happened here?"

"We had a break-in," I say shortly, no longer sure who I can trust. "It's been reported."

"You sure? I haven't seen a report and I checked your file before we left the station."

My file? They've got a file on me?

"Nothing to do with me." I shrug. "What do you want?"

"Shall we go inside?"

"No." The bald refusal hangs there for a few seconds. I

don't back down.

DS Peters sighs. "Have it your way. Here." She hands over the Jiffy bag. "We've been advised that you're Mr Knowley's next of kin. These his personal effects. It appears he emptied his pockets onto a desk when he lay down to sleep in the office. Mr Knowley's father released the keys to Mr Ferguson before we knew they should have gone to you."

"It's OK. I've got them."

"I also have to advise you that Mr Knowley's body has been released by the Coroner's Office. " She hands me her card. "If you can let us know which funeral parlour you would like him taken to, I'll get that organised."

"What about your investigation? Do you know who did it yet?"

"The enquiry is still open; we'll let you know when there's any information."

She turns back to the car. For the second time today, I'm dismissed.

Miss Dressing Gown, from last night, makes a beeline for me from across the road. With a hasty wave and a mumbled 'Sorry, can't stop', I dive through the gate to the back yard, and bolt it behind me.

Safely inside, I go in search of my little-used wide angle lens. I couldn't promise Leon I'd find his mother, but I can start looking. With the lens mounted and the camera stowed safely in my bag, I'm ready to go. My keys lie on the table, where I've thrown them, next to the Jiffy bag with Rob's stuff in it. I tap my fingers against it, unsure whether to open it or not, then quickly rip it open.

There's not much – Rob's wallet, leather cracked and scuffed, a couple of bookie slips and his watch. Inside the wallet, my own picture stares back at me, a selfie I had taken for him. Driving licence, lottery tickets and odd scraps of paper are stuffed in the back compartment; a series of credit cards in pockets at the front.

A memory surfaces of Rob, scratching on the bottom of the carriage clock that sits on the mantelpiece. Sure enough, when I turn the clock over, he has written his pin numbers on the base. I scribble them down on a piece of paper from the wallet, replace it and put the wallet in the back pocket of my jeans. Then, picking up my keys, I leave the house by the back door, locking it after me.

When I get to the QMC for the second time that day, I am greeted by the same nurse who had tried to help me earlier in the day.

"I'm sorry, love, but you can't see Leon at the moment. The social services conference is taking place, and he's in the room with them."

"Do you know how long they'll be?"

"Not really, these things can go on forever."

Disappointed at not being able to see Leon, I reluctantly hand over a small bag.

"Can you give this to him, when he gets back on the ward? Tell him... just tell him Jilly was here, I bought him a present. There's a note inside."

"Of course I will." She takes the bag from me and bustles off, back to her station.

"Thanks," I say to her retreating back.

My paper map directs me to the hospital cafeteria, where I eat a sandwich, drink tea and think over my next move.

CHAPTER FORTY NINE

The city streets are nearly empty, cleared of home-going workers and tourists, the evening revellers yet to appear. I pass Maisie's bench, now occupied by a couple of teenagers, wrapped in each other's arms, oblivious to the rest of the world. My steps slow when the Old Mill looms up out of the dusk, the windows dark; even though I'm pretty sure Noel isn't there any more, it still takes a few minutes to summon up enough courage to walk past it.

The garage door is closed, but not locked; the metal hinges screech as I ease them open with my gloved fingers, revealing the dark interior. No Jaguar. Although I've only a hazy recollection of the garage's contents, it seems less cluttered to me. The petrol can is still there, lying on its side in the furthest corner, as if it had been kicked there. I adjust my camera to cope with the low light levels, wary of drawing attention to myself by using a flash, bend down and take a close-up of the can. Back outside, I fire off a long shot of the interior before pushing the door shut, teeth clenched against the metallic complaint of the hinges.

Darkness creeps over the rooftops, far above my head, casting long shadows over the narrow streets. Instinctively, I raise my camera and take a photograph of the

Old Mill exterior, focusing on the windows where Tina lived. I don't know why. It doesn't hold any good memories for me, but it's where the ill-fated sequence of events began. And the streets themselves – silent witnesses to the first time I came here and met Tina and her fractured family; Tina and I fleeing through them to escape from Noel; and Leon and I stealing through them to return the petrol can. A germ of an idea blooms in my mind, unformed but insistent. I spend half an hour shooting in the dark streets, searching out different angles and following the shadows as the moon rises ever higher, aware of time ticking away but also sensing that I may never come back.

The Duke of Clarence serves as a pitstop for the girls who work on Forest Road, a place to rest their aching legs for a few minutes or to avail themselves of the washing facilities. More than one girl has sobbed in the toilet while her friends dab at a cut from a disgruntled punter. or administer to an emerging black eye from a dissatisfied pimp. Tim, the landlord, turns a blind eye, as long as they keep buying alcohol. He only draws the line at them actually doing business on his premises.

I slide on to a barstool. "Evening, Tim. Large white, please."

"Not seen you for a while, Jilly. Heard you had a bit of trouble."

His face is sly as he pours the wine, hoping for some juicy gossip.

"No, not me." I won't give him the satisfaction. "Any of the girls been in tonight?"

"Couple in there." He nods towards the snug. "Candace was in a little while ago, so I know she's working tonight."

"Thanks." I head for the little room at the back, carrying my drink. Two women, Helen and Sue, who both took part in my photography project, are slumped on the velveteen seats, high-heeled shoes off and feet up on low stools. They look up when I enter and, without a word, put their shoes on and leave.

"Hey, girls." I call after them but they keep going, the door slamming shut behind them.

Tim has come into the snug behind me to collect glasses.

"What was that all about?" I ask him.

"Well ..." He draws it out, like he's about to tell me a secret. "I have heard that you're ..."

"What? I'm what?"

"... shall we say ... unwelcome round here."

"Is this Noel? Do you know where he is? Where Tina is?"

He lays a finger against his nose, shakes his head and disappears back into the main bar. I follow him, but he refuses to tell me anything, just keeps shaking his head.

Back out into the night, I stop to take a few photographs of the pub. This brings Tim rushing outside.

"Here, you can't do that!"

"Yeah, I can, actually. I'm standing on a public road."

To wind him up more, I carry on shooting, including him in the picture as he shakes his fist at me.

Petty, but it makes me feel better.

A few hundred metres along the road, Helen leans on a tree, engrossed in her phone. I quicken my step, reaching her side before she sees me.

"Helen." She jumps at the sound of my voice and looks around her, panic in her eyes.

"Go away. I ain't talking to you." She raises her voice. "I ain't talking to her!"

"OK, it's OK." I back off. "I understand."

I retreat to the other side of the road, into the shadow of a building, and click off a picture of Helen. A quick glance in the monitor shows a dark figure emerging from the gloom behind her.

Further up, Sue stands chatting to a girl I don't know. As soon as they see me, Sue nudges her friend and they melt into the darkness.

I call after them, "Please, I just want to find Tina. Do you know where she is?"

They're gone. I walk the length of the road twice and don't see another girl. I reach the Clarence for the second time and sit down on the low wall surrounding the car park. Without warning, someone punches me in the back and sends me sprawling to the ground.

A voice says in my ear, "Take this as a warning. Fuck off and stop asking questions, if you know what's good for you."

I curl my body up and put my arms over my face, waiting for the onslaught. It doesn't come and, after a few moments, I crawl back to my feet, feel for the wall behind me and sit down again. My breath comes in short gasps, heightening the pain in my back. I'm afraid to look up, in case my attacker is watching me. My every impulse is to get up and run, not stopping until I get home. I have to dig deep to resist giving in to the fear that consumes me.

"Jilly."

I lift my head, searching for the source of the soft voice calling my name.

"Over here." No more than a loud whisper, it comes from the dark recesses of the car park.

I'm on my feet, pain forgotten. "Tina? Is that you?" I

stumble through the cars, searching for her. I've found her! "Where are you?"

"Ssshh! It's me. Candace."

My heart drops. I was so sure it was Tina. The disappointment slows my feet and Candace calls to me again. "Jilly, I've got to go. Here, quickly." I respond to the urgency in her voice and stumble through the parked cars in the direction of her voice. She starts talking as soon as I'm within a few feet of her.

"What the hell was you and Tina thinking? Noel's been like a crazy man, looking for her." Loud voices ring across the car park as a group of men leaves the pub and she shrinks further into the shadows. "Sam – my man – he were on the phone to Noel, making arrangements to look after Noel's girls for a while. I heard him say, 'so, you boxed the bitch down' – something bad's happened to her."

I groan and stuff my hand in mouth to stifle the sound. Candace says, "I like you, Jilly, you was always nice to me, so I'm warning you. Don't come round here no more."

With that, she's gone, leaving me alone and even more frightened than before.

My phone vibrates in my pocket. A text has come in from an unknown number.

tx. u rock followed by a smiley emoji.

In spite of my fear, I smile. Leon got my present and my number on the bit of paper.

i told you id always find you

I wait for an answer.

hv u found my mum?

The pub door opens, spilling a group of men out onto the pavement. Acutely aware of the painful warning meted out to me just a few minutes ago, I get up from the wall and walk quickly off towards the city.

Leon's last question is still displayed on my phone. Instead of an answer, I send him another question.

where does lainie live

Leon has never admitted to either Tina or me that he has been to Lainie's house, probably to spare his mum's feelings. I cross my fingers he'll come through for me.

A message pings back.

big hse @ btm oak rd b careful

I send him a thumbs-up and cut down a side street towards Hyson Green. Oak Road stretches upwards away from the city, dominated by semi-detached Victorian houses, now largely given over to bedsits. Two large houses anchor the bottom of the hill, one converted into a block of offices, the other divided into flats.

There are plenty of vacant on-street parking spaces, but no sign of Noel's Jaguar. I stand outside the flats, frustrated by the double doors, which will only open if one of the occupants buzzes me in. A padlocked gate leads to the back garden, too tall for me to climb.

I pick a buzzer and push it. No answer. I push another.

An angry male voice crackles out of the speaker. "Who the hell's that? It's one o'clock in the bloody morning."

"Uh, sorry to bother you. I'm looking for Lainie. It's urgent."

"Who?"

Another voice sounds faintly in the background and, in a few seconds, he's back. "Oh, her. Yeah, she's gone and good riddance."

"Do you know where she went?"

"Her and that black git smashed the place up and she did a runner."

"Wait! The black guy, is he still here?"

"What am I, his keeper? He's gone. Now piss off."

A distant memory surfaces of Tina talking with disdain about the girls who work in the Meadows area; the Forest Road girls don't mix with them. Perhaps Noel's tentacles haven't reached that far. It's too late to go there tonight so, after taking another series of photographs, I turn towards home.

CHAPTER FIFTY

The bench is cold and damp beneath my legs. The grey drizzle stopped about an hour ago, but the skies remain leaden. Lights come on in the shops across the way and assistants roll up shutters and unlock doors. The trickle of people on their way to work becomes a flood.

Sometime after ten o'clock, the sun breaks through the clouds. Steam rises off the wet streets and my spirits lift a little.

Here she comes, puffing up the hill, pushing her trolley in front of her, one hand balancing the assorted carrier bags, which seem to have grown since the last time I saw her.

"Good morning, Maisie," I greet her and budge up before she can tell me. "Do you remember me?"

"Of course I remember you, I'm not senile. Come for your coat, have you?"

"How did you –"

"I'm not daft, either. I saw you put it in me trolley. You need to get up early in the morning to fool Maisie."

"I didn't mean to fool you. It was just to keep it safe for a while."

"Mmmm." She looks sideways at me, eyes calculating. "So, what's the story, then?"

"It belongs to my boyfriend. We had a big argument and I took it, to make him pay for the things he said."

"And?"

"And we've made it up, now, so he can have it back."

"Ha! That's a cock-and-bull story, if ever I heard one. But, here –"

Maisie fumbles through the carrier bags and drags out my black bin bag. I reach out to take it from her, but she hangs on, refusing to let go.

The old bat smiles. "What about my storage fee?"

A few minutes later, my purse ten pounds lighter, but with the coat tucked safely under my arm, I'm on my way home. Once inside, I fold the coat, with the earring visible, still stuck in the sleeve, and seal it into a clear, plastic bag.

I'm ready, but nervous. My fingers shake so much, I have trouble tapping through my contacts to find the number for Ferguson's Print Shop. It rings five times before an answering machine kicks in and Nige's voice says,

You have reached Ferguson's. We're sorry we can't take on any orders at the moment, while the factory is being refurbished. Should you wish to make a delivery, there will be someone on site to receive it. Thank you for your understanding.

Oh yes, Nige, I want to make a delivery, if I can summon up enough courage to go through with it. A deep breath in and a long breath out. And repeat. I walk through to the living room, where Leon and Tina's rucksacks lie, side by side on the floor. I'll deliver Leon's to him this afternoon at the hospital and hopefully find out where he's being placed. But, Tina's … my heart constricts and tears threaten. I force them back. No more tears.

Noel is going to pay for taking Tina away from me.

The factory is shrouded in scaffolding. Workmen are everywhere, repairing brickwork, installing new windows, mixing cement in the car park, sluicing the ground with water. I pick my way through them to the office to find Nige tearing a strip off a guy in overalls about supplies that haven't arrived. Conversation over, he glares at me.

"What the fuck do you want?"

"Can you come outside?" I nod towards the door, indicating I want privacy.

He swears under his breath and follows me. I stand near a couple of workmen, just out of their earshot.

"What is it, then?"

I remove the coat, encased in clear plastic, from the black bin bag.

"Remember this?"

"You lying bitch. You said you gave it away." He looks nervously towards the workmen. "Let's go back into the factory."

"You must think I'm stupid." I sneer. "We'll stay here, where people can see us. Make sure you keep your hands to yourself"

"Go on, then. Spit it out. What do you want?"

"I'm thinking of taking this to the police."

He laughs. "No, don't try that one. Me and Rob used to wonder why you didn't go to them when … you know. We reckoned you've got a criminal record or summat."

"No, nothing like that."

Calm, stay calm.

"I was a bit of a tearaway when I was young, didn't trust the police. But, you know, since Rob … they've been really understanding. I've made good friends with Sergeant Peters and, uh, Sergeant Wilkins. I feel like I can trust them, tell them anything."

Am I over doing it?

"Maybe it's time to tell them about the rape." I swallow as I force myself to say the word. "And, this coat … you were wearing it when you attacked me, remember? My earring was ripped out of my ear and got stuck in the sleeve, so I'm guessing there's DNA on it. I'm just giving you a heads-up, you know?"

Nige's face leaches colour. "Why would you do that? Rob's gone, God rest his soul. He only wanted to teach you a lesson. And I didn't really do anything, did I?"

"You bastard, you beat me, you set me up for Noel to …" I forget my plan. Fury overwhelms me as I remember the terror, the helplessness of that night. I've got to get a grip or I'm going to blow it. Deep breath in, slow breath out. My world steadies again, the anger drained. It's an effort to carry on, but I focus inwardly on the pictures of Tina and Leon, their ravaged faces, and I grow strong.

"Anyway, are you willing to take the chance?"

Nige begs. It's a sweet moment for me.

"Jilly, please don't do this, I'll do anything, just don't go to the police."

And I tell him what I want.

CHAPTER FIFTY ONE

Midnight. The Meadows.

There aren't many girls, it's a slow night. I show them Tina's photograph.

"Sorry, duck, I don't know her."

I wait until I see girls return to the street, get out of cars and take up a stance under a streetlight.

Same response.

"Aw, she looks nice. Is she in trouble?"

"No, I've never seen her round here."

....

At QMC, I'm told, "Sorry, love, he's gone. He's in a place-ment."

I ring him, over and over.

Number not available.

....

Foggy, eerie light, no girls on Forest Road.

I don't linger, frightened of the faceless person who threatened me.

....

The Women's Centre.

I can't get past the door.

"You know we can't tell you anything."

....

Leave a message, I'll get back to you.

"Christie, it's me. Where's Leon? Call me back."

....

For three days and three nights, I walk miles across the city, ask questions, return again and again to the police station, try to contact Leon and Christie, all with no result. I guess they've all moved on but I'd hoped Leon would text me.

Everywhere, I take photographs, poring over them when tiredness or despair drives me home. They don't have any clues to offer me.

Tina's family are untraceable. She once told me her mother was dead, and on another occasion said her family lived in Clifton, but I don't know their name, anyway. Tina always used Lloyd, Noel's name. The only posts on her Facebook timeline are pictures of clothes, models and animals, culled from anonymous websites, nothing personal.

CHAPTER FIFTY TWO

Mid-morning on the fourth day. A knock on the boarded-up door.

I shout, "Who is it?"

There's no answer for a moment, then a gruff voice says, "Letter for Ms J Graham, needs to be signed for."

What now? I've completed all the formalities with the solicitor's and have an appointment with the funeral parlour this afternoon.

"Take it to the back gate. I'll be there in a second."

Preoccupied with thoughts of where my search will take me today, I plod through the house and unlock the back gate.

Christie stands there, smiles all over his face. He holds a stack of white boxes.

"Can I come in? I've brought lunch."

I fight against anger and relief. "Where the hell have you been? Why didn't you answer me? I've been going out of mind."

"I'm sorry, I can explain." He sobers and gestures with the boxes. "Please?"

"OK." I stand back and open the gate wider. "But this had better be good."

He walks in and, before I can close the gate, Oliver follows him, also laden with white boxes.

"Good morning, Jilly," he says, in passing.

"For God's sake, what is this? A party."

"Well, it *is* my birthday." My heart leaps at the sound of Leon's voice and there he is, drawn and with tired eyes, but managing to smile.

Tears of joy prick my eyes and I can only stutter, "Leon, but how …"

He looks at Christie and Oliver. "Can I tell her?"

"Sure." Oliver nods. "But shouldn't we go indoors first?"

Leon can't wait. "They're my foster parents!"

Christie smiles. "Well, we will be when the paperwork's done."

A shadow falls across Leon's face, "Just until Mum comes back, yeah?"

"Yes, of course," Oliver assures him. We all troop indoors and, while Christie and Leon unpack the food, I draw Oliver to one side.

"I'm sorry we didn't let you know what was going on, Jilly. It's been a very fraught few days and we only got confirmation this morning that we could be his temporary foster parents."

"And Tina?" In my heart, I know the answer, but I ask, anyway. "Is there any news of Tina?"

"I'm afraid not. Social Services found her mother, but she didn't want to know Leon."

I'm not surprised. In my experience, families aren't all they're cracked up to be.

I look across to where Leon's laying out plates of cakes, sandwiches and vol-au-vents.

"How is he?"

"He only came to us last night and he was pretty subdued. He alternates between being a bit hyper and giving in to grief. He's holding on to the hope that he'll see his mum again, but in reality, I think he knows –"

"No!" I cut in sharply. "There's *always* hope."

Oliver lays a hand gently on my arm. "Jilly, the social services are in constant touch with the police. They're not treating Tina as a missing person any more; they're looking for a –"

'Don't, Oliver." I jump away, as if his hand were red hot. "Don't say it. She's out there somewhere, I know it, and I'll find her."

Leon glances across at us, alerted by my raised voice.

I force a smile and join him at the table. "Wow, look at all this food. It's wonderful. Where did it come from?"

Christie grins and lays his left hand across his chest. Oliver walks over to him and adopts the same pose.

"What?" Then I get it. They're both sporting gold wedding bands. "When?"

"Yesterday morning," Christie says. "It was quiet, because we had appointments all day with various branches of the social services before we could pick Leon up."

"Congratulations, guys. I'm really pleased for you both."

"Thank you," Christie beams, as he puts one arm round Oliver and the other round Leon. "Looks like we've got a little family going here."

I smile back, trying to ignore the small pain that stabs in my chest. They're already a closed unit that doesn't include me.

Be happy for him.

And I am. I will be.

We heap up plates of food and carry them through to the living room. The newly weds sit on the sofa, with Leon perched on the arm, one hand resting lightly on Christie's shoulder. I turn on the radio. The bittersweet sound of Simon and Garfunkel fills the room with words of comfort and hope. Christie hums along, Oliver joins in and Leon starts ribbing them, calling them old men. I remember the first time I tuned it in for Tina and how Leon complained that the house was like an old people's home.

The small pain deepens. I slip out of the room to fetch my camera and bounce back in with a bright smile.

"Come on, guys, let's get some wedding photographs for the album," I say.

Laughter fills the room, as they pose and mug for the camera. Nobody laughs harder than me.

Ollie says, "Don't forget to send them to Christie, so we can get some printed. Our first family photographs."

"I want a set of pictures for in here, like other people have."
Tina's voice tears at my heart. I lower the camera and turn away, pretend to fiddle with the controls.

Oliver's phone rings. He checks it, raises a hand. "Sorry I have to take this."

Christie takes my camera and scrolls though the pictures while Leon looks over his shoulder.

"That was Head Office," Oliver says. "There's going to be an announcement on the news tonight."

He hesitates. "It's about your father, Leon. The police have apprehended him in Birmingham. He's been charged with arson and manslaughter; apparently, they have evidence to tie him to the fire at Ferguson's."

Leon looks at me, eyes wide with fear. I shake my head, the smallest of movements, narrow my eyes and telegraph to him, *don't say anything.*

"Did they say what it was?" Christie asks the question. I don't say anything, in the hope they'll read my silence as shock.

"From what I can gather, they got a tip off. Someone sent the police a couple of photographs of a petrol tin, presumably the one used to set the fire. His fingerprints were on it."

Christie's puzzled. "But how did they connect it to the factory?"

"There was a smear of printer's ink on the petrol can. They matched it to an empty tin in one of the wheelie bins."

"My mum? What about my mum?" The hope on Leon's face is unbearable.

Oliver shakes his head. "I'm sorry, mate. He's clammed up."

Leon is visibly shaking, his body rigid in the effort to control it. I put my arms out and he stumbles into them, clinging to me as he mumbles in my ear.

"How did the ink get there? There might be some on our shoes or something."

"Christie, can you give us a minute?" I ask. He nods and follows Oliver out of the room.

"Keep your voice down," I whisper. "Forget about the ink. Nige put it on the petrol can and then put the tin in the wheelie bin for the police to find."

"Why would Nige do that? He doesn't even know Noel."

"Don't worry about Nige. Don't talk about it. Not to anyone. That way, you can't make a mistake."

"Will my dad – Noel – go to prison?"

"Very likely, if the police can make it stick."

I hold Leon as he shudders.

When I feel his shoulders relax, I say, "OK, we're going to call your dads back in." I tip his chin up in an effort to make him smile at the small joke. "They're the good guys, Leon. You're going to have a great life with them.

A new school, friends … but promise me …" I falter. "Promise me one thing. Never give up hope on seeing your mum again, whatever they tell you."

His eyes are flooded with tears as he promises with a nod of the head.

"You should go home now. It's been great seeing you, but you look wiped out." I muster a smile. "Go get your new life."

"All right, Jilly. I've got my phone back now, they took it when I was at the children's home. You'll call me if … when you find her, won't you?"

Now I'm the one unable to speak. I tighten my arms round him and kiss his cheek. That will have to do.

I call Oliver. He comes into room, takes one look at my face and puts an arm round Leon, easing him gently out of my arms.

"Come on, old chap. Time to go."

They walk through the house, past the ruined door, through the dining room and kitchen. I watch every step they take until they vanish into the back yard.

"Jilly."

I turn with a start. Christie stands behind me, my camera still in his hand. He clicks to bring the monitor live and holds it up in front of me. It shows a picture of Oak Road at night.

"What's this?"

"It's …uh, it's an old picture from my project. I forgot to delete it from the card."

"Don't lie to me, Jilly. I can see the time and date. Two o'clock this morning. What the hell are you doing?"

I have no answer. "You're playing a dangerous game. Noel's locked up, but he's still got friends, bad friends."

I stay silent and he sighs, "Look, there'll be a media campaign now to try and find her –"

The word *body* hangs unspoken between us.

"You should go now, Christie."

He puts my camera down with a shrug and says, "You understand, don't you, that if you persist with this search or whatever you want to call it, that we can't have Leon involved? His safety and well-being are our priority. He needs stability and …"

"I know."

Please, just go. I need to be alone.

We walk through to the back gate and Christie tries once more.

"You can still go to London, put all this behind you."

My throat is too full to answer and he turns away. As he reaches Oliver's car, the back door flies open and Leon runs towards me. One last hug, a muttered 'Don't forget me' and he's gone.

I stand at the gate for the longest moment before going back indoors.

A text message pings, as I clear the table and put the left-over food in the fridge.

It's Nige.

It's done. Where's the coat?

I block his number and delete it from my contacts. I'll probably give the coat to Maisie to keep her warm in winter.

....

Dusk falls.

I turn off the radio, shoulder my camera bag and walk through the empty house.

Tomorrow I'll get that door fixed.

Outside, wispy clouds scud across the moon. It's going to be a clear night

I start walking.

CHAPTER FIFTY THREE

Black smoked glass stretches from floor to ceiling, turning the dark street outside into a smudged palette, spiked intermittently by starbursts of lamplight. The room is filled with people holding catalogues and drinking wine, as they view the photographs hung on the gallery wall. I mingle, already buzzed on the cheap plonk, listening to the comments.

"Great depth and insight."

"Bit grim, aren't they? Why are they all taken at night time?"

"A stunning metaphor for today's lost society."

"Just old houses, you can't call that art."

"Did you see she got a write-up in *The Times*?"

"What are the missing person posters all about, then?"

"So evocative ... and the title, *Forever Night*, gives me goose bumps."

"Here, I think that's my gran's house. Wait, I'll phone her."

The Mayor of Nottingham beckons me over. I join him and Alastair James, the curator of the art gallery. Time for the speeches.

Alastair speaks first.

"It's a great pleasure to welcome you here tonight to the inaugural exhibition of Jillian Graham."

He drones on about my degree from Nottingham Trent University, how I worked to fund my photography and how proud he is to host this local girl's exhibition. I see a few women in the crowd purse their lips at this and smile inwardly. It's not the worst thing that's ever been said about me.

The Mayor's up next.

He wants to make sure everyone knows he was a prime mover in raising funds for this innovative and progressive gallery. Alastair whispers in his ear and he moves on to briefly praise my work, before asking me to say a few words.

I grab another glass of wine from a passing student, press-ganged into waitressing for the evening, and mount the small dais to address the great and good of Nottingham.

"*Forever Night* has been a long time in the making, nearly five years. Many of you will never see – or want to see – these places. I'm quite sure the Mayor here –" I gesture widely and my wine splashes on the pristine floor. "– would like to see the area round the Forest bulldozed and *innovative* and *progressive* buildings raised in their place."

A few nervous titters.

"See that Missing Person poster on the pillar by the door? That's Tina, my friend ..."

I forget what I'm supposed to say next, who I'm supposed to thank for their generous funding. A surge of the old anger spurs me on.

"None of you would have given her the time of day –"

Alastair puts a warning hand on my arm that says, *Don't do this, Jilly, don't make a scene.* The Mayor's face is an interesting shade of puce.

I tip my head back to drink what's left of the wine, mutter 'Fuck it, anyway" and leave the dais. Alastair leads a hasty round of applause.

The local papers will have a field day tomorrow and the Sheriff will be able to say, "I told you so." He opposed my photographs being used tonight, but was over-ruled by Alastair.

The student with the tray of glasses approaches me. I wave her off and shoulder my way through the crowd, ignoring their whispers. It's cooler at the edge of the room and I lean against the distressed brick wall, looking out into the murky night. My focus shifts and the reflection of the room behind me spreads across the dark glass, obscuring the outside world.

I wait. I've played this game many times before.

The crowd ebbs and flows, forming groups, breaking part and coming together. Ever changing patterns. Colours. Dancing light on wineglasses. The chatter and laughter of the guests recedes. I hold my breath ... and she emerges from the shadows, blonde hair gleaming and with Rob's old tee shirt falling off one shoulder. She holds my gaze with the faintest of smiles. My throat closes, swollen by a pain that claws its way down to my heart.

Her lips move. I can't hear her but the words burn into my brain.

Enough, Jills. Let me go ...

We both know I can't. Sometimes, as evening draws in, dusk calls me away from my computer and the golden oldies that play softly in the background. I walk all the old haunts, knowing it's futile but unable to stop. Occasionally, one of the girls will speak to me, but not for long and with nervous glances over her shoulder. Men catcall when I pass the Duke of Clarence and a couple of times someone throws a stone at me. Once in a while, I see her fleetingly – reflected in a darkened window, disappearing among the trees, in a car window as it passes beneath the lamplight.

How can I stop?

A precious few moments tick away, until my beautiful illusion is shattered by the reflection of a tall figure, dark hair in dreadlocks, who materialises beside her.

My breath hitches.

Noel?

Tina shimmers and disappears; noise creeps back in and the outside world merges once more with the reflection of the room behind me.

He's still there.

"Jills?"

"Leon!" I whirl round and look up into his face, hardly daring to believe my eyes. He's nearly six feet tall, strikingly attractive, dressed casually in tee shirt and jeans. Unsure whether to hug him or not, I dither until he laughs and sweeps me up in a bear hug.

"Are you glad to see me?' he asks, depositing me back on the floor.

"God, yes!" I peer behind him. "Are –"

He sobers. "Sorry, they're not here. Christie didn't want me to come, either, but I couldn't leave without seeing you again."

"You're leaving? Where are you going?"

Leon nods toward an empty bench. "Grab a seat. I'll get us a couple of drinks. I haven't got long."

He walks confidently across the room in search of wine. I sit down, only to be accosted by a reporter from *The Evening Post*. She has an iPad with a list of questions and settles beside me, ready to read her way through them.

"Congratulations on the exhibition," she begins. "Can you tell me a little more about your inspiration for it?"

"No, sorry. Just read the handout."

I walk away in search of a quiet corner to wait for Leon, confused as I try to make sense of his unexpected appearance and the news that he's leaving. Many times in the last five years, I've been tempted to respond to his texts, but my unspoken promise to Christie always stopped me. That, and because I couldn't bear to admit I had no news of his mum.

"There you are. I thought you'd done a runner."

Leon's back with a couple of plastic glasses, half-filled with tepid white wine.

I raise my eyebrows. "Well?"

Leon drinks, shudders and puts his wineglass on the floor. "Me and the dads, we're moving to London – permanently."

"You're going to London?" My laugh is brittle, laced with anger. "Now, where have I heard that before?"

He avoids my gaze, studying the dark streets beyond the glass. "I know, it was our dream. I remember the plans we made … there's not a day when I don't think about … her."

That makes two of us.

"I've got a university place in Kingston-on-Thames and Christie thinks it's a chance to make a permanent break, so they're both re-locating."

"Re-locating? Christ, listen to yourself. You even talk like them."

His jaw tightens. With a visible effort, he says, "There's something else."

"Well?"

"I told them."

He did what?

My legs give way underneath me and, somehow, I'm sitting on the floor, drinking from Leon's glass and screeching at his back. "You idiot. You fucking idiot. How could you be so stupid?"

He hunkers down beside me. "Keep it down, don't make a scene."

The reporter from *The Evening Post* raises her iPad.

"Shit, she's taking pictures." mutters Leon and hauls me to my feet, one hand outstretched to block the woman's vision. "It's OK, she just slipped on some wine," he reassures her and she melts back into the crowd.

"Listen to me." Leon speaks rapidly, his eyes scanning the room for curious glances. "I wasn't coping. I *needed* you. You're the only other person who knows what we did. And you cut me off."

"I didn't. Well, I did, but Christie –"

He's not listening. "They sent me to so many therapists. I kept hoping Mum would turn up one day, especially after Noel went to prison. I even wrote to him, begged him to tell me where she was. He never even answered me. And you didn't answer my texts ..."

I wanted to.

"Anyway, I got wasted one night about six months ago when the dads were out and started walking to your house. They found me at the bottom of your street with a bloody nose. My wallet and phone missing."

"And that's when you told them?"

"Yeah. Christie was furious, ready to go to the police, kept saying he couldn't believe you would burn down the factory, let alone take me with you."

Who does he think he is, coming here in his expensive

clothes, talking like Christie, looking down his nose at me? "I didn't want to take you, in the first place. And who lit the match, eh? Who started the fucking fire?"

"Please, Jilly, keep it down, people are watching." Leon moves to stand between me and the crowd. He raises a hand as I fight for breath. "I'm sorry, but I was a kid, albeit a damaged one. It was always going to come out at sometime. Ollie and I talked Christie down, but he won't live here any more. He wants a new start ..."

A new start.

The anger drains from me. A memory surfaces, so strong that I lean against the wall for support. A sunny morning in April, laughing at Candice and her brazen antics, happy because my new life was just a few weeks away. Christie, outside the computer building, asking me to do him a favour. Is that where things changed? Or the day Rob found the picture of Tina?

Leon leans beside me, gives me a minute, then takes my hand and leads me to a photograph of the Old Mill. In the image, it's dark with rain sleeting down, bouncing off the pavements. A small, indistinct figure is just visible as it nears the far corner.

"That's not her, Jills. She's not coming back. All this –" He takes in the exhibition with a sweep of the arm. "It's got to stop, now. You're not going to find her."

I won't listen. "Oh, this one was funny. I had a carrier bag on my head to keep off the rain and my camera stuffed inside another one, with a hole cut out for the lens ..."

Leon tries again. "She's not there and it's not the way I want to remember her. Please, for my sake as well as your own, give it up."

We both know I won't.

There's no point in prolonging the moment.

"Go, now." I take his arm and walk him to the door. It slides open automatically. A misty rain falls softly and he looks ruefully at his designer tee shirt.

"Gonna get wet."

I manage a laugh and push him out of the door, repeating the words I'd said the terrible night Tina disappeared from our lives.

"Go on, go get your new life."

Back in the room, I'm buttonholed by the young reporter.

"Please, Ms Graham, my editor can be a right bastard …"

I sigh. "OK, get me a drink and we'll talk."

While she rushes off in search of wine, I drift over to the smokey glass wall, now stippled with tiny droplets of mist. If I half-close my eyes, I can just see a distant figure, disappearing into the night.

THANK YOU

My thank you list is short and of enormous importance. As a new author, I received endless advice and encouragement from the members of Scribophile, the online writing workshop and writer's community. I thank those who critiqued my work on an ongoing basis and those who answered my questions with patience and courtesy. Of particular note are three fellow authors who followed Jilly all the way through Circles of Confusion – Ann Dudzinski, Mirri Fnurrstrom and Valerie Shay. On the home front, my eternal thanks and love to Jan Wyer, who has always believed I could do anything I set my mind to.

ABOUT THE AUTHOR

Jj Grafton

Jacqui Jay Grafton was born in Ulster and lived there during her formative years, moving to Nottingham, her adopted home, as a young woman. She wrote Circles of Confusion, her first novel, at the age of seventy-six, fulfilling a long held ambition. Jacqui is an award winning photographer  and lives with her partner of forty two years. She is currently working on her next novel, Ashes on the Tongue, set in 1950s Ireland, just before the outbreak of the Troubles. For more information or to read more of her work, visit www.jjgrafton.com

Printed in Great Britain
by Amazon

11443581R00185